"I will not leave y[...]

"Nay." The word was forced out of the wounded man. "You must leave me."

Not a reproach, not a plea. It was a command.

"You must go. I will bring you danger."

Danger. Gemma's skin, the very air around her, shivered with it.

"No." She tried to hold the shifting brightness of his eyes. There was more to this than a chance meeting of strangers. A bond had been made, of what kind or how was beyond her understanding.

"No…" she began again, but the gaze was gone, into some realm she could not follow. She watched the thick lashes drift closed, cutting her off. She could not hold his gaze, could not hold him.

Gemma looked at the cut on the muddied swell of his thigh. He was not her responsibility. She could not bring an unknown warrior—an Englishman—into the Viking camp. She should leave this warrior creature to his own fate.

But how could she?

Helen Kirkman

A Fragile Trust

HQN™

ISBN 0-373-77077-4

A FRAGILE TRUST

Copyright © 2005 by Helen Kirkman

For Tracy Farrell and Jessica Alvarez

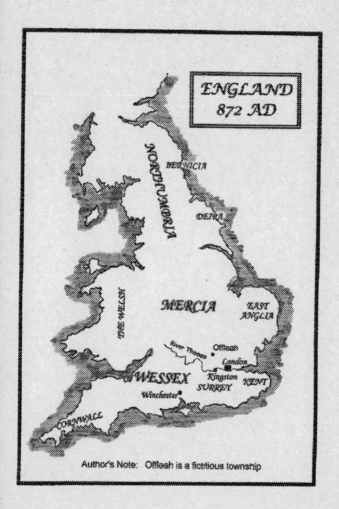

ENGLAND
872 AD

NORTHUMBRIA

BERNICIA

DEIRA

THE WELSH

MERCIA

EAST ANGLIA

River Thames

Offleah

London

WESSEX

Kingston

SURREY

KENT

Winchester

CORNWALL

Author's Note: Offleah is a fictitious township

A Fragile Trust

PROLOGUE

Wimborne Abbey, Wessex, England—871 A.D.

"I SWEAR."

The heavy air inside the hundred-year-old walls deadened the words. Cold seeped through his body, through the stone reliquary that held St. Cuthburg's bones. Through the dark.

Then the shadows parted. A hand, quick and unhesitating, touched the carved and painted casket beside him.

"I swear."

The echo of his own words beat against the darkness. The sound swelled, taken up by other voices. Other hands caught at the stone lid. But he saw only the hand of his brother, beside him as always, like a sign of trust.

Across the chamber, torchlight outlined the pale, arresting face that commanded the fate of a kingdom.

I swear. The sound rose and died. But the meaning did not. It was no ordinary oath of fealty. It reached beyond life and death, beyond the shadows gathered round the newly crowned king and the banner of the golden dragon.

It was irrevocable.

CHAPTER ONE

The Mercian border, England—spring, 872 A.D.

"STOP," shrieked Gemma. "The man is alive."

The horse and cart lurched to a halt so abrupt it nearly threw her.

Gemma's gaze fixed on the heap of rags beside the track. She could make out the startling breadth of the man's shoulders under the torn wool, glimpse the bare thickness of a muddied thigh.

She leaped down while the cart was still rocking, landing light-footed in the remains of last winter's leaf mold.

"Don't! Lady, stop. You do not know who he is, or what. An outlaw, most like, a wolf's head. There could be others, waiting for you to go near the trees—"

But the figure of the man drew her, as though she were caught on an invisible thread. She watched the dark shape: motionless, damaged, infinitely mysterious.

She kept walking.

Still, damp-laden air closed in around her like a heavy curtain, cutting her off from the road, from the angry, fearful shouts of the boy, Boda. Such sounds and the ordinary world had no meaning. There was only the man lying beside the forest, half concealed among the trees as though he were part of them.

Only that and the sense of danger.

Her feet made no sound at all, not a rustle. She knelt down amongst the wet bracken.

He was a mess. Her breath choked in her throat. There was blood mixed in with the mud, some dried against the skin and the clothes, turned rust-brown and black. Some oozing fresh, as though he had been moving, quite recently. That was what had drawn her attention: the movement. Movement and the pale gleam of uncovered flesh.

He did not move anymore. The patch of naked skin belonged to the strong sinuous length of his leg stretched out in the damp bracken beside her. She stared at the gaping cloth, the taut swell of muscle exposed beneath; at the blackened slashing line of what could only be a sword cut. Her hands clenched.

Naught about him was what she had expected. She had thought him one of the poor, starving wretches who haunted the countryside in the wake of the Viking raids. Heaven knew there were enough of them.

But swelling muscles did not belong to starving men and while his wounds could be those of a robber's helpless victim, she felt in her bones that this man had fought. And there had been a skirmish, quite recently, which the Vikings had won. She had heard their boasts.

She touched the crushed cloth of his tunic. It was poor and coarse enough for the lowest cottar. He was filthy. He was completely alone.

All of that meant nothing. She knew what he was.

He was lying facedown, his body slightly twisted, one arm stretched out in front of him. The broad battered width of his hand was wrapped—nay, clamped—round a tree root, as though if he could no longer walk forward, he would crawl. She fancied she could still see the whiteness of his knuckles caused by the sheer unadulterated power of that grip—a legendary Beowulf with the strength of thirty men in one hand.

A warrior's hand.

The poor stuff of his tunic grated against her fingers. She despised warriors.

Something thudded onto the earth beside her. Boda. She could hear his hissing breath.

"I cannot see anyone. There is not a sound." His voice shivered.

It was so strange, the dense waiting silence. Dampness seeped through her knees from the cold earth.

"I still say you should come away, Lady. Leave him. He could have pestilence, anything. There is little enough you can do for him. You have next to naught yourself. Gemma, please…"

The gruffness in his voice caught at her. He almost never used her name. Half man and still half child, he was her brother's boon companion, not hers. She did not even know where he had come from. She had just found him, running wild round the Viking camp, alone. Because he had no parents. They were dead.

He touched the edge of her cloak.

The temptation to give in to that mixture of pleading and rough good sense was almost overwhelming. The battered man was a stranger, worse, a soldier. In truth, she could take nothing for granted. For all she knew he could be Danish, some Viking ambushed in revenge, set upon and left for dead.

She let go of the man's sleeve, wiping her hand clean. Dried leaves shed cold and dampness against her skin. Mud and...blood.

What if he died?

Boda's nervous breathing at her shoulder struggled against the silence, an intrusion like her own breath. The very shadows of the trees pressed against them.

"Come away."

She could not tear her gaze from the stranger, from the heavy outstretched warrior's hand.

Her own hand slid forward, evading Boda, reaching out until her fingers touched the stranger's flesh. She could feel each separate knuckle of that fierce grip. His skin was freezing. She could not pry his fingers free.

"I cannot leave him." She scarce knew whether she had spoken aloud.

Boda's eyes widened as he saw the sword cut across the bared thigh. In that moment, the stranger moved.

His eyes were the color of the forest, dun shadows and green light, so deep they did not seem to belong to a world-dweller but to a spirit, a *wood-wose*. Deep beyond imagining.

Gemma had the sensation of falling. She was leaning low, close to him, her body stretched out across his. Now the rolling movement as he turned brought her nearer still, so near they touched at almost every point.

Sudden fire seemed to erupt around her, despite the cold—wild, fast forest fire. The wood-dark eyes burned into hers. The spine-crawling silence of the air beat against her ears.

"Who are you?" The English words, deep as the earth's fastness, seemed not to break the tingling silence, but to be part of it. His voice demanded an answer. Yet it hurt him to speak. She could tell that from the tautness of his mouth, the heaviness of his breath. His speech was not Danish. It was as Mercian as hers.

That did not take away one iota of the danger.

"I am Gemma."

Her own voice seemed bright against the stillness, yet not out of place, part of the dangerously charged air between them.

"Gemma?"

Gemstone. It was not a usual name. It was, had been, a proud father's choice. The choice of a master goldsmith.

Her mouth tightened. None would believe that now from the clothes she wore: a plain blue tunic over a gray underdress of undyed wool. Her head and her face were almost completely hidden, swathed in a linen veil so coarse she would once have considered it scarcely fit for a cleaning cloth. Only the cloak was good. But the brooch at her shoulder was of iron and copper.

"A jewel, then."

His gaze held hers. Heat scorched across her skin, deep and disconcerting.

Her appearance appealed to no man. She did not want it to.

"It is well."

It was all that the man said. But then his face, scratched, bearded, coated with dirt and dried blood, smiled. She saw the gleam of even teeth, the bright, taut rise of his cheekbones dappled in sunlight. And his eyes.

The strange wildfire inside her kindled, coursing through her veins, making her whole body burn, so that sight and feeling and sense dizzied with the power of it. It was like the rush of the strongest mead. Nay, deeper, like the force of life itself, like the strength of spring that quickened the trees' growth and all the world's fairness.

The mysterious male creature under her hand had made her feel that.

All around him were tiny stars of green that she had not noticed in the cloudy light, the first signs of spring's power, a green haze creeping out from the forest's eaves. But the promise and the brightness of that were less, so much less than all that lived in him.

She gasped and the sound was lost in the suddenly shimmering air and the dazzling pools of his eyes.

Beside her the lifeless fronds of last year's bracken crackled and the sharp snap of winter-hard twigs broke the spell.

Boda. His grubby fingers tightened on the edge of her cloak, trying to draw her away. A kind of panic leaped inside her. She was mad to linger here beside the dark bulk of the forest filled with outlaws and thieves and the bitter dispossessed.

"Lady, come away."

At the sound of another voice, the hazel gaze flickered past her to the grimness of Boda's face. She caught the gleam of…what? Acknowledgment? An admission that Boda was right?

The deep-earth gaze turned back to her. She saw the bloodied mouth move, trying to form the words. All at once, the strained face seemed not that of an other-worldly spirit, but man-kindred, human and therefore vulnerable despite its evident will. The painful breath swelled mortal lungs, so that the laboring chest brushed her breasts through the layers of her clothing and his.

She felt the touch of another person's flesh and she felt the pain he felt, through the inadequate barrier of her skin. It reached inside her as though all that tortured effort hurt her body as much as his.

He would ask for her aid. He must. She knew, with a startling completeness, that she would not refuse him. The urge to reassure him, to respond to the humanness that she saw, to tell him he was not alone, cut through mind and flesh.

"It is all right. I will not leave you. I will help you—"

"Nay." The word was forced out of him, like an act of will, and she understood what she should have known the moment she had seen his hand. He would not beg for anything.

"You must leave me—"

Not a reproach, not a plea. It was a command.

"No—"

"You will. Gemma, Jewel. You must go. I will bring you danger."

Danger. Her skin, the very air around her, shivered with it.

"But I cannot…" Her voice seemed breathless, strengthless. She still had hold of his hand. Her fingers tightened on the frozen flesh. She might as well have held stone. But then the strength came to her, out of the stillness of the air.

"No." She tried to hold the shifting brightness of his eyes, to tell him without words what the breathless tingling air told her. Things she did not know herself. That there was more to this than a chance meeting of strangers, that a bond had been made, though of what kind or how was beyond her understanding.

But the forest-green gaze slid beyond her to fasten on Boda.

"See her away—"

"No…" she began, but the gaze was gone, far beyond both of them, into some realm she could not follow. She watched the thick brown lashes drift closed, cutting her off. She could not hold his gaze, could not hold him. She let go of his hand.

She stood up, the brown earth rocking beneath her feet, Boda beside her.

"Leave him." The words were vicious, laced through with a fear and an anger she could almost smell.

It was not Boda's fault he was harsh. The world had been harsh to him, more harsh than he could well bear.

As it was for her.

She could not afford to upset her Viking masters. She could not bring an unknown and dangerous fighting man into the camp, an Englishman.

She looked at the cut on the muddied swell of his thigh. He was not her responsibility. She had more responsibility than she knew how to endure. She should leave this man, this stranger, this warrior-creature to his own fate.

Boda saw the truth of that.

Even the stranger had seen it.

She knew what her decision was. She straightened up. She would have to be quick. Very, very quick.

IT WAS NOT QUICK at all.

When Boda turned the cart between the high wooden gates of what had once been a royal estate of Mercia, it was gathering dark. Rain had started, thin and dismal, and it fell on the Viking camp with the bleak, bone-numbing chill that said winter's grip would never end.

Gemma's heart beat so loudly she thought the foul-tempered guards must hear it.

Boda's hands pulled on the reins.

"Perhaps I should just turn back to the crossroads," he muttered. "It would save time."

Boda was the kind of youth who was born to be hanged. She closed her mind against the thought of the empty gibbet where the roads met.

"No one is going to hang you." *Unless it is me.* "It will be all right." Her mouth twisted and bile rose in her throat. "How could it not be? I am in Erik the Bone-breaker's pay, after all."

The cart stopped. Boda shot her a furious look. But then the shaggy head turned and the jests rolled from his mouth, rough-edged and cheerful against the gloom. There were advantages to Boda's kind of impudence.

She breathed, lowering her eyes in humble deference.

Most of the Danes would be in the great mead-hall by now. The rest would be wishing they were. They would not want to bother with two peasants and a cart. They would be swilling their looted ale, defiling the carven oak benches that had once held the proud hearth-companions of King Burgred.

She kept her face impassive and her gaze fixed on mud churned by the hoof prints of stolen horses and the ceaseless footprints of an army.

Burgred's men were all gone from here, those arrogant, reckless, high-hearted warriors whose shouts and boasts and songs had made the rafters ring with noise. They huddled round their now-powerless king in Tamworth, or held on grimly to whatever of their estates remained to them.

Or were dead.

Dead as this wounded stranger would be if she had left him.

She heard the hearty falseness of Boda's voice. Her hand tightened on the heavy shoulder that was jammed against her thigh in the back of the cart, among the stacked wood, hidden by sacking and the folds of her cloak. The rain dripped down her neck.

Stay still, my forest-spirit. The silent words burned through the cold air as though the unconscious man could hear them. She thought she felt him stir restlessly.

What had she done?

One of the guards stepped forwards and her breath caught. But at that moment the horse shied in bad temper, shaking itself and showering the man with mud and freezing rain. He cursed, but the others only laughed.

Now.

She leaned forwards into the moment of confusion, elbowing Boda. The cart lurched through the gap.

They would let her go. They must. They were used to her going out to gather wood for her fires, and the plain goldsmith's wench and the half-wild boy held no more charm than the snows of Sol-month.

She got inside the gates. No one yelled. No one followed. She made Boda pull the cart to a halt in the blackness on the far side of her own small bower. *Bower.* A tumbledown hut no one else would live in: one room divided into two by a rotting wooden partition.

She would not have put swine in it for choice.

She and Boda unloaded the cart in the dark. She thought Boda's resentment would strike sparks through the hissing bleakness of the rain.

They put him beside the fire. She straightened her back. She had one panful of hot water and the last of the nettle soap.

She thought he would die.

"Will you stay and help me?"

"Reckon I have done more than enough already."

Boda glared, hunched up against the cracked door timbers like a savage animal poised for flight. There was silence.

She nodded. Then she turned away and knelt down in the rushes. She would manage alone.

Where did she start?

She stared at the cold, dead-white skin, the darkness of the rough-spiked beard, the stark lines that made up the face of a warrior. She could see the power in him so clearly, it seared through her bones.

She hated that. She hated what she was doing. She was supposed to be the clever one. But this time Boda had the right of it.

The silence of the small hut closed round her, filled with coldness and shadows different from the bated pulsing quietness of the forest. That had been life held back, waiting. This was empty. Like her world. Something that would freeze out the force of life.

By the saints. She would not let it.

She reached out. Fire crackled behind her, flames

sending light shooting up the rough wattle walls. Her head whipped round.

Boda dropped more wood on the fire.

"Suppose I had better help you with him. He might come round. Happen you could want another man here then."

Her tired muscles tensed. Such a thought had not occurred to her. At least, not in that way. What she had felt, the burgeoning, frightening heat inside her when she looked at the man, when he had spoken, had seemed quite a different kind of danger. Something that came from inside herself as much as from him.

But Boda was right. The strength in the body she touched, the limbs that made up the deadweight she and Boda had carried into her miserable hovel, were lethal.

She licked parched lips.

"He is too badly hurt."

"Mayhap."

"Then we shall have to see."

She closed her eyes for an instant against what she would see, and yet her mind shivered with the anticipation of it.

"Heat more water. He...he needs washing." She turned back to the mess. Her mouth tightened. "He needs help."

There was no one else to give it. Behind her, Boda shuffled his feet on the packed-earth floor.

"Fetch me some more water and some dry wood for the fire."

"Sure, are you?"

"I am."

The heavy feet moved towards the door. She heard the latch, felt the rush of cold, rain-laden air.

"Will you—will you light the torch before you go?"

The air swirled. Pitch hissed in the fire. Boda's shadow wavered and then light raced along the wall as he stuck the torch into the iron bracket. The flame trailed black smoke in the wind and then the door shut.

She was alone.

She did not know what to do. She had never undressed a man in her life. Her hands hovered over the unconscious form sprawled across her floor. She had never seen a creature like him.

No one could be an object of beauty smeared with dirt and dried blood, their body spilling out of muddied rags. Yet he was. Her eye had been trained to study beauty, to see how its lines would emerge from rough metal and uncut gems. She could see it now, even though she did not want to.

The thought of his beauty frightened her as much as his power. She reached up to adjust the torch in its holder. Her hand was shaking.

This was mad. The man was no more than she had described him to Boda, another human being in need. He could not make her so afraid and heated and... He did not even know she was here.

How could he have such power over her?

She closed her mind against the memory of his eyes

and how they had looked at her, how the very air at the forest's edge had pulsed with the aliveness of spring's new life, with the aliveness of *him*. Now the stark whiteness of his face beneath the dirt seemed to stand out so sharply. Suppose that life faded under the cold's malice while she hesitated?

She could not bear to be responsible for that. She seized the stranger's belt buckle.

Her hand brushed the taut flatness of his lower belly, her arm rested against the hard rise of his hip bone. She could sense the soft movement of his breathing.

She could not get the buckle undone.

She bit back a surge of hysterical laughter. Here she was, about to tear the clothes off the Lord of the Forest, Herne the Hunter, Frey the Prince of Spring and carnal concupiscence, and she could not get his belt undone.

She bit her lip and lowered her head for one dizzying moment against his disgusting tunic.

She could hear his heart beat, steady, firm and strong. Living. The pull of that pulsing life was shocking. She wanted to bury her head in the filthy material and let Boda's surly antagonism and the entire carousing herd of Vikings outside her door find their own road to the outer reaches of hell, or wherever else they would go. The urge was so strong it hurt.

She wanted to weep.

She wanted to pound her fists against the unwelcome stranger's beating heart and scream.

She wanted to lie here and sleep. Because the hard-earth, rush-covered floor and the man's body were the most comfortable place in the world.

She felt so weak.

Her breath surged. She could not remember the last time she had eaten properly. Neither could she remember the last time she had slept through a night. Because of all that depended on what she did. It was all her responsibility, just like the stranger's life, and she could not manage it.

The door slammed.

She raised her head.

Boda was staring at her, his arms full of wood. The stranger was still lying on the floor. She had her arms round him. Her breast pressed against his. Their breath matched.

"Stoke up the fire in the hearth, and then fetch some more water to heat. We will need it."

Boda kept staring at her. She did not have the strength to explain further, indeed she did not know how. After a long pause, he bent to set wood on the fire. Her fingers began the process of wrestling rain-swollen leather through an iron buckle.

The thin strap pulled against the stranger's wet woollen tunic, showing the contours she had touched, the flat tightness of his belly, the powerful flaring line of his chest.

She dropped the buckle as though the metal had scalded her.

"You are afraid." A bucket thudded to the floor beside her.

"No."

But she was. There was something in the very air around the stranger that affected her so. Something she could not define. She ripped the damp veil off her head, because the heat from the replenished fire was unbearable. The heavy mass of her hair slid forwards over her shoulders, falling, spilling across the stranger's chest. She stared at it, lying pale and fine-stranded against the mud and the wet darkness. Her father had said her hair was as fair as any thread he could spin out of gold.

He had been proud of his daughter. Once.

She shoved the hair behind her neck. She would cut it off, all of it, if such a thing would keep her safe in the vipers' nest outside her door.

"I could still get rid of him. Leave the body somewhere—"

"*What?*"

Boda shrugged. "No one would ever know. And he would not be telling any tales."

"No…" Her voice trailed off.

She shut her eyes. Her mind saw the Vikings outside the door and the impossible life-price she had to fashion before the moon waxed full and its owner came to claim it. The thought of everything that depended on what she did frightened the life out of her.

She could not take on this burden, as well.

"Gemma?"

It was a way out. *No one would ever know.* Boda was talking sense, and it was not just her life at stake.

Cold wetness and the roughness of coarse wool stung at her fingers. The stranger's tunic. She had no recollection of burying her hand in it. Her hand was fisted, white-knuckled and immovable.

She thought of how the stranger's hand had looked. Clamped like a fist, as though it belonged to someone driven beyond what it was possible to endure. But he had not given up.

"No. Get me some more water."

The slam of the door made the crumbling wattle walls shake.

She got the belt undone.

The man did not move. It was only she who started backwards like a scalded cat, choking on her own breath. There was no change in his breathing. At least, she did not think so. Her hand reached out to touch his chest, felt the gentle rise and fall of his breath. It was so smooth compared to when he had been conscious, watching her, trying with all that hard-locked strength to speak.

His face dreamed. He would not feel his hurts now. He would feel nothing. It was a blessing, such silence and such stillness, not feeling anything.

A release.

She could not find that now, even in sleep. Perhaps no one could in this wasted land. Her heart tightened.

"May you find healing and peace. May—" She

stopped. She was speaking her thoughts aloud, the way she did sometimes because she was so alone.

She took her hand off his softly breathing chest.

She had to get his clothes off.

She caught the fraying end of the belt and pulled. It stuck.

She slid one hand underneath the slight, springing curve at the small of the man's back. Wet wool filled her fingers, the material soaked through, freezing, and under it a sheet of muscle, thick and subtly flexed against her palm.

He weighed more than she would have thought possible. Certainly more than was reasonable for one man.

She pushed, hauling at the leather with her other hand. It came free. An absurd stab of triumph shot through her.

"Done," she said to the unconscious face.

She untied the laces at the neck of his tunic, peeling the wet material away from his skin. She tried not to stare at the shadowed hollow at the base of his throat, the firm rise of his collarbone. The neck of the tunic was torn, as though someone had tried to rip it away from his shoulders.

Or strangle him.

There were bruises darker than ripe sloe berries at the side of his throat.

A shudder started somewhere deep inside her and began radiating outwards.

"Who are you?"

The question burning her mind mirrored the very first words he had spoken to her, with those forest-deep eyes holding her trapped like some helpless creature in a snare. She had blurted out her name. But he had said nothing.

What was his truth?

He had wanted her to go away, but she had been foolhardy, nay, reckless enough to ignore that warning. If it had been such.

It was too late to heed the warning now. Her hands clenched on the wet wool until they hurt, until the coldness of it seeped into her bones.

The cold.

She pulled at the tunic with ruthless hands, yanking the torn and muddied wool high over his head, trying to work it up under the weight of his body. His arm got stuck. She pulled at it. Even the arm seemed to weigh as much as a tree trunk and to be just as unwieldy.

She got the cuff over his hand. Almost. She pulled. It gave. His elbow hit the wall of the cramped room with a thud she could feel as much as hear. She winced. Suppose she had added to his collection of bruises?

She eased the tunic very carefully over his head. That, at least, was easier. Because of the torn neckline. The legacy of whichever kind soul had tried to strangle him.

"So that much is done. Now—"

She did not want to look at what she had uncovered. She did not want to know or see anything of him.

He had body hair on his chest.

In the firelight it seemed made of the deepest, darkest gold imaginable, like the thread that was created by the nearest thing to magic: the melding of fire and the most precious of metals.

It dusted lightly over the surface of his skin, blossoming out across his chest below the collar bone, narrowing down the flat line of his abdomen to plunge below the waistline of his trousers.

She touched it, that coiling dark-gold thread, and its human strength sprang back against her hand. Because it was alive and…and virile, not some cunning mechanical creation of the artificer's *cræft*. Like him. A breathing world-creature. Real.

Male.

Her hand flattened out, feeling both the soft-roughness of the fine-woven hair and the smooth skin. Her fingers slid over the hardness of ribs beneath, over the taut curve of muscular flesh. The dark bead of one tight nipple brushed against her palm.

Her teeth clamped on her lip to stop the scream caused by the power of the feeling inside her. It was the spell she had seen in the deepness of his eyes, in the light of the forest. It had a life of its own and it had taken her, like a spear thrust.

She snatched her hand away, doubling over and gasping as though truly pierced through with the spear's point. A faint moan escaped her lips and she staggered to her feet, backing away as though the unconscious man could touch her, drag her off into some primeval fastness of the wood and have the soul out of her.

CHAPTER TWO

She was by the door when it banged open to admit Boda carrying buckets.

She stared at him as though he were something from the Otherworld. His hard-boned face scowled with temper and his copper-brown hair bristled. He set the buckets of water down with a thud. One of them steamed.

She did not know how he had managed to find such a precious commodity as more hot water. But that was Boda. She did not know the half of what he did or where he went. It was best not to know.

"Thank you."

She got that strange look of his, the one that was almost hungry. Perhaps for all the things Boda had never had in his life, like the common human exchange of small courtesy. And kinship.

"We have to help him," she said. She never knew what Boda thought. "It is not right to leave a person to die."

Boda grunted. Boda, quite probably, thought nothing.

She knelt down again. It was not high charity. It was

weariness. To her surprise, Boda thumped down on the other side of the unconscious man, extending one grubby finger like the child he still was to poke at an equally grubby shoulder.

There was no reaction.

"Ought to be dead," said Boda, "if he is that wet and cold. Wonder why he is not?"

She suppressed the faint glimmer of a smile.

"It cannot be his fate." *Or perhaps he would not allow it.*

Boda's thick fingers straightened an outstretched knee.

"Looks bad, that."

Her gaze was drawn to the long arcing line of the cut, swollen and ugly and crusted with blood. It looked worse than bad. It looked sickening and painful. Shame rose in her like bile. So much for the Good Samaritan. So far she had had more in common with Jezebel.

She and Boda worked together. She did not ask why he had decided to help her. She was just grateful that he had. They worked in silence. Boda managed to lift the body to get the trousers off. She tried not to look any more than she must. She tried to concentrate only on what she had to do. But whatever she tried, it availed nothing.

The stranger was as beautiful as she had known he would be. The mud and the bruising and the cut made no difference. Whatever there was of him, whatever quality was in him, in the shape of his flesh and beyond it, affected her like a spell.

"Wolf's head," muttered Boda.

But trying to pretend that the man was some brute felon left by the wayside, some lifelong vagabond or outlaw, was like trying to pretend the sun was a candle flame.

All the dirt washed off. She could not even feign surprise. It was not the ingrained dirt of someone who had known nothing beyond the forest's fastness all his life. It soaked away, and all that was left was the glowing wealth of his skin. And hardened muscle.

She had not been wrong. The muscles in his arms and his back stood out like cords. He was bigger than Heremod, who had been King Burgred's champion swordsman. The damaged thigh was thickened with saddle muscles. His hands were callused across the palms. She would swear that was from gripping a sword hilt, not a plow handle. There were little purple and silver nicks across the knuckles that came from constant fighting.

He was a warrior.

She had no time for warriors.

He was not Danish.

What in heaven's name was he doing here?

She stared at the face that was now becoming visible. They had decided the beard was beyond saving. Boda was shaving it off. But she had rebelled when Boda had wanted to chop off the tangled hair that slid across the naked shoulders. It was too rich. The color, under all that mud, turned out to be nut-brown with red lights. Stronger than a hazelnut. Deeper than an acorn. Like the fruit of a chestnut tree. A forest color.

The face that was emerging from Boda's ministrations promised to be as arresting as the body. She caught a glimpse of high cheekbones, a wide jaw. She looked away.

The injured leg concerned her. The other injuries, and they were plentiful, were just on the surface, the kind that would heal with rest and good fortune. But the cut… It was not as deep as she had feared, but it was long and snaking.

She had applied herbs: agrimony, garlic and elderflower in a salve of her own. She was binding it with clean cloths. Her hands were shaking. She wanted to tell herself that it was from the pure and anxious concern of a healer. It was not. Although that was there, too.

She had to face the truth that she wanted this exotic and frightening stranger to live. She wanted it with a force that unnerved her, as though the danger he might bring meant nothing by comparison.

Such danger. She knew what it meant. So did Boda.

The strips of clean linen slid through her fingers. She hated wounds.

"Will be the death of him, that," predicted Boda with a certain savage satisfaction.

Yet his eyes watched what she did and she could sense the boyish fascination with something as heroic as a battle wound.

Dangerous stupidity.

She yanked at the bandages.

She had set her back to all the violence and misery that was inflicted on her country in unending waves. It was something she could do nothing about. It was foreign to her nature, utterly senseless. She could not understand how there could be such ugliness in the world when there should be so much beauty.

That was the only thing that made sense to her: creating beauty, a beauty that lasted many lives of men, a beauty fashioned out of metal and precious stones. It feasted the eye and ravished the touch and was imperishable. And incorruptible. Unlike men. Warriors. People who came and destroyed the innocent because they knew they were stronger.

There was naught she could do to turn back the tide. There had been naught that King Burgred and his entire army of arrogant thanes had been able to do.

She tried to get her unsteady fingers under control.

This stranger would be no better. The beauty of his form was a lure and his strength was nothing but a trap. She knew that from experience, from…she would not think of the past that had torn her family apart.

This man would be what he was: strong, willful, mood-proud and eager for gain.

She did not understand how the kind of mortal, untrustworthy beauty that was in him could affect her so.

It was something she had never experienced. It brought an inner terror because of its power. She felt as if giving in to that power might unlock some masterless unknown need inside her that would have no limit.

Her face burned. She hoped Boda could not see it.

Her reaction to the stranger's nakedness was something she was ashamed of. It had made her behave badly, and for all the man's formidable strength, at this moment he had no defense.

He did not know what she did, or that the savagely fine curve of his thigh, the dense, foreignly masculine arrangement of his hips made the heat glow inside her and the sharp claws of hungry need score through her.

Her breath came hard and her painfully inept fingers fumbled over the linen strapping.

She was never clumsy.

Her wrist twisted. The side of her hand touched… touched that darker, denser hair that shadowed the heavy thickness of his sex. She tightened. Her whole body ached, as though it strained helplessly for… She did not know, *could* not. Because she had never known a man.

She had never wanted to. Her father had not given her into wedlock at fifteen winters to become the property of some preening dolt, some vain profligate's bed-servant.

He had not wished that fate on her. He had wanted something better for her. He had kept her safe and taught her all the secrets of his craft. She had followed the interests of the mind. At twenty winters, her skill, her knowledge as a goldsmith, were matchless, because she had dedicated herself to it. The needs of the flesh had not mattered.

A drug for fools. That was what her father had said.

He had been right. She swallowed, blocked down memories.

She would not look at the stranger, at his maleness, the shape of him, the way the thigh under her hand swelled into the densely fashioned curve of his buttock beneath, the tight-stretched hip bones above. Most of all, she would not look at his naked sex.

Because if she did, the wanting in her body, worse still, the wanting in her mind, would fashion knowledge that she did not have. Of what all that carefully placed symmetry could do. Of what it would be like to know that body completely in the most fundamental way of men and women. How it would be to feel the power of what she had despised, know the magic that lived in the unknown man; the magic she had seen not just in his body but in his eyes.

She would not be able to bear that. She would be overwhelmed by it, enslaved to its treacherous spell, just like—

She pulled away. The last knot in the bandage locked tight under her shaking fingers. She stumbled to her feet, desperate to flee, unable to move. Her gaze watched the rich body, the brilliant lines of the clean-shaven face in the torchlight.

"Holy saints—"

"What?" Boda looked up, the sharp-edged shaving blade in his fingers. "What is it?"

He stared from her face to the stranger's face under his hand. "Do you…do you know him?"

She pressed herself flat against the wall. The torch-light flickered in the air currents from the roof-hole over the fire pit. Light and shadows fled and reformed over the dreaming, unconscious stranger's face.

"No. I do not know him."

The likeness was an illusion, a trick of firelight and fine lines. This man was different. Too young. The shock had come from memory.

"Oh," said Boda in disappointment. "I thought may-hap he was some famous warrior you could get a ran-som for."

A warrior with blood on his hands and a face to be-guile women who—

"No."

"Or—"

"*No.*"

"Or someone you knew," persisted Boda, who was born to be hanged.

She thrust the memory of Lyfing aside. She turned her face away from Boda's narrowed suspicious eyes, from the stranger who had no right to such beauty, to such power over her and all that she was.

"I could still drag him outside, leave him…."

Yes. Yes, yes, yes.

She turned round before she could say it. She walked away towards the hearth.

Boda could finish off now that he was done with shaving the stranger's face. He would know what to do. Indeed, there was nothing left to do.

Her breath came in uneven gasps that both frightened her and wounded her pride. What had happened to her? How could this dirt-streaked forest-creature, this false warrior, this wolf in rags, have done this to her?

He was naught but a man. An unconscious man, a helpless man.

A man who was not able to do any miserable thing at all.

She turned back.

"Gemma?"

For answer, she snatched the soapy blade waved around the stranger's face in a way that was likely to cut off the disputed hair after all. Or perhaps an ear.

"I will wash the blade." Her voice was quite steady. She looked down. Two ears still, a nose, lips. Eyelashes... That the unknown face was as fine as the body seemed like a deliberate insult. Or perhaps it was justice for all her vile imaginings. She set her teeth.

"You...you take him to..." Well, there was no choice in this cramped apology for a bower. She had known that all along. "Put him in my bed. Carefully."

"What?"

"You heard. He is ill. There is nowhere else. Besides," she added, feeling the heat flushing her face, "I will not be there. I will spend the night in here, beside the hearth."

She should not have to explain so much, not to a mere boy. Or if she did, it should not embarrass her. Boda was simply voicing what he saw as the obvious. Boda was good at that. He was very basic.

Perhaps, when it came down to it, she was, too.

She could not stand that possibility. She bent down over the stranger who had a false likeness to someone else. She twitched the edge of the sheet over his unconscious form to cover it. Pathetic gesture. But it seemed like some sort of reparation for the dubious way she had handled him, for her thoughts.

Boda took the weight of the body. She took the feet, decorously wrapped in linen. She could not feel his flesh. She did not want to. Boda dumped the burden in her rickety bed.

She turned away to look for the precious amber bead in her treasure box to put under the bolster. It would charm the stranger's recovery as much as the herbal salve. That is, if you were foolish enough to believe such things.

She hesitated over a fox's tooth. She did not like it. But then it might be appropriate for him, something from a forest creature.

She shoved them both under the pillow. Over the bed was a wooden cross. The influence of that was greater than anything.

She pulled the covers up round his shoulders. There was nothing more she could do.

Boda gave the unknown warrior one last baleful look.

"I shall be around the camp," he said with immense dignity. "I will hear if you scream."

That was a comfort.

She shut the bedchamber door on its dangerous contents. There was a lot of clearing up to do in the other room. Boda left without a word. Clearing up was women's work, and besides, the lure of the night doubtless called him to whatever it was he did in the hours of darkness.

She took her time. But one could not leave an injured man alone forever. She doubted he was conscious. She had not heard him stir. Yet she hesitated with her hand on the door latch.

She was not a coward.

She flung the door back and marched in. Into *her* room.

She looked across at the bed. It was the one item of relative comfort in her appalling hut. Her back ached and her eyes burned with tiredness. She had never felt more like sinking onto the straw mattress, dragging the covers over her head and never coming out again.

Fine chance.

Unless she wanted to share. She stalked farther into the bedchamber.

Did there have to be so much of him?

She sank down on the wall bench beside the bed and turned her head away.

Now what?

She got up and checked the ancient brazier. It was hot. Really hot. She shoved her finger in a bowl of cold water and swore.

She sat down again.

The hair Boda had wanted to chop off really was a mess.

But even that could not detract.

"Do you have to be so very—" She could not find the word.

She glared.

Perhaps she should have let Boda cut the hair off. It might be alive with something.

She knew it was not. She had washed it. Just as she had washed…everything. She got up and slammed her fist into her palm.

"Ouch."

She searched for her gilded comb in the carved oak chest that had once been stuffed with such trinkets, and fine clothes, and… She had one more underdress and tunic as shabby as those she now wore, and a spare pair of shoes. Broken.

She slammed the lid.

She sat down again. She was not going to comb that disgusting mess. A bird's nest would be in a better state.

It felt like silk thread, despite the tangles, and she could smell the clean tang of the chamomile she had used in the rinsing water.

The hair coiled round her fingers. It could not do that since he had not moved his head. But it did. The snarls unfolded under her hands' skill. She had learned that deftness over years. But she had never used it on anything living.

"What a waste."

She had not said that. She could not feel the barren strands of her artificer's life unraveling with the whisper of each magic thread across her skin. Such a thing was not possible. She would not think it. Her life had been exactly what she had wanted, what her father had trained her for in the high and ingenious mechanical arts. It was a calling. Not some ordinary, pathetic life dependent on another's whim.

Her clever fingers trembled under the weight of living silken threads.

There was no one left now to wear her ingenious creations, her thick torqued arm rings, and her brooches so delicate they seemed made of gossamer. None save the Danes.

Her father would have said it hardly mattered, that the purpose lay in the creation itself, not in the human frailness that borrowed its unquenchable lustre for a short life span.

But…but suppose that was not true? Suppose… What she wanted was to have her little brother with her once more. Safe at her side, under her protection, never to leave her again.

What she wanted was a person to love, not a thing.

What she wanted was someone she could talk to, another adult who knew how to answer when she spoke. Someone who would share the burden.

She could feel silk threads under her cheek. She could feel skin. She had no recollection of burying her face in the stranger's hair. His skin was freezing. Still.

Despite the heat of the brazier, despite all the covers she had that could be put on the bed, even her cloak.

As cold and beautiful as a statue made out of gold. But he was not some empty creation of mechanical art. He was real. Just as she was.

He was so cold, as cold as her heart felt. The thought frightened her. A heart should not feel that cold. A person should not. That was death-cold.

She would not allow it.

There was no one to see, no one to know what she did, least of all the man in the bed.

Sitting up, she undid her girdle and dragged off her tunic and her patched stockings. Leaving her underkirtle on, she slid under the covers.

She was moon-mad, of course. She was shaking, so hard it could not only be from the cold. She did not dare to touch him, only the very edge of his hair spread out against the bolster. But he would feel her warmth, in the bed. It was there and it would reach out to him and he would no longer be so cold.

She could not stop trembling. She curled up into a ball, like a small child. Her foot touched him. She nearly shrieked. But nothing happened.

He could not harm her, her dangerous stranger. He was lost, struggling in his dream world of illness and pain.

He was alone.

She crept across the bed.

The fullness of his body in her arms glutted sense. Her head swam and her body cleaved to his glorious nakedness through the coarse barrier of her dress. She could feel through the darned and mended linen, through the pores of her skin, every nuance of the shape she had tended beside her fire.

Her body fitted against it like something fashioned for the purpose, as though she had been meant to be the counterpart to each strong line, each lithe mysterious hollow.

His flesh filled her hands, dense, rich, fiercely curved and angled, so strong.

So very close to death.

"I could not have left you," she said to that forcefully muscled skin, the smooth sweep of his hair.

"Just as I cannot let you die." Her voice faded to a whisper that choked her throat.

Outside, she could hear the keening of the rising wind, its icy death-cold breath finding every chink, every gap in the poorly built walls. Winter's malice. Even more terrifying were the yells of the Vikings in the hall.

Her hands tightened. Her body pressed itself harder against his, as though she could make its small animal warmth flow into him.

"You will not die." She clung, her body rocking against his and her words whispering against his hair.

Shadows raced across their heads where the single rush-light flickered, and she did not know whether she gave comfort to the stranger or took it.

SHE HAD HAIR the color of purest gold, deep and rich and abundant. He had known she would have. Just by the shape and the color of her eyebrows.

He could not move because of the pain. All he could do was look at her.

She was a beauty. No, not that. She was something much more dangerous, this woman who had appeared like part of a dream.

She was fascinating.

He had known that, too, deep inside him, from the first moment of seeing her. It had been a pointless ruse on her part, trying to hide such a quality under rags and a hideous veil.

She was real, not part of the feverish madness brought on by wounds. Gemma, the bright jewel, was real. He could sense the warm curving weight of her against his skin, smell her sweet scent: warm, bed-scented woman. The scent that would drive a man mad.

He watched her and sensed all that she was.

Gleaming hair spread in undulating waves across his chest. One of her hands lay on his leg. The other was buried in the curve of his neck. She breathed very softly and the fine sinuous length of her body curved around him as though it was meant to. Because it fitted him, just as he had known it would from the first blinding sight of her. Even the coarse dress she wore under the bedcovers could not stop him from feeling every richly female curve of her.

He knew so cursed much, but what he did not know was what he was doing in her bed.

His lips twitched.

Under other circumstances the answer to that would have been obvious, *was* obvious. If she moved the delicate warmth of her hand one span farther over, she would have the proof: that his blood heated from her, despite wounds and exhaustion and the crippling force of pain. The thought of that fine, slender hand touching white-hot, already engorged flesh hardened him further.

His throat tightened and the searing bolt of need, burning like flame, striking like lightning, cut through muscle and bone.

More than he could bear. The depth of his anger at that took his hard-won breath, shocking by its force.

He controlled both, the lust and the rage.

Control was something he had learned the hard way, in a life where every move he made was examined and judged.

His own judgments were made alone.

Fairness told him that the woman had saved his life. Yet there was an edge of witchery in her beguilement, something that pulled on the tangled web of fate and he would not have that.

He belonged to no one. For him it was not fitting.

He shifted his weight against the straw mattress. Pain stabbed at him, bringing the edge of death's blackness.

The woman should not have taken him from the forest. He had told her so. That was the only thing that mattered. He could bring nothing but danger to her, to anyone.

He bit back the fierce, unexpected spurt of desolation that thought caused. There were things to be done.

He turned his head and the hand lodged in the curve of his neck brushed against his skin, causing jolts of aching sensation.

His skin.

She had shaved off his beard. He fought the urge to curse and swear like a madman. She had taken whatever chance he had had of blending into the Viking war band. A clean-shaven Dane did not exist.

Why would she have done such a thing? What game did she think she was playing? Her body wound round him in its open and heated seduction, trapping him with its subtle, seemingly helpless curves as surely as iron bands. He was naked in her bed, with no memory of how he had got there and no knowledge of what she had done.

He moved. But he must have been too abrupt because the pain splintered into light and then there was darkness, like the pit of hell.

SHE SHOOK HIM out of it. Her hands scrabbled at his shoulders, nails raking at his skin. Her face, bent over his, was terrified.

She was still lying in the bed with him. Behind her shoulder was the well-grown youth who had been with her in the forest. Behind him was a Viking *hersir*.

Everything slotted into perfect hard-edged clarity, the way it did before battle. Fatigue, pain, the appalling lack of information he had, were all forced aside by the need for thought. His mind assessed every possible makeshift weapon in the pitifully furnished room, the way out for the woman, the sounds outside the thin walls, the light. He caught hold of her arm because she seemed to need that. He willed her to wait, to see.

The next move had to be the Viking's.

He watched the man's bloodshot gray eyes narrow. But the expected assessment of him was blunted by— what? A night's carousing? Probably. But something else. There was suspicion, quick and uncertain temper, but—not enough surprise.

It was not entirely unlikely then, that the woman would have someone in her bed.

He beat back the primitive bolt of feeling, of anger, of *possession*, that tore through him. It was something utterly irrelevant, out of place. There was time only for thought, not the misplaced instincts of some stag in the rut.

The woman was not his. He did not want her to be.

But there was an unsuppressible feeling of claim as he slid one naked arm around her slender shoulders. His grip must have felt more like a jailer's than a lover's. But he did not know how she would react, and the wildly out-of-place instincts were still there. The challenge in his eyes as he stared at the *hersir* was far greater than he had intended.

He would not back down.

He could not stomach anyone's terror in the face of the Danes. This woman's struck through bone. He would allow no one to touch her, even at the price of his life. There was no way she could know that, yet she sank back against his shoulder, as though it were a ref-

uge. Her face turned towards him and the heavy eyelashes fluttered against his skin as though she would
swoon.

The Viking warrior glared. His hand rested on the
hilt of a *long-sax*. The woman clutched the bedclothes
round her.

"That is him?" The English was poor, heavily accented. Perfectly comprehensible to him. It was exactly
how he had spoken. Once. He would never be free of
the memory of that.

"Not what I was expecting."

The shock was raw, though it should not have been.
The witch had betrayed him after all, taken him into her
bed and then she and the youth she ran with had sent
for this creature. He wondered how much she got paid.
And in what kind.

The woman's blue eyes stared at him in a kind of
entreaty.

The warrior shifted his weight, the decorated wooden
scabbard nudging against his leg. He would have preferred most weapons over a *long-sax*, even a sword. But
the chance was there, always, and that was what he lived
by. One thing alone was certain for him and the Viking:
only one of them would leave the room with his life.

"So that is him?"

There was more impatience, this time. The woman's
full, curving lips, softened and blurred with her sleep
and the shared warmth of their bed, formed the answer.

"Aye."

Her hands still clutched at him beneath the bedcovers, but her small strength would be no impediment at all.

The *hersir*'s fist dropped away from the hilt of the three-foot-long single-edged blade. He crossed his arms over the width of his chest, slid one booted foot in front of the other and leaned back against the door frame. A stance from which a moderately nimble three-year-old could have knocked him over.

"So you are the smith who is going to do the work for me. You took your time."

CHAPTER THREE

THE MAN WOULD deny it.

Gemma knew it with every breath in her body and every petrified beat of her heart. She was touching him and she could feel each tensed muscle, sense the raw energy that fed all that strength, gathered, leashed in. At any moment it would break free.

The man was a warrior. Warriors were not capable of thought. He would attack the Viking and they would all be killed. Even if a naked, unarmed man could possibly win, the noise would bring an entire army down on their heads. He did not know they were in the middle of a Viking encampment.

She had committed the foolhardy indiscretion of oversleeping, sleeping with a man in her bed. And now Erik was here, in her chamber, a place he never came. She was lost.

The man.

Her hands scrabbled uselessly at bruised and hardened muscle. Her eyes beseeched him, but she could see nothing in the green eyes but the glaze of a terrifying heat. Anger leached from him in waves. He did not understand anything. There was no way that he could, and she could not tell him.

Over by the door, the foul creature they called Erik Bonebreaker stared: at her, at the molten volcano in her bed.

"You had better be worthy of your trade."

The molten green eyes did not so much as flicker.

"You may believe it."

She swooned.

Nay, she did not. It was just the dizziness in her head and the closeness of so much furious, uncomprehending, thick-skulled…quick-witted maleness. He still had his arms round her. Probably because he wanted to kill her, as well. She could feel so much of his hot, hard-muscled body that her senses started to swim again. Her head seemed jammed against his shoulder. She could not move.

He did.

She grabbed at the bedclothes so that Erik would not see she still had her dress on, and clung to the terrifying form of the shape-shifting goldsmith because there was no other choice.

Erik laughed. The warrior-goldsmith in her bed smiled. It did not change either man's eyes.

"Then it will do no harm for me to expect miracles. I want the work finished inside two weeks. Before its owner gets here. Let us hope you are as good at smithing as you are at…" The rest of the words were in Danish, but the meaning was universal.

Erik's avaricious gaze, tinged with a new interest, slid over her. Then clashed with green fire. The heat of that took the breath from her lungs. But then Erik was gone, his heavy-booted feet beating against the earthen floor. Boda went after him.

Boda had looked at her as though she were indeed a lust-hungry Jezebel.

The door slammed.

Fast as thought, she levered herself away from the molten maleness in her bed. He would not let her. A small scream gathered at the back of her throat. Never had she been in such an intimate, vulnerable, utterly terrifying position with a man.

"Let me go."

"Why? I thought we were lovers."

His body covered her. Most of the bedclothes had slid down in their brief struggle. She could see the long, angled lines of him, the thickness of his muscles, the scattering of dark-springing body hair that had wreaked such havoc with her yesterday. She could see the bruises that came from fighting. She could see the heat in his eyes. It was in him, everywhere, where yesterday there had only been coldness.

She could feel him.

"Let me go."

"It is too late for that now. It is you who should have let me go yesterday beside the forest. I tried to tell you and yet you did not. Why?"

She stared at his face. It was just as handsome as it

had been last night when it had emerged from the dirt and the blood and the matted beard. The beauty was still there, all of it. What she had not counted on was the ruthlessness. That came from the spirit, from what lived inside him.

How could she say to that face that she had pitied him, that she had been afraid for him? That she had believed he needed her help? She should have known what he was, that he did not need her. The sight of that broad hand clamped round the tree root as though it would drag his body forwards should have told her.

"I made a mistake."

"Aye. A bigger one than you realize."

Her breath came in quick, unsteady gasps. His matched it. His hands gripped her shoulders and the lithe, lethal weight of his body uncoiled over hers, a heavy sinuous arcing line holding her down, trapping her.

"If you harm me, I will scream. Boda will come."

His eyes told her that neither Boda, nor the whole Viking encampment would avail her against this man's will.

She would not allow him to take her. She would kill him first. Or herself. Her muscles tensed. Her eyes narrowed and became sharply focused. Her heart beat hard, and then she felt the blood, through the inept bandages she had wound round his leg, through the rumpled linen of her dress.

His eyes held her and she stared straight into them.

"You might have died but for me."

"So might you, just now."

There was a silence so heated that she could not breathe through it. All she could feel was the press of his body. The press of his mind. That was worse, the power of that quick-thinking mind that had deceived Erik with such rapid and dangerous ease. His mind wanted the truth out of her.

"Why did you do it?"

His voice was rough, deep. The air of her small, cramped room became very still, heavy, tingling with the power that had been under the forest's eaves.

Neither of them moved. She stopped trying to evade him. There was no sound except for the ragged pain of his breathing. She thought she could see all that pain reflected in his eyes, and then she thought that the pain was something different, something of the spirit.

She could feel the warmth of his blood.

"I did not want you to die."

He placed her back against the moth-eaten bolster. His hands were very gentle. She had not guessed they could be gentle. She stared at them. Her gaze took in the recent scratches and the scars of the small cuts that must go back to the very start of his manhood: wielding a sword with which to kill people.

Or defend them.

"Why did *you* do it?"

His head was buried in the bolster beside her, face-down. All she could see was the vibrant hair still tangled from sleep. The silence stretched out and she was frightened. Perhaps he had swooned because of the wounds and the pain and all the blood. She touched his hair. He started as though she had hit him.

"Why?" she said, when she had not meant to say that at all. If she could just see his eyes, she would know. If he would just look at her. The formidable shoulders under her forearm bunched. He raised his head.

"What is done is done. I will get you out of this disaster if I can. But do not seek to know who I am, or what I do here. That is the only thing I will ask of you." His eyes were utterly blank, shuttered from her with a darkness that cut out light. She watched him take the breath to speak.

"You have my word, such as it is." The fine lips twisted in the bruised face. "I have naught else to give."

She lay in the bed beside him. He breathed like a savage, he was marked like one. She thought he was quite capable of being one.

She thought of her brother, Edgefrith. She thought of the deception she had started with Erik. She thought of all that depended on her and the terrifying nature of her vulnerability.

Then she was not thinking of that at all. She was thinking of what she had seen in the depths of his eyes.

"I accept."

"YOU HAD BETTER tell me who I am supposed to be."

It was not a reassuring beginning to a partnership in crime with a desperate outlaw.

She was dealing with the leg wound. This time, she had the desperate criminal decently covered with the bedclothes but it hardly seemed to help. She had to hitch herself onto the edge of the bed beside him in order to get close enough. The only thought in her brain was that somehow she had to get out of the bed before she told him who he was.

The covers slipped.

"Will you hold still? You only have to pretend that you are the smith. You do not actually have to do the work, just make it look as though you are."

The covers slipped farther. She swallowed a certain dizziness. It came from hunger and tiredness and…no other cause at all. She tried glancing away, to get her breath back.

He had very fine knees. She blinked. Scratched, of course.

"Perhaps you could tell me your name," she said. "If that is not one of the forbidden questions?"

"Ash."

She should have expected it. A forest creation. The tree that produced the strong, straight wood used for spears, or the shafts of battle axes. It was also the most beautiful of trees and full of magic, a connection to mysterious worlds. Her hand slipped.

"Ah."

She gritted her teeth. So did he.

"I am sorry."

"Think nothing of it. It is only a leg." *Only* did not apply to his legs. "I will still be able to hammer plowshares and remove horseshoes and…accomplish other things."

Other things. She swallowed.

"No one is going to ask you to hammer plowshares," she snarled.

"No? I thought you had been bedding the blacksmith and I was the substitute."

"You thought *what?*"

She fought to steady her hand.

"I said I thought you had been—"

"Yes. All right. I heard what you said and what you thought. I just did not believe it."

"No? You mean you have drawn me into this web of deceit with false inducements? I am not to replace your bed-companion after all?"

She breathed through flared nostrils and refused to blush scarlet. She refused to even consider how it might be to have a bed-companion like him. She refused to be angered in the slightest over the fact that he thought she was a trollop and a *hor-cewn.*

"I am not bedding the blacksmith," she yelled.

She thought the breath tore at his throat. His skin gleamed with the faint sheen of sweat.

"I—I am sorry," she forced out, because she had made even him flinch. She loosened her grip on the mangled flesh.

He did not scream. He did not make the slightest sound apart from the deepening of his breath. She found that rather frightening.

"Then who are you bedding?"

His eyes were narrowed like slits of green fire.

"That is none of your business," she snapped. Because she was not going to admit to this man that she still had her maidenhead. That she knew less than nothing about bed sport and the kind of dark, earthy carnality that seeped from his sweat-sheened skin and his narrow-slitted eyes in waves.

"So I could be anyone?"

"Aye," she said, meeting that green flame with a fire of her own. "You could be anyone I choose. But as it happens, the Viking believes you are my husband. It will be all over Offleah by now."

She really had hurt him. She could hear the intake of his breath hiss like a deadly snake's.

"I'm sor-"

"*Offleah?*" His voice cut as sharply as the blade that had marred his flesh.

"Aye," she said, and the rest of the words came tumbling out of her under the force of the tension she could feel in his corded muscles and the brightness of his eyes.

"I told the Viking that I had a husband in order to keep him away from me. He will not be here long, so I thought he need never know the truth. Or that I could get away from here. But I did not manage to get away and now—now I cannot." Some remnant of self-preservation left under that terrifying gaze made her stop before too much of the dangerous truth came out.

"He believed me but I—I have to fulfill all the work he wants done." She paused, thinking of Erik Bonebreaker's commission and the complexity of it. She took a breath.

"I can do the work and I will." Her spine tensed. "I tell you now, that there is no power on earth that will stop me."

The words were fine. She meant them. But the brightness of his gaze made her feel lost.

She would not give in.

"I shall do what I must. But…but the Viking would not believe that a woman could accomplish the work he wishes and you…my husband…*you* are not some bull-brained blacksmith shoeing horses and beating plowshares."

She took a breath and said it.

"You are a goldsmith."

THE FEMALE VOLUPTUARY was gone.

Ashbeorn the Goldsmith stared up at the roof of her bedchamber and tried breathing through the red-tinged mist.

Offleah. He did not believe it.

He shut his eyes against pain and the wavering view of a badly thatched roof. But that was worse because then he could see the all the dead faces of the Wessex border patrol around him, the staring eyes and the wide-stretched mouths. The Vikings had known just where to find them.

His eyes stared behind closed lids and his nostrils filled with the tang of wet earth, as though it were there, under his face, his hands, the rich life of it slick and tainted with blood. The dead men's blood. And his.

The mud slid under his grasping hands and he was fallen, unable to gain his feet, the pain and the darkness claiming him.

But that had not been the end, even though the Danes had been victors. As he had moved, no more than half-conscious, the heavy weight of the betrayer had hit him, chain mail crushing his torn flesh, and the hands at his throat, choking breath.

The last word he had heard had not been Danish, but English.

He ripped his eyes open. But the dead faces were still there in front of his sight. They would not fade because they were unjust deaths. Treachery.

He knew all about betrayal. None better.

He swallowed bile and stared at the roof. But his mind went further back, to the full-scale disaster at Wilton.

No, not to that impossible battle fought against the combined might of two Viking armies, but to what had happened afterwards. To the fate of the one who had not escaped, who had been taken prisoner and then…butchered like a beast. His breath choked off in his chest.

It should not have been he who had survived the lost battle at Wilton and its consequences. He was not worth as much.

And yet even though he lived, that other death had taken its place deep inside him. It was not life that filled his mind but revenge. For treachery. On the man who had butchered his brother. On Erik. Erik the Bonebreaker.

He would find the man and vengeance would be his. He had sworn it. The breath filled his lungs with a gasp the goldsmith woman must have heard through the thin walls.

The present swam back into focus: the squalor of the Viking camp. It was an unlikely setting for the sense-ravishing Jewel-creature. She was a high-class artisan's wife—no, not wife. There had been no husband. That was a figment of her imagination.

So she said.

She said a lot of things, his Jewel-woman, and not just with words. His skin tightened from the remembered feel of her heated voluptuous curves spread out beneath him on the bed, open to the slightest move of his body.

Ashbeorn forced the thought aside. She was not *his* woman at all. The rutting stag feelings of this morning had no place in why he was here. Ending up in bed had just been…convenient for both of them. She apparently needed a husband and she had picked one up beside the road and dumped it in her bedchamber.

The husband she had chosen needed to be in the Viking encampment.

If she had saved him from death, it had been for his usefulness. If he had not betrayed her deception to the Viking, it had been to fulfill what he must do.

There could be nothing else.

He stared at the crumbling thatch in the empty room. But it no longer seemed empty, it seemed filled by fate. *Wyrd's* working and the power of things unseen.

Unseen. He sounded like the dark Briton who stood at the throne's back and saw things no mortal eyes could.

He stirred in the bed. He had to fulfill what he had sworn. Before he could think of personal vengeance. Or any other thing.

He had no right and no cause to think of any other thing. The heated temptation of the Jewel the Deceiver had no part in the rootless, shadowed half life that was his, the life of a damned spirit driven eternally onwards. No one could break that, least of all, him.

He slid out of the woman's bed.

An amber bead and a tooth fell out from under the bolster.

He was too tired to think about it.

He straightened. But as soon as his foot touched the floor the dizziness took him. The writhing darkness and the red edge of pain washed over him in waves.

SHE WOULD HAVE TO FEED him.

That was what was wrong. His injuries by themselves were not enough to hold him. He was already stirring back to consciousness as she and Boda maneuvered him back onto the mattress. He did not seem feverish, or only mildly so, and the wounds, both large and small, seemed clean.

But he had had only water and a herbal draught made with willow bark to sustain him since she had taken him in. True, he had not asked her for anything, but she found that restraint more nerve-racking than reassuring.

"Careful with him."

She saved the supple length of an arm from tangling with the wall bench. Boda shoved, anyway, nearly pitching her on top of her false husband.

Lover.

That was what Ash, the lord of the forest, had called it. The remembered deepness of that rough-smooth voice shivered her spine. *Lover.* She reached out with her other hand to steady herself. It touched flesh. Something sharp and demanding blossomed inside her, untried and waiting. For what?

She jerked herself upright, pulling away from nakedness, from the thick curve of a bare shoulder, the blatantly masculine scent of heavy skin.

Boda's feet shuffled behind her.

"I still do not see why you had to get into the bed with him last night. He is not your real husband."

The sinful need stabbed at her.

"I have told you."

But her explanation had hardly been convincing. She tightened her lips.

"Give me the bedclothes."

She grabbed the covers out of the boy's hand. She

wanted the stranger decently covered before those earthily vital brown-green eyes fixed on her, before—

"What are you doing?"

The voice was fathoms deep. Rough. Blackly and sinfully exciting.

She jumped, dragging the bedcovers over the most heatedly disturbing aspects of her new husband before he could realize that— The piercing, newly wakened eyes fixed on her. The blood left her veins. Nay, raced through each one of them, burning.

"Gemma?"

Who had given him such a voice? Dark as rich black loam, clear as stream water running over murmuring white stones. The sound made her so…angry. It was anger that made her glare with a viciousness that should have delighted the boy beside her.

"What you thought you were doing trying to get out of the bed was more to the point. You cannot walk yet."

The eyes of the man called Ash held hers. She could see all the way down through the sunlit woods to the clear, unyielding stones beneath. She was reminded that this was a man who had crawled across heaven knew how many miles of cold, wet ground because he could not walk.

There was silence, the assessing kind of silence that produced cold sweat. She tried straightening a piece of tattered wool around a thickly muscled rib cage. She avoided a bruise.

"I have made some food."

Its sense-dizzying aroma invaded the room: stew

made with the last small piece of bacon she owned. Probably the last meat she would have until Erik Bonebreaker paid her. She could scent it like a desperate hound on the track of its quarry. Her belly clenched. She suppressed the primitive urge to haul the pot from the fire in the next room and snap her jaws round the meager contents, savaging anyone or anything that got in her way.

She went and ladled out a small wooden bowl full of bacon stew. Boda followed. She usually fed him because he had no one and nothing. He snatched the bowl with a look that must be as wolfish as hers and dropped down beside the hearth to eat. Nay, gobble.

She got another bowl and went back into the bedchamber to feed the stranger. She sat on the wall bench and watched him eat.

The color came back to his face. She had not seen that before. It gave a finely shadowed depth to the fierce planes and angles. His eyes stayed just the same, as though their brilliance were something apart.

His hunger matched hers—nay, must be greater in its need because of the wounds to his body.

But he was not like Boda. He ate slowly. What he had was poor, not nearly enough. He asked for nothing more.

He had manners. Or a will fashioned out of steel. Neither possibility gave reassurance.

I will get you out of this disaster if I can. She did not know quite what that meant.

He set the bowl down.

But do not seek to know who I am, or what I do here.
"What are you doing?"

His question, not hers. She was not permitted to ask. She had her answer ready.

"I fashion fine things, jewelry, weapon fittings…"
And this other object of great price, the secret.

"For the Vikings. Out of what they have plundered?" Anger, fierce and undisguised, sharpened the beautiful voice.

"Aye." Her mouth hardened. She was alone. She had no one to help her. There was only herself. And Boda, the unruly dregs of the camp, who was more trouble than help. She had no proper food. She was giving away what little she had.

She had once had everything.

Before the fighting.

"What else would you have me do? Refuse what the Vikings ask, act as though I were some boastful, witless, self-absorbed warrior and get myself killed? It is the blind arrogance of warriors that began this strife, the same blind arrogance that now perpetuates it…."

Could he not see common sense? But she was watching his eyes and the words dried up.

She knew with sudden conviction that what he thought held none of the compromise she had had to adapt to. What he carried in his heart was not the burgeoning force of life as she had believed, but only finality of death. His eyes held it and in them she could see stone hardness, not the bright warmth of sunlight.

What kind of creature had she let into her house, her life?

No, not her life. Never. That was hers and hers alone.

"Let me make one thing clear, false smith." *False husband. Heart of stone.* "I have no interest in this war between Danes and Englishmen. Nothing in it was of my making. I have no part in it and I wish none. I do my work and that is all that matters to me. I do not expect you to understand that—"

"No."

Fury flared inside her and with it the crushing consciousness of all the burdens that had been set upon her unasked. She glared into the overbright eyes.

"Then you fulfill exactly what I expected of you."

But it was not true. He had only to look at her with those eyes and she expected all kinds of things that were impossible.

Things she did not want.

"My work is an act of creation," she insisted. "It does not depend on anything so pathetically frail and… corruptible as the flesh that wears it, or carries it. It has its own beauty and its own purpose. That is all that I care about—" She stopped, gasping after breath. She sounded like her father at his most fanatical. She sounded like a madwoman.

She sounded like a liar.

"All that you care about?"

"All." But her voice shook. She saw her father's face

bending over his work, the fierce light in his eyes, the beauty that took shape under his fingers.

She saw Edgefrith's eyes as they had looked in her last glimpse of them: terrified, begging her for help. She saw Boda scavenging for scraps round the camp, like an animal. In her mind's eye she could see all of Mercia laid out, mile after vulnerable mile, to the Viking hordes who would destroy it. To the north, Northumbria was conquered, to the south, only Wessex stayed free. And Wessex was isolated, vulnerable, its king young and desperate. But one year crowned.

Inside her heart was a smoldering anger she had not even known was there.

She blanked it out. She blanked the vision out. It was not her fault. And she had to survive. Everything depended on that.

Then she could see nothing except the stranger's face: the warm life mixed with the flint-hard stone.

"That is how things are," she said. "You had better get used to that if we are going to deal together."

She took a steadying breath. She could not afford to make a fatal misstep, not with this man. He had come to her out of the air at just the right time, but she could not forget how dangerous he was. They had an agreement. He had to hold to it.

"I will work for the Vikings as long as I have to. Soon they will be gone from this place, back to join the host in London." She took a sustaining breath. She thought of her brother. "But I will be here. I will be alive and I

will have my work. No one will be able to touch me or
what is mine again and I will not care who buys what I
create, Mercian lord or Dane."

She did not know why his eyes were so impossible
to look at.

"All you have to do for your life until that time comes
is let me do my work. Then you can go, and none will
be the wiser and nothing will have changed." *Nothing*.
It was what she repeated to herself every night. But she
could feel the familiar certainty slipping away from her
so that there was naught left to cling to. Her mind dizzied with a frightening emptiness.

She got to her feet. But that only made the dizziness
worse, physical, enough to make her sick except that
she had not eaten anything. She had to get out before
he noticed her weakness, took advantage of it.

"You had best think on what I have said. You had best
remember what lies outside these walls."

"That much I am not like to forget." The deep voice
held quietness and beneath it a relentless force that
could eat through steel.

She stumbled back into the main chamber. Boda had
eaten her food and gone. She was alone. She shut the door.

BUT BODA CAME BACK after a while. She heard the
scrape of a door latch, but she did not look up, because
she was trying not to weep.

She did not want to weep, particularly in front of
Boda, who was a child. She straightened up and tried

to pretend nothing was wrong. But she was sitting on the floor and even Boda must think that was odd.

He did. She could hear the hesitation in his heavy tread.

It was not possible yet to turn her head, but she steadied her voice and said, "It is all right. There is nothing to worry about." At least she had thought that her voice was steady.

But nothing was under control in her world. It was all beyond that. The stranger had made it so.

He could not. She would not let him. She tried again. "Boda? Wait—"

But he did not wait. He kept moving around. Shuffling. He would still be annoyed. Anxious. She gritted her teeth. She had to get her face straight. She had to look after him, the way she had always looked after Edgefrith. The shuffling approached her.

"Boda—"

She put a hand on the floor to lever herself up but there was a heavy thud beside her, as though he had sat down on the floor like her.

"This," said a voice like the deep living earth, "is the last of the food. For you."

She froze. She had her head turned away, but out of the corner of her eye she could see a bare foot, the edge of her own thick blue cloak…the one that had been on the bed. She looked at the foot again. It was large and clean and delightfully supple. She had washed it herself.

She could feel a rush of heat in the dead, cold air of the room.

"You cannot walk."

"So you keep saying. You are going to eat this while it is still hot."

"What—"

"—is it? Hard to say. In a former life it might have been bacon stew. You might have learned goldsmithing, but did no one teach you how to cook?"

"Of course I can cook. If I had the—" She stopped. He was goading her with his so carefully offhand comments. He had made her admit that she lacked the food to make even one meal palatable. It was deliberate. It was…clever. She looked up. Second mistake. Those bright, intelligent eyes were watching her.

He would see she had been appallingly close to crying.

His face, stark lines and smoky shadows in the gloom, was impassive. He held a wooden bowl. It steamed gently in the cold draught that came through the holes in the wall. She caught the scent. The last of what had been left in the cooking pot.

She shivered. Because of her hunger. Because of *him,* so close to her.

"Come on. Eat."

His voice was almost…kind. No one had ever brought her things or tried to look after her since her mother had left. She had been the one who did things for people—for her father, for Edgefrith.

She imagined eating the food, taking the rough bowl

out of the strong steady hand of the unknown stranger, the unknown *man*. Perhaps their flesh would touch. Perhaps...perhaps he would be warm, the way he had been in her bed; and she would see those vivid eyes brighten and feel his strength. The warmth would turn to heat, and she would know.

She would learn how it was to feed the other desperate hungers of the body. He could teach her that because the knowledge was in him, in the life that flowed from him in waves.

"Take it."

His eyes were clear, very bright. They watched her as though they could see straight through her, past every defense to the turmoil inside her, as though their owner could see the disintegration of her whole life. As though he could sense that other hunger.

There was no surprise in his terrifying eyes, just an age-old knowing.

But that way was madness.

"I...I cannot." She did not know what she was answering. What he had said, or what lay in the ancient man-heat of his eyes.

Mad. She did not want carnal love. She did not want a man, to *belong* to a man. She could not. She swallowed the dryness in her throat. Licked her lips. Saw the flare of heat in his eyes. She slid backwards until her spine hit the dried mud and wattle of the wall.

"I will not."

"Yes, you will." It was not so much a command as a

statement of fact, based on some immutable law she would not acknowledge, something as fundamental as life. His gaze was like flame, touching hers.

"No…" But she could not get the word out. It would not make a sound.

He set the bowl down on the floor. "If not now, then when you are ready."

He stood up, in a movement of strength that had a fluid grace beyond the marring of pain and wounds. He walked over to the sad remains of the fire and picked up his clothes that she had washed and mended and set out to dry.

She found her voice.

"Where are you going?"

She sounded desperate. She sounded…alone.

"To see what lies outside these walls, in case I forget."

"But the Vikings. You cannot. You are not well. They must not guess you are wounded. You…you said you would pretend that you—"

"That I am the goldsmith? That I am your husband? We have a bargain. I have said so. I would not break that. You hold my word."

He spoke with the quickness of sudden temper, as though his words should be beyond challenge. As though he were the most mood-proud thane that had ever walked through King Burgred's hall. He was a warrior. His eyes held all that, and something else, something forged in the heat of the fire that had passed between them.

Still unfulfilled. But waiting, biding its time. She could feel the burning wonder of it, but also the weight of fear: fear that such a thing would never survive, fear of believing in it. Fear of wanting to.

Moments of wonder like that did not survive in this world. They were not strong enough.

"You must take care."

The burnished chestnut head turned. The harshness vanished and he smiled. She thought the strength of that was greater than anything. But still she said it, because she wanted him to know, so that he would keep himself and the strange magic of the unknowable wonder between them safe.

"He is very dangerous."

"Who?"

"Earl Guthrum's man, the one I am doing the work for. Erik Bonebreaker."

The smile died. She watched it shatter like crystal touched by too much fire. She saw the darkness replace it, a darkness she had not fathomed in him. It was something that ate the light until there was none left.

She was terrified by it.

"What…what is it?" The darkness seemed to hold the power of death. He turned away from her. She watched his back, broad, straight and lethal.

"What are you going to do?"

CHAPTER FOUR

SHE HAD HIS WORD.

A man's word was a stronger bond than a fetter of iron. It should always be so, otherwise there was no justice and no rightness left in the world. Otherwise one became a savage.

Ashbeorn walked outside into the viper's nest of oath breakers. The cold struck at him through the threadbare tunic. The sound of many voices tore through the east wind. The only light came from King Burgred's hall.

He walked towards it. The sound surged and writhed with the wind and the black shadows, grotesque, distorted, *overdrunken*. It was a sound without the spark of grace that made men human.

How was the bond of a person's word to be measured against the laws of revenge?

He walked up the seven paved steps that led to the massive oaken doors.

The hall was fine, not the largest of the Mercian royal houses, but fine. In the darkness and the torchlight it seemed vast, like a roofless cavern. The flames caught the gleam of brass and copper, the fugitive slashing glitter of many painted colors. The tapestries were gone. The pillars were defaced with Nordic runes.

At first he could not find the man he sought. He closed his lids for a moment against the burning ache of his eyes and when he opened them the Viking was there, twice as large as the rest. Jarl Guthrum's man, shouting.

His hands clenched and the great bull-neck turned, as though the man had sensed his presence, as though the power of what he felt could cross the distance between them, striking through the stale smoke-laden air of the hall.

But it was not so. The shaggy head turned away, mouth stretched wide in what could have been the grimace of his own death-mask. He was still shouting, oblivious.

It would be easy, if it were done now. So easy. He moved through the doorway, the weakness of his leg unfelt. He kept to the shadows, the stealth and the quietness of that movement both natural and trained. He had no weapon, but he would not need one, not to take one man. What followed would not matter.

Something lurched at him out of the dark recess of the wall. Fast. Low. He caught an arm, smashing it back against the doorpost, the speed and the balanced force of his weight driving the other man's body back into the wall. A russet head smacked against a pillar. His foot found where the small six-inch *seax* blade had hit the floor.

He need not have bothered. He thought the man must have blacked out from the blow. His attacker's body slumped against his arm, the weight heavier than he had expected. He shoved backwards once more, just to be sure.

"Ahh... Do not..."

He stopped. There was a space of silence, broken only by the harsh rasp of their breathing. The silence in the entranceway had been unbroken apart from the sound of the man's body striking the wooden wall. He did not think the drunken sots inside the hall had noticed.

There were faint choking sounds. He eased off the pressure just slightly, so that the man could speak. Not man, boy.

"Did your mistress send you?"

"No—" The sweating face of Gemma's companion turned purple.

"Sure about that?"

"Gemma...does not know I followed you."

He slid the blade across the floor with one foot.

"This was your idea?"

"Yes." To the boy's credit, he looked up, his gaze straight. Beyond the shock and the terror, Ashbeorn could believe he read truth, and an edge of desperation that went beyond the fear of the moment. The boy's mouth worked. "I guessed what you were going to do."

He almost let go. The lapse was enough to allow Boda to slip out of his grasp, the speed completely boylike, despite the bulk that could have belonged to a man. Ashbeorn kicked the knife aside, training blurring over instinct. His body followed. The blade was in his hand before the boy could straighten up.

The blue eyes stared at him, terror mixed with pleading and behind it a courage that struck a chord somewhere inside him.

"Do not do it. Do not kill him."

"Kill who?"

"Erik. I saw you looking at him. I saw what you were going to do. You must not."

His hand fitted round the worn hilt of the knife like a second skin. Erik had done murder, and not cleanly. "Why not?"

"I cannot say. You just must not…." The voice trailed off into a sullen silence. The youth glared at him out of his filthy rags, like a savage, no more. Except for that spark of determination that outpaced his fear and his surliness as surely as it lacked the ability to find words.

Ashbeorn might have looked like that once—

"You will hurt Gemma."

The knife handle dug into the flesh of his palm.

Gemma the goldsmith, the woman who cared not who she worked for or why or what any of it meant, except her own act of creation.

Her face took shape out of the flame-streaked shadows, taunting him for blind arrogance, for caring to the depths of his soul what he did and why. He could feel the anger of that, merging with the fathomless, endless anger of now.

"You owe her."

I did not want you to die. He could no longer see her gem-hard eyes denying all that gave life any worth, just her face swimming above his when he had lain at the forest's edge with the life slipping away from him, the terrible aloneness of her sitting on the floor in the meagre rushes, with only a child-man for a protection and the Danes outside her door.

He had given her his word. Just as he had given it once before in an oath that transcended everything. His duty was not only to the dead. It was to the living, to the clever, overburdened and desperate man who was responsible for an entire kingdom.

He had sworn his loyalty to King Alfred. He could not jeopardize his mission by killing Erik now.

He would not break the pledge he had given, as the dead man had not. Surely the dead man would understand. He did not know. The blankness where once there had been an understanding beyond thought defeated him.

He stepped back into the shadows. The fierce, desperate gaze of the youth followed him, but he no longer saw that.

His mind was suddenly full of the woman. He could see her tear-streaked skin, the vulnerable turn of her head. He sensed the warmth and the wild entrancement of her body, remembered the scent of it and the subtle sheen of her hair.

She held his word.

It should have been simple. It was not. A death payment and the whole kingdom of Wessex lay between them.

The knife left his hand, striking naught but the defaced wood, harmless. But the blade vibrated in the rank air of Burgred's hall.

Like a promise that would be fulfilled.

HE HAD NOT COME BACK.

Gemma tried to feel surprised. But she had known it in her heart from the beginning. She did not know why she had thought the man would stay. She did not know why she had believed, when he had dragged himself out of the bed to follow her and bring her the last of the food, that he was capable of pity.

She did not want his pity.

Neither did she want what had sprung between them afterwards, that wild-hot unspoken need like summer fire. She had refused that. Doubtless that was why he had gone, why the wild heat had turned to anger.

The savage turn of his body as he had walked out, the soul-dark hardness of his eyes, were scored into her mind. He had said not one word.

He must have thought that the pretense of being her husband entitled him to what he wished. She had disappointed him. He had left. It was what such men did. Only a fool went crawling after them, staggering along in their arrogant footsteps like some helpless unregarded thrall, until death brought an end to it.

She closed her mind against that, against the past and

the woman who had died alone through her own folly and helplessness. No one aided the helpless.

She had to find her own way through this. She had deceived Erik the Bonebreaker into thinking she had a husband who would work for him.

Now she would have to explain why she did not, then convince a furious and vicious Dane that she alone was capable of doing the work he wanted, that she could be trusted to do it.

If she did not convince him—

She got to her feet. It was late.

She went back into her empty bedchamber and closed the door. She got into her bed. Fatigue and sickness and despair clawed at her. She buried her head in the covers.

But it was no longer her bed. She could feel every hollow where the false warrior had lain, catch the clean, sharp scent of chamomile from his hair. She writhed and her body remembered the heated touch of him, his weight, the rough-smooth heavy-satin touch of his skin.

She thought about how she had felt in this very bed when the stranger had so unexpectedly saved her from Erik's wrath. She remembered the intoxicating surge of his strength, the power she had felt in every muscle of him, touching her, warming her in a way that had as much to do with the heart as the body. She had thought—

The bed was empty.

She stared at the blank wall.

Every sense screamed for him. Worse than that, her mind did.

She closed her eyes.

GEMMA DROPPED to her knees on the floor.

"Why?"

The word that should have had the power to shake the high rafters came out as a grating whisper of sound. The false warrior did not hear it.

He was asleep beside her hearth, wrapped in her spare cloak. As though he belonged there.

Gemma stared at the dark shape in the shadows cast by the dying embers and the grudging dimness of early dawn.

Her heart beat so hard it would burst. Because of the measure of her fury, because… She reached out and her fingers twined in the soft silk of his hair, touched the warmth of skin.

He was real.

Her eyes burned and the warmth seeped through her hand, deep inside, dizzying. She sat, her hand on his flesh, and her fear of his power over her feelings was far, far greater than her fury.

But nothing mastered the warmth. It blossomed in her veins, in the deepest pit of her belly. Her hunger for that warmth was stronger than her hunger for food. It held a need deep and primitive, stronger perhaps than her will to survive.

She wanted to snatch her hand away. But at that moment he woke and she was caught, caressing his face and his hair like a desperate wanton. Caught in his eyes.

"What—what are you doing here?" She could not get away from his gaze.

"Bedding."

It could have meant he was sleeping. Or it could have meant so much more. The warmth of him was heat, scorching her, flesh on flesh.

"What else?" he said. Then "What are you doing here?"

The flames caught. She slammed backwards. The hand that had been caressing his face balled into a fist. She could not stand that look in his eyes.

"I live here," she shouted. "This is my hearth, my home." *My life.* She stood up, seeking space, desperate for that much protection. He moved. The cloak slid off a naked shoulder. She fought for control of her voice.

"Why did you come back?"

"Oaths."

The green eyes, she realized, were not hot at all. They were as opaque as the cut glass she set into gold.

"I thought you had gone."

"Why?"

"Because— It does not matter. Where did you go?"

He sat up. She saw the full length of a bare arm and took a step backwards.

"I told you, outside to look at what is in the camp."

"But—"

He stood. The patched wool of her spare cloak slid across skin. She flinched. The wall bench jammed painfully against the backs of her knees. She stared. At least he had had the minor decency to keep his trousers on.

She sat down and her gaze fixed on his battered skin. He would see she was staring at him, as he saw everything. But she could not look away. He was still here and yet— A thousand forbidden questions writhed in her mind, amongst the anger and the helplessness and the fear, and the humiliating heat of what he made her feel.

"Who did such damage to you?"

She had stepped perilously close to the forbidden ground. Nay, she had stepped onto it. The green gaze bored through her. There was silence. She did not move and the silence stretched out. Then he spoke.

"Erik Bonebreaker's men."

The life flowed out of her heart, just like the hope.

"*Erik*— Battle?" The skirmish. Near the river they had said. Erik's men had won.

He did not reply. He did not need to. She had known all along that he was a warrior.

"But the marks that…the marks on your neck…"

"Where someone wished to strangle me?"

She nodded, her mouth dry and the sickness like lead inside her.

"That was no Viking. But then an Englishman may work for a Dane like Erik. It is easy. So very easy."

There was a blight in his voice like the sudden coldness of death.

Working for the Vikings. Like she did. But him—

She looked at the bleak, implacable green of his eyes. "That's why you stayed. You want vengeance on Erik."

"Yes."

Her gaze moved across the large, capable hands held loosely at his side, traveled across the naked torso, examined each particular muscle under the sleek taut covering of his skin.

"Will you kill him?"

"Yes. One day."

She tried to moisten her lips, but her tongue seemed clamped to the dryness of her mouth.

"Why will you not kill him now?"

"Oaths."

"*Oaths?*"

"You hold one yourself. I am bound by them."

He moved away to pour the last of the washing water into a bowl.

"Is it not time we made ready to go to your workshop? Do I not have work to do? For Erik."

Oaths. I am bound by them. She did not believe him. She had put her faith in the hands of a warrior who was hell-foot, a trained killer who wanted revenge. She stared at the naked width of his back. He would try and kill Erik Bonebreaker when the chance came, and then what?

He would kill her and all that she tried to protect. Even if it was not his hand that touched her, the result would be the same.

"Ready to go?" said the false warrior, her executioner.

She got to her feet. She did not have a choice.

IT WAS BETTER in the workshop. This had been her world. Always. She could pretend it still was, that the deadly warrior-creature was not pacing the floor like a caged animal two feet away from her.

Gemma pulled the polished brass oil lamp closer, because the sheer power of his movements made the flame flutter. She tried to focus her eyes on the slender thread of drawn gold, setting it precisely against the grooved tool that would bead the thin wire.

She could not afford mistakes. She concentrated. The creature whirled past her in a flicker of black shadow, then turned away. But his left leg was still not strong enough, throwing him slightly off balance. The skirts of his tunic brushed the edge of the table. The dark, bright-edged mass of his body almost touched her.

"By all the saints!"

He looked around. She swore again, shaking her finger where the edge of the stamping tool had scored the skin.

"You have hurt yourself."

"No. Go away."

But, of course, he did not. He closed the small distance between them and she thought that his presence in this room would send her mad. He stood, looming over her with that savage beast look.

"Give me your hand."

"No."

But he had hold of it and there was nothing she could do. Fury ripped through her and with it an edge of despair. This was her room and her craft and her life. Yet he had come in to it and he would take it all and ruin it with his wild creature's power.

He would kill Erik. And then he would be gone.

"Let go of me."

The words were no more than one long snarl of sound. She had the grooved, stone-sharpened, double-edged stamping tool in her other hand.

He did not know what was in her heart.

He glanced at the razor-sharp metal and she read naught but indifference, tinged with slight exasperation. As though anything that she could do would count for no more than an insect bite against the strength of a wild boar.

"You need some cloth. Over there."

He leaned across her. His outstretched arm brushed her shoulder and she felt the shock of it deep inside. His face was so close she could see the darkness of stubble growing back already across his jaw, the thick sweep of his lashes hiding the disconcerting eyes.

She could gouge those eyes out right now with what she held. She could ruin the sight of that brown-and-green flecked beauty with one blow.

Perhaps.

The solidity of his arm moved.

"Open your hand."

He did not so much as look at the jeweler's tool held so tightly in her right fist. He was oblivious.

His own hand utterly engulfed her damaged fingers, surrounding them. He would force her fingers apart.

He held her and she could feel his warmth, not just through their joined hands but through the largeness of his body so close to hers, leaning over her.

She remembered what it was like to lie with him. He opened her fingers.

Then he wrapped the cloth round the cut. She watched.

"Help me hold it tighter. It will stop the blood."

No. The word existed only in her head. He took the jeweler's tool out of her other hand with scarcely a glance.

"Put your fingers here. That is it. Keep still. You can rest your arm against me."

No. Oh, no. But the warmth of him was there, in a rush, unstoppable.

"I said hold still. I presume you wish to be able to carry on with your work."

She found her voice.

"There is naught that would stop me."

Each word came out like stone. She knew the sharp intake of his breath. She felt it through her arm where it rested against the solid wall of his chest.

"Does it mean so very much to you, creating your own perfection?"

There was something she could not identify in his voice. She wanted to hear the bitter chill of his harsh-

ness, but all she could feel was the warmth of him,
the power.

She wondered what it would be like to tell him, to
actually say to another human being all that pressed on
her mind. She watched his hand round hers. It was
bruised, covered in small scars.

"Yes," she snapped. "I have my skill and naught else
has meaning for me. I doubt someone like you would
understand that."

"Someone like me?"

"Aye. What I do is a craft. An accomplishment of the
mind learned over years. What would someone like you
know of that?"

She could scent the edge of danger in him, feel it in the
moving, softly breathing wall of muscle under her hand.

"Indeed I could know naught. Who could expect
otherwise?"

"Not me. I can see it. In the way you pace my chamber like some savage beast—" The sudden tightening
of the muscle beneath her fingers was not imagination,
nor was the sharp intake of his breath. She felt all that,
though he did not speak. He might catch her with his
warrior's strength but she caught him. She understood
him. She knew what was in his mind.

"You must despise what I do, because it is beyond
your scope."

"Aye." She felt the push of his breath. "I must."

She moved her hand. He would not let her. The oil
lamp flickered in a sudden draught, and the likeness to
Lyfing was unmistakable.

"Let me go. Nothing will take me from my *cræft*."

"No. I see that."

The thick, brown lashes veiled the keenness of his eyes as he looked down at her bloodied hand.

"Have a care for yourself, Gemma, in where your craft may lead you, in what you do."

"Have care?" Her own breath strengthened in answer, with the same wild force. "You mean as you do?"

His sudden laughter struck sparks in the lamplight. Its recklessness and its life vibrated in the air, inside her skin, making it tingle.

The darkness, the edge of danger, were subsumed in a different feeling, rich and mysterious, a feeling that made her heart quicken and her blood sing.

She had meant to taunt him with his hurts, which were many, with his furious pacing round the room despite the injury to his leg. Most of all with the arrogant uselessness of his warrior's strength.

But what she saw in his tipped-back face, in the brightness of his eyes, held some other quality she could not define. It went beyond the much-prized physical strength, beyond simple recklessness of either body or mind.

She realized with a strange thrill that held both fear and a savage sense of recognition, that it was a strength far beyond consciousness of self.

"Then we both have that which we will do and naught will stop us."

"Aye."

She watched the brightness of his eyes and both the recognition and the fear tore at her. It was for the *fæg*, such single-minded power, for the fated. Or for those who would take the threads of the fate-web in their own hands, light and dark, good and ill. Life and death.

He sat down. Her bent arm rested against his side, the elbow just brushing the tight line of his belly below the band of leather at his hips, her hand, their joined hands, close to his heart.

The whole world had narrowed to that, to the feel of his big body so close to hers, the smooth swell of his breathing against her arm, his fine strength. The faint clean tang of herbs from his hair. His warmth.

"Gemma."

It was said against her hair. He spoke again, so low she could not catch the words. It did not matter. She only needed to hear the deep, loam richness of his voice, feel the faint vibration of that dark sound through her body. His size and his strength, no longer seemed something to fear, but something she could melt into, like his warmth.

So she let the warmth take her because that was his trueness. He was made for life's strength, not cold death.

He held her while the pain ebbed out of her hand, and for long miraculous moments, her fierce, potent, fate-starred stranger did not move. It almost seemed as though the warmth and the strength that lived in him could give her what she craved most: rest. She shut her eyes.

"What are you doing to her? Let her go. Or I will make you."

The shouted words jarred her out of dreams. Her mind felt numb, her confused senses unable to adjust to the familiar shapes of her workshop, the ordinary light of the brass lamp. But the heavy warmth of the stranger's body was already sliding from her grasp. He found his feet, the pain of the damaged leg obliterated.

"Boda…" she gasped.

"What are you doing?" demanded Boda in the overloud voice that belonged to those who have committed themselves too far. The smoothly balanced stranger, each muscle controlled into one fierce wall of strength, would kill him.

Her hurt hand reached instinctively for the punching tool on her table, though what she would do with it— The lethal force beside her did not spring.

"Boda," she said into the tight silence, "you know you should not come in here—"

"I will come in here when—"

"Hush." The deep voice cut across both of them. "There is no cause for concern." The green eyes flicked across her hand, clamped round the tool, with what could only be a gleam of amusement. But it was gone when he turned back to Boda.

"The lady hurt herself when she was working. That is all." The voice was as unyielding as his face, yet the mockery she expected was not there. Only the kind of grave courtesy one warrior might extend to another.

Boda swallowed, his gaze turning to her, his uncertainty as clear as his obstinacy.

Something made her bite back the scolding retort.

She put down the punch and showed her hand and the bloodied cloth.

"It is true."

"Well, if *you* say so." Boda managed to hide the relief almost completely. He swaggered a bit over the top of the uncertainty. She had to stop her jaw from dropping. She had never seen Boda look like anything but a cornered dog that had been beaten, all fear and teeth. He shot a glance at his opponent, head back.

The warrior called Ash blinked and bit his lip. She was so close she could hear the catch in his breath. He held on to the gravity.

Boda sat on her bench, his gaze roaming over the workshop he was not allowed in.

He had a bruise disappearing under his matted hair.

"Boda? Did you hurt yourself, as well? What—"

"No! It is naught." His gaze flicked once more towards his antagonist as though under compulsion.

"Naught," agreed Ash, as though anyone had asked him.

She could have sworn the color in Boda's face heightened under its covering of dirt. His fingers drummed on the table, scrabbling through all the arcane instruments of her craft.

"Have a care. You will—"

She saw it.

The sightless eyes stared up from her table where Boda had disturbed her work.

"Boda, will you leave that."

He had only to move his great ham fists one fraction and he would touch the faces. And then he would speak and the rapid-thinking, fast-moving creature Ash would see—

"Boda—"

"What are those masks? They look like faces."

"Leave it—"

"Look. They change with the light and the way you look at them. There were two faces before. Now there is only one. It was frowning and now it looks as though it smiles."

"Give me that." Her injured hand snatched the mold out of Boda's grasp with a force that brought more blood. She tried to hide it, to control the savage movement of her hand, the viciousness of fear in her voice.

"It is naught," she said. "A mold for a pattern. But it is old and easily broken. It is naught to do with the jewelry I am making now. Just…something old."

"It is fascinating." The power of the deep voice of Ash the stranger, the power of the deeper mind behind it, beat at her. She could trust nothing about him, not when it regarded her commission for Erik. When it regarded her brother's life.

"It is nothing." She held the dangerous shape-changing mask concealed in her hand. But she did not think anything could hide the ancient beauty of it, the image dedicated to Woden, the shape-shifting god. It had been imbued with the power to confound evil spirits by changing its appearance. It was dangerous and full of strange powers no one remembered now.

She could not hide such a thing. She put it down among all the scattered materials of her craft as though it were indeed nothing. She picked up the gold thread she had been working on.

"I have to get on with this bead-making." She turned to the quick, hard-bodied creature beside her. She refused to look at the green eyes that held more mysteries than Woden's masks. She reminded herself he was only a warrior, a man who knew nothing beyond the worth of a sword's blade.

"You had better watch what I do to make the bead string. Then if Erik should come and expect to see you working, you will know what is done." She would have to heat the furnace for the soldering. She got up and the weariness and the ache in her hand dogged at her.

"Is there anything to eat?" said Boda.

"No." She bent down to stoke the small furnace behind the fire screen fitted with its leather bellows. "Why do you not go out and look at the snares we set?"

"That is what I came to tell you. Someone found them and cut the cords and took the catch. There is nothing. No hares, not so much as a blackbird."

She picked up a piece of wood.

"Then you will have to set some more."

But she knew what she would really have to do.

She would have to ask Erik for some of her payment now. Erik wanted her to do that. She thought it had been for the pleasure of humiliation. But now that the stranger had come, she had seen something different in Erik Bonebreaker's eyes.

The stranger took the wood out of her hand.

CHAPTER FIVE

IT WAS THERE.

Ashbeorn had known it would come. He had read its tracks, new and old, and he had known it would be drawn by the lure of the water.

It stood motionless in the shadows, testing the air. Flecks of blood and foam flicked from its jaws, remembrance of some small creature it had killed in the eternal chain of the hunt. Thick muscle moved under the dark bristling hide. He held still.

It did not sense him. He was part of the forest.

The heavy head, the thick jaw, the twisted tusks bent to the water. Dark trails swirled out through the clearness of the pool. He could hear its snorting breath, the sounds of its greed. Its concentration.

He moved. Thin reeds slid over his naked flesh, over the linen bound across his thigh. Cold damp earth yielded under the soles of his feet. Closer. Ever closer, until he could not be concealed and speed mattered more than guile.

He struck. The great head raised at the last moment. The creature's gaze was pure heat-fury, instinct and strength combined in the mindless urge for survival. The snare of that primitive drive caught them both. The death that had to be taken or given.

His body twisted with trained speed to avoid the crushing weight, the tusks aimed low at the vulnerable flesh of his belly. Pain shot through his leg, weakening the movement that should have been lightning fast. But the spear was grounded in the immovable force of the earth, impaled in the creature's flesh.

He caught balance, the magical state that meant more than strength, his whole will centered on holding the spear, avoiding the killing rake of the thrashing tusks. The savage, bone-snapping movement stopped. There was no sound, only the tearing harshness of his own breath.

Nothing felt but the sweat on his body, the burning pain in his thigh. And the blood. His and the creature's mixed. His head rested on the cool earth the way it had after the battle five days ago, against the dark soil that gave life and received it again.

It took the same effort to move as it had after the battle. He slid naked into the blessing of the pool. As the water closed in cool silence over his heated skin, he heard the voice. Beyond the curtain of the reeds and the trees.

It spoke the Norse of the Eastern Danes. That did not matter.

So did he.

SHE WAS PACING the floor of the cramped bower when he got back, small fists clenched at her sides. He could see the whiteness of the linen still wrapped round her left hand. Her heart-shaped face was whiter, like some frightened youth about to face a Viking shield wall.

He shut the door carefully.

He was fully dressed in the cleaned and mended clothes he had preserved from the primitive ritual of the hunt. No mark was visible on him from the death struggle.

"I thought you would not come back."

Her eyes were wide. Her soft lips parted on the quickness of her breath. He reminded himself that he still looked perfectly civilized. No one could see inside him.

"Were you about to go out?"

Her hands moved to the folds of the cloak that covered her dress, the smothering veil on her head. Her gaze turned opaque.

"Aye."

"Looking for me?"

"No. Why would I do that? I told you. I did not think you would come back."

He moved very slowly to set his burden on her wooden table. The spoils of the chase cleanly dressed, neatly wrapped, acceptable.

She stared at it.

"What is that?"

"Food. I killed a boar."

"*What?* But how did you…how… One man would not hunt a boar alone, even if he were well."

She was staring at him, with the coldly familiar look

of disbelief, the look people reserved for something alien and unwelcome that had invaded their world. He told himself that there was no mark of savagery that she could see.

"You killed the boar…."

She sat down, in the cloak and the veil she must have donned to meet Erik the Bonebreaker. She looked at the food he had provided for their keep.

"You had no weapon," she said.

"This is a Viking camp. It is full of weapons." The Danish voice he had heard while the water slid over his skin, echoed in his head.

Her damaged hand reached out to touch the wrapping.

"Why would you have done such a thing?"

The unsteady tone of her voice and the small wondering movement of her hand confused him. His mind had readied itself, as ever, for the rejection of that part of him that was not acceptable, for the wall of impenetrable English distance.

"Why would you have risked so much?" asked Gemma. "For me?"

Her eyes were the color of the evening sky. The time of shifting balance between day and the mystery of night. Her gaze was fixed on him, full of brilliance over unknown depths. If he looked at eyes like that, he could believe what he wanted to.

Ashbeorn sat down. He stared at the spoils of the chase, the blood and the danger still fresh in his mind. And the Viking's voice.

"We had an agreement—to work together until your

commission is complete. You hold my word." *Yet you believed I had gone, and you have your own agreement with Erik.*

She touched his hand. Her fingers were small and cold against his flesh. One hand perfect, the other still wrapped in linen bands.

His own fingers were scratched from the death-struggle in the forest. He tried to draw his hand away but she caught at him, and he realized her hands were not perfect at all, but marked with other small scars from her work. It was not usual to see a Saxon lady's hands so.

But she was an artisan in her own right and she had to fight for what she had, just as he did.

Yet she had no bodily strength for such a fight, not like him.

He turned his hand, covering hers with the warmth and the strength that coursed out of his own body like a force that could not be stopped.

He watched their joined hands. The quietness in her bower was the kind that begged to rest. Yet he asked, "Where were you going just now?"

He looked at her eyes that might or might not hold so much: the color of the sky at the moment of change. Their skin touched and the warmth flooded through his veins, striking heat inside, cutting through flesh and bone.

"Will you not tell me where you were going? Why?"

There was a moment when the smoke-scented air hung still and heavy, tightened to the same pitch of expectancy that thrummed through his body.

Then her eyes froze. The moment of change shattered, even before she spoke.

"Nay. There is naught that I need tell you. Any *agreement* we might have does not impinge on that."

He kept hold of her scarred hand, stopping the small movement to escape him without using one quarter of his strength. They stared at each other, so close that he could see the wild beating of the pulse at her throat.

When he went to speak, their breath mingled. "He should be back by now. He will be waiting for you."

The blanked-off eyes widened.

"Who do you mean—"

"Erik."

He let her go.

HE SHOULD NOT have expected the woman to trust him.

Yet he had. Beyond reason or the experience of anything he had never known.

He had expected more of her than he had expected of the beleaguered king who held his oath. Just because of the sound of her voice and because of what he thought he had glimpsed in her eyes.

He had expected more than any rational being was prepared to give him. The fault was his.

"Why would you say that…?" began the woman, but then she stopped. Her shoulders squared beneath the cloak that reflected the color of her eyes.

"How did you know?" Her directness met his like something matched.

"I heard Erik Bonebreaker say it."

"What? When?"

"In the forest. After I had made the kill. I was washing the blood off. I heard him through the trees, speaking to someone. He was conveying a message back to Jarl Guthrum."

She flinched at the sound of the Viking earl's name. The small movement was discernible to him. But she did not look away. Her courage cut at him.

"What did Erik say?" she demanded.

"That the jarl's gold-work would be completed on time. That he was sure I would finish the task because he was holding my brother-in-law hostage."

It made her bow her head. Her gaze slid away from his. The thin shoulders hunched under the deep blue wool of her cloak. She would not look at him.

Erik the Bonebreaker and a hostage. Erik the butcher.

"Why did you not tell me?"

"It was not for you to know. You wanted to kill Erik. You still do. You are a warrior and filled with pride. I could not tell you."

He got to his feet, dragging his useless leg across the small space of her chamber. The rotting window shutters gave under the force of his hands. Cold air touched his skin, raw, heavy with the scent of rain.

Erik with a prisoner. He could not see the chilled remains of Offleah. Nothing but charred and beaten flesh and the expression in dead eyes that would never leave his mind as long as he lived. That was Erik's use for those in his power.

Erik. And Guthrum, his master, who had the will and the intelligence to take all. His mind's eye saw all the battles won and lost, all the battles that were still to come. And only Wessex left to fight them.

That was where his duty lay. He should have left Offleah and tracked Jarl Guthrum's man through the concealment of the forest. Not come back here because Erik held one more hostage.

The chills ran across his skin. Erik was his fate and there was more in this place than he had yet fathomed. The clever, frightened woman held magic in her workshop. She had tried to hide it. She had said that the face of the heathen shape-shifting god was naught.

He had to unravel what was in her head.

"YOU HAD BETTER tell me about your brother."

Gemma had not expected him to speak again. She had lied about her debt to the man he wanted to kill.

"Edgefrith is only a child." She could not keep the heated desperation out of her voice. "It is not his fault. None of this was his doing."

She stared at the broad back, the meaty hand clenched round the window frame. He would not understand.

She began again. She had to *make* him understand. Her brother's life-price. She would beg if she had to. For Edgefrith.

"Our father died last year. He had always traveled. For him that was part of the magic of his craft." Her voice was stammering, getting the words in a muddle.

"My father would not stay at one workshop, or at one royal estate, not even in London-wic—"

"You never had a home?"

"A home?" What was he talking about? "I needed none. I…" She tried to get her thoughts into order. The rigid, warrior's back moved not one corded muscle. There was no way he could have the slightest conception of what it meant to take the precious gift of skill and learning through the breadth of a kingdom. Always seeing new things, learning more—

"I had my craft," she said. "Why would I want a home?"

"Some people do. They love what is theirs."

"I—I do not know what that would be like. I…" He confused her unbearably with his ideas, with his sudden terrifying anger and his equally terrifying warmth. She stared at the solid wall of his back. "Do you—"

"Nay," said the unfathomable voice. "It is as well not to have a home in these times."

Then at least they matched in that. But there was a strange emptiness round her heart. A home was one of the things her mother had wanted, one of the many things she had blamed her husband for not providing. It was one of the things she had never got, even after she left.

Chasing after a man like this one—

"We came here to Offleah. We did not intend to stay here, but my father took sick. There was naught I could do, naught anyone could do and he died. It was so quick. Only two days and all that had been healthy was dead."

She looked away, even from the immovable back. But she made herself go on speaking.

"Erik came. He wanted a goldsmith. Someone had told him my father was here. All he found was the body to be buried. He was…put out. He had some work to be done. He decided I could do it instead. He took everything that I owned away from me."

It was not as though such words had the power to move her anymore. Not many things did. The only thing left to do was to survive, and that took all the thought and the energy that she had.

There was no need for him to turn so that he could see her, to make his way so painfully back from the biting air of the open window. The cold made her shiver. She felt its power more than he did. He was so warm.

She did not want him to be so warm because he was naught but a danger. She could not cope with another danger.

His chest was like a solid wall. He smelled clean. His hair was damp. That was because he had washed the blood off after killing the boar. She did not want to think of the strength it had taken to do that. Or the will.

Warrior's arrogance.

He had his arms round her.

He should not do that. She could see his hand where it fastened round her arm. It was scratched. Just flesh. As vulnerable in the end as hers. He felt all the pain of his hurts and he was weary. She could feel that in the slight hesitation with which he moved, in the rhythm of his breath and the touch of his skin against hers.

It was not arrogance that had let him do what he had. It was courage.

She did not want to know that.

She shut her eyes so that she would not have to look at his face. If she could just get the last words out, he would leave her alone.

"Edgefrith, my brother, is younger than Boda, only ten winters old. Erik took him from me so that I would do his work. If I do not do all that he wishes, he will kill my brother."

She lay very still in the deceptive, remorseless tenderness of an embrace she could not break.

"If any harm should come to Erik, it is a ten-year-old boy who will pay."

She felt the sliding heat of his body against hers as he moved. It was over. He would let her go. She must make him let her go. She did not want him.

"There is naught else to say. I made up a story in front of Erik when he first came that I had a husband who was due back any day. Someone to protect me. I panicked. I thought I would get away from here before I had to prove my words."

His warmth kept her, enfolding her in its generosity and its strength. She could feel both the bated power of it and the unexpected vulnerability. She realized she could feel the harsh unevenness of his breath, the heat and the dark edge of exhaustion because he let her.

It was like a gift, raw and intimate. It was something given, she would guess, almost in spite of that formidable will. Yet given all the same, out of a source deep beyond her imagining.

She could not take that gift. Duress and force she could have dealt with in her own way. Mayhap. But not a gift. It…it involved something shared. That made her feel vulnerable, too.

She tightened muscle and sinew turned weak and pliant by the power of rich beguilement. By need—

"It was naught but pretense. I am alone. There is my brother and there is Boda who made a friend out of him. But Boda is no more than a boy, just a leftover from the Viking raids who comes and goes. I have nothing more, but I do not wish it. I do not wish for—" *warmth, protection, false gifts.* "I am alone because that is how I wish to be."

Her head came up and her eyes opened. But that was a mistake, because she could see the dark depths of the forest in his gaze and green heat. She could feel that heat reach deeply inside herself the way it had when she had first seen him. It burned her.

The moment hung still, charged with awareness and the gift of his touch and his held-back strength. She saw his bright liquid gaze fastened on the shape of her mouth and she knew what he would do.

Her heart thudded. No man had ever kissed her. She

had not wanted such a thing. She would not permit such an intimate invasion of who she was.

She watched his relentless face bend to hers, the harshly drawn lines blur because of his closeness. She felt the heat of his breath. His mouth stilled above hers, the strength and the power of his body held her, its shadowed mass pressed against her. She felt every tight line and every dark hollow of its shape.

Her mind filled with the knowledge of the heated heavy weight that had lain with her in her bed, trapping her with its size and its power the way the strength of his arms held her now.

But just like then, she could feel so much else, his realness and his courage and his life. She wanted the burning life that was in him. She wanted all that she did not understand.

She could have moved in that hot fractured moment when he held still. She could have pulled away despite his strength and he would have let her. Something made her believe that.

But then she would have been alone.

She took his heat. She took all the force of the life that burned in him.

His mouth covered hers.

The sensation of his lips against her mouth sent sharp jolts of that white heat bursting through her. It was terrifying. And then she realized what the heat and the fierce feelings meant. Pleasure. It tightened inside her and broke, cascading in waves through her body with the smooth seductive movement of his lips across hers.

A small startled sound escaped her and was lost against the power of his mouth. The kiss deepened, and with it the pleasure. The fire burned through her, pooling low in her belly, sharp, more than she could bear.

Her body writhed, not avoiding his touch but craving it, touching all the fierce brilliance of the form she had seen, seeking its fine lines and its heavy-shadowed fullness through his clothes. The feel of his shape fired her blood, dizzying mind and sense, bringing a wild breathless hunger beyond reckoning or control.

She imagined all that she had seen spread out on her floor in this room before her gaze. Her skin remembered what she had felt in her bed when she had held him, what it had been like when all that savagely made perfection had moved, crushing her body beneath his, making her feel his heat and the vital grace of his strength.

This was what it meant, all the love-craft with a man that she had so despised. Its beauty and its power ravished sense. Her body opened itself against his and his arms tightened, taking that involuntary movement with his strength, subsuming it with his heat, the fierce sensual turn of his upper body, the glide of his hips.

Her back was pressed against the wall, stretched out under the finely drawn line of him, so that she could feel the straining power of blood-thick muscle, the harshly ripened fullness of his manhood.

But she did not want to draw back from that. Her hands sought his body while her desperate, ignorant lips sought to match the maddening, sense-aching movement of his. She must have done something in her blind hunger and her helpless desire because the pressure of his mouth opened hers wider and she felt the first tantalizing movement of his tongue.

Her body spasmed but his hands held her, sliding down, smoothing the line of her side, tracing the sharp hollow of her waist and the flare of her hips, heating the flame inside her until she could not bear it and then moving up to the swell of her breast.

She gasped and her mind seemed to dizzy as though she would fall, except that he was holding her and the strength of him was beyond her knowledge and beyond aught that she could match. A fighter's strength. The sharp, cold fingers of alarm started in her head.

He could do all that he wished and she would not have the strength to stop him. More terrifying than that, she might not have the will. And then he would leave, abandon her; and she would be betrayed and left yearning like a sick woman after all that she had lost, all he would take from her.

His lips moved from her mouth to the naked skin at her throat, burning with the same power that would take her body, all of it.

She could not allow that.

Her small muscles went rigid with terror, with fury, with the urge to strike out and protect herself. She would do that, she must.

"Let me go."

She would strike out if she had to. She would kill him. Or he would have to kill her.

He was sitting back, staring at her. His body was one single feral line of power. The tension of it cut the air. *Warrior.* They were takers, destroyers.

Her breath came in great sobbing gasps.

"I know what you are," she said.

His eyes watched her. Fighters always watched before they struck. The terror of him clutched at her. In her fear-blinded mind, the clear lines and the black shadows of his face merged with the memory of Lyfing.

"You would take from me. I know that. I know all that is hidden inside you—"

The beautiful face went blank. There was not one human expression left on it. He moved.

She slid back, lightning-fast, far faster than thought. Her hand caught one of the rough branches laid out for the fire. Splinters of bark dug into her skin. But what she did was pointless. He did not even see. He had gone. Out into the cold black night, like the forest creature he was.

She put the piece of wood down. She was safe. She looked round the empty room. The booty from the chase caught her eye. The means to save her from starving, from having to crawl to Erik the Bonebreaker.

A gift.

She went into the inner chamber. It was empty. She shed her clothes and got into her bed.

It was all right. She was safe from the glittering-eyed stranger. He had not sprung at her with all that lethally held strength when she had refused him. He would leave her alone now. She had seen the emptiness in his face.

She crawled into the coldness of the bed. She had all that she could reasonably expect, more. She had only to finish her work and Edgefrith would come back to her. They would travel again and things would be just as they had been before—

Before death and destruction had come. Before—

She shut her eyes against the image of the glittering eyes, the touch of burning heat against her skin. Most especially, she closed her mind against the bleakness she had seen in that last glimpse of the stranger's face.

But she had preserved her future. It stretched out before her in an endless line.

It held the same emptiness she had seen in him.

"THEY ARE ALL dead, Lord."

Osmode, thane of Wessex, watched the fury gather in the handsome, youthful face. He stepped back. It was a chancy business, bearing bad tidings to kings. Even to the fool who thought he could hold his kingdom back from Guthrum the Dane.

"All?"

A faint movement of shock traveled round the small group of men, thanes and bodyguards, gathered in the great hall at Kingston. Osmode was aware of that. But he kept his eyes on the king.

"The border patrol. We were too late to save them. It was as though the Vikings already…" He let the pause hang. He heard the faint gratifying rustle of movement again.

"What would you say, man?" demanded Alfred of Wessex.

Osmode bowed his head, letting the reluctance show.

"Lord, it was as though the Vikings already knew where those men would be."

Behind him, someone made the faint sound that spoke of a blade partly unsheathed by a guard's impatient hand. Sweat started at his back.

But they were fools, these West Saxon warriors, prey to their fears, quick to suspicion because outside the bounds of this kingdom every man's hand was turned against them.

"All we could do was count the bodies. All dead save—"

"What?"

The king's voice was deadly. He was not so easy to predict, the young creature who held Wessex.

"All save one, Lord." The ice-sweat pricked at Osmode's spine beneath the war-padding and the muddied chain mail. He said it.

"I saw the Lord Ashbeorn."

The rustling behind him became a murmur. The

sound was cut off by one slight movement of the king's hand.

"Speak."

Osmode dropped to his knees as a reluctant bearer of ill news should.

"He survived the massacre. He alone. I tried to come up with him but I could not. He vanished into the forest and—"

"So you did not have speech with this man or see him close?" *Close.* Osmode could feel his gloved hands round the thick neck of Alfred's dangerous thane, the terrifyingly fierce struggle of the wounded body under his hands. A doomed struggle. The man was dead.

True, Osmode had not had time to recover his sword and use it. But no one could have survived that struggle. And he had dragged the corpse into the trees before anyone had seen what he did.

"If you were not close, how do you know this man was the Lord Ashbeorn? He could have been a Viking."

"Lord, I would swear to what I saw on that day amongst all those slaughtered men."

Dead men told no tales. All that mattered was what the living could be made to believe.

"The man I saw fleeing towards Offleah was Askr-" He choked off the Danish syllables of the man's name. He must not be too obvious.

"Lord, I may have been wrong." He lowered his voice, humility laced through with duty. "Forgive me for bringing such tidings. All I know is that the man fled into the forest and that although we gave chase, we could take neither him nor the Viking war-band."

"I see." The words were slow, measured. They hung in the air with more questions than Osmode would have wished.

"We were too close to Offleah." His voice cut into the dangerous silence. "Lord," he added quickly. He looked up. "You have given us no authority to raid into Mercia."

"No." Just that single word and the suddenly inscrutable face. Could the fool not see?

Osmode surged manfully to his feet, open, eager. Loyal.

"Lord, if you take my rede." Advice would be what the West Saxon king craved. He might be clever enough, but he was nine winters younger than Osmode and overburdened with responsibility.

It would be like leading a bear.

"Then give your men the word. We would rout out that viper's nest at Offleah and the borders of your kingdom would be safe. I would do that, or…" The young always thirsted after glory. "You could lead the raid yourself. Then naught could make us fail."

Osmode held his breath, the eagerness pinned on his face. No one spoke.

He had gone too far. He knew it. Erik and his plans, his greedy confidence, were wrong. He sought frantically in his mind what to say. He should never have risen from his knees until the king gave him leave. He should—The pathetic bastard clapped him on the back.

"Lord—" The word came out high-pitched, too strong. Relief.

But the king smiled. Alfred of Wessex had the kind of face that would have caught attention out of stone. The ability to show the sort of interest in other people that left them helpless. Osmode could feel the reaction to that in himself. It made him furious.

There was naught for him in a land that antagonized the new rulers of the rest of England. No profit to be gained in a land bled dry by war. He had never received the favour that was his due from the house of Wessex.

The broad hand bedecked with rings fastened on his shoulder. Comradeship. The warmth of a brother in arms. The young king held the aura of confidence without limits that drew devotion out of those who should know better.

Osmode would not be fooled by such mock heroics. Never.

"Come and tell me more."

The king of Wessex, the last son of Ethelwulf, arrogant enough to risk all their futures against the invincible power of the Danes, led him away.

CHAPTER SIX

ASHBEORN CROSSED the courtyard at Offleah.

It was madness, the ache in his blood for the Mercian woman, the fire that sprang between them whenever they were in the same room. A madness that had no future.

The Lady Gemma had seen that. With the same completeness as him. His pace quickened, abused muscle in his leg protesting from yesterday's hunt. It had to heal. He had to finish what he had come for. He had to get back to Kingston.

"Wait." It was the lady's belligerent companion. That was all he needed.

"She told you. Gemma told you about Edgefrith."

He turned. Sharp eyes measured him, torn between suspicion and whatever force had compelled the boy to run after him across the yard.

"Aye." He waited.

Boda's bare feet scuffed at muddy grass.

"Erik will not let her see him. No one ever talks about him. Not even Gemma." And there it was, bared to the sunlight, the reason he could not leave the difficult Lady Gemma.

Boda attacked more of the grass.

"Edgefrith is younger than me. I used to make sure that he was all right. You know?"

Ashbeorn studied the mangled grass. He would not think about the person who had attempted to look out for him.

"Then Erik…" Boda's deepening voice stopped. "There was nothing I could do." The grass disappeared under a vicious spurt of mud.

"Will you show me?" The wild copper head shot up. "Will you show me what you did back there in the hall when you took the *seax* blade off me? I need to know." Eyes full of the anger of youth and the bitterness of a fifty-year-old stared at him. He could not speak.

"I am old enough. The Lady Gemma thinks I must have sixteen winters, or thereabouts." Boda's considerable shoulders squared.

"I s-see what you think." The belligerent voice stuttered. "You do not believe I am f-fit to be taught. Because I do not know my age or how to behave like Edgefrith and Gemma."

"Why should I think that," inquired Ashbeorn mildly, "when I do not know my own age?"

"*You* do not know?"

"If anyone asks, I say I am the same age as the king of Wessex."

"Twenty-four winters?"

Ashbeorn shrugged. It was as likely as anything.

Boda's eyes took light. "Have you ever seen King Alfred? Is it true that he won the battle at Ashdown when his brother was king? That he began with half the army and would have carried the day while his brother was still thinking about it?"

"So they say. It is not a tale I would tell here."

"I would have started the battle rather than wait. I bet you would."

"Mayhap. But you have to judge when it is right to do that and when you must hold back. That is the first thing a warrior learns."

"You mean like…like with Erik? I suppose…I suppose we both did the same thing then, held back?"

"Aye."

Ashbeorn clamped down on the burning unslaked drive to avenge what Erik Bonebreaker had done, what he did now. He did not think he had learned that lesson at all.

Like Boda, he was not fit.

The prescient Lady Gemma had seen that.

"Come, I will show you what you may do against a man with a knife."

HE HAD SOUGHT HER out in her workshop, the wild creature who could enchant the same wildness out of her. It should not have mattered. She had no desire to repeat last night's disaster.

Neither did he.

That much was plain.

Gemma stared at the engraved fine-grained wood of

the die. The design was precisely laid out. Correct. All was going well. *She* was well. She might not have slept much but, miracle beyond price, she had eaten.

She could work.

She put down the measuring compass that mapped out the carefully spaced circles in the wood.

She stared at her workbench, littered with gold beadwork and glittering fragments of rock crystal and cut garnet. Such beauty as kings dreamed of.

She could not even see it.

All that filled her mind was the living beauty of the man beside her. He was all that her delicately attuned senses could feel. Her fingertips touched not fine wood or the smooth coldness of gems, but his skin. She could not see the daylight, hear the sounds of the Danish voices outside her window. Her eyes saw the smoky darkness of her room, her ears heard the rustle of his clothing, the tightness of his breath. She felt its heated whisper. Felt *him*.

"What is the matter? Does your hand trouble you?" The creature looked up from his examination of a piece of quartz.

"No."

There was not the slightest need for them even to speak, certainly not to touch. All he had to do was be in the room in case Erik came. He knew that as well as she did.

They were being appallingly polite to each other.

"You are tired."

"No."

He put down the piece of quartz.

If only he would sit still.

He picked up the die.

"Leave it!" She wanted to snatch it out of his hand but she did not dare in case she touched him.

"You will use this on the gold foil."

"Yes." She did not like the quickness of his mind, the way he could turn and adapt to things with the speed of the shape-changing image she had hidden.

Yet she should be glad of it. Because of Erik.

"The foil is set under the stones and the crystal so that the light will reflect through them."

"So the true colors can be seen."

Her mouth opened and shut. People outside her world of knowledge did not guess straightaway all the hidden artistry that was needed to produce the beauty they craved. Particularly not people who made their living destroying things.

His scarred hands moved to touch the carefully shaped gems. She reclaimed the die.

"But how do the gems stay in place?"

"I have glue of wax clay and powdered quartz, but the real secret lies in the way the gems are cut."

"I can see the facets."

She watched the intentness of his eyes below the thick brown lashes, the way the large hands that should have been clumsy moved with such care. He understood.

"It can take up to three days to cut one gem if it is

done properly," she said. "Five months to cut the gems for one brooch, depending on the design, perhaps a year to complete all the work."

"And you have done that?"

The fascinating lashes flicked up.

"Of course." Did he think fifteen years of training from a master counted for naught? He would learn. "Even though I did not have to do any cutting now because—" She held her tongue.

"Because you are refashioning, not making something new? But if the design of what you are making now is different, how do you manage with the stones that are already cut?"

His eyes were brighter than any gem she had ever seen, cleverer than those of any artisan she had ever known. They would draw out all that she hid because they were so clever.

He was not interested in the intricacies of her craft at all. Only in trapping her to find out what she did with so many riches.

The design of what she did was not different from the original. Letting him think so was a ruse.

He put the gemstone down.

"You need more light."

"No—" Her hand shot out at the instant he moved the brass lamp. She touched him.

"It is hard to work in shadows."

The small touching of her fingers on his reached all the way through the tightly wound tension of her body.

He watched her.

His eyes did not hold the greed that followed those in her craft. His hand stayed quite still. It was as though the touching reached through her mind.

The fiercely focused brilliance of his eyes no longer seemed a snare, but a promise. He had understood about the power and the needs of her artistry. What if he understood about the needs of her life?

She did not think of his terrible strength then, of his dangerous secrets. He stayed unmoving. His scarred hands touched hers over the stem of the brass lamp on her table littered with the scattered threads of beauty.

His own beauty had far more power.

The urge to tell him, to blurt the truth and the confusion and all the frightening misery was more than she could bear. She was not meant for deception and the power games of the world. She hated it.

"Ash—"

He turned his head, the bulk of his shoulders. It was a movement of controlled grace. But the light shifted across the handsome planes of his face and the strong line of his body, and the fugitive likeness to Lyfing was there.

"What?"

Her throat seized up. Her heart pounded.

"Naught." She forced her voice through the painful constriction. No missteps. Not ever. Too much was at stake. She was not a fool. Or a weakling. She moved her hand.

"I have my work to finish. I have all that I need to do it. I need nothing else." She turned away.

"All is as it should be. I only have to match the shape of the cells to the shape of the stones and the task is complete."

She put down the carved die.

"You would not understand."

She stared at the needle-sharp point of the engraving tool.

"All complex objects are fashioned in such pieces. The process is the same whatever you do. You can make any ornament you wish."

She looked at the sinuous shape of the backward-biting beast. It could have been a brooch, an ornament for a belt buckle or a scabbard. He would not have a clue what she was doing. He might have fine eyes. He might be as clever a hunter, as guileful and greedy a warrior as ever stepped on the earth, but he would not guess.

What she worked on was only a small fitting on the object she fashioned. The rest was hidden away from his ruthless gaze. No shape-shifting masks, no powerful stem fashioned with grace out of ageless bronze. Naught to betray what she did. Naught to fear and—

The door latch burst through. She dropped the die.

The noise of strained metal and breaking wood faded into silence.

"Erik."

It was Ash who spoke. Ash who watched the grinning figure in the doorway with eyes that calculated everything, down to the small splinters at the booted feet. He had not moved, but she was close to him and the hard-leashed power in him frightened her more than if he had been on his feet yelling.

Her hand reached for the engraving tool. But Ash had it. And the die that would stamp the gold foil.

Erik slammed the door shut and leaned against it. His gaze moved in rapid appraisal across the contents of her table and the half-finished gem work. Then he looked at her. His gaze lingered. She thought she hid both the fear and the loathing.

Then he looked at Ash.

"Hard at work?"

"As you see."

Beside her was the subtle movement of coiled muscle. He must be closer. She could sense his heat. The trailing edge of his hair caught her skin.

Erik's grin widened. "After the first time I saw you, I thought you might have been hard at…" Erik lapsed into Danish.

Ash answered him.

The barbaric, sharp-edged sounds poured out of his mouth. Unhesitating. Erik's eyes widened. The clear air of the workshop became still, stretched and then it shattered under the sound of Erik's braying laughter.

She kept very still, even when Erik's gaze returned to her face and her body and his laughter beat against her ears.

She said nothing. She was supposed to know her

husband spoke the same language as the heathens who
had taken her land. That he could share jests about her
with the man who held her brother prisoner.

She looked at the vibrant face half-turned away from
her, sharing Erik the barbarian's laughter.

She was supposed to know. She picked up the pair
of compasses, just to have something in her hand, something to look at. Anything so that she would not have
to see her husband's face.

Above her head, the alien sounds continued unabated. There was no mistake, no stumbling in the deep
earthy voice beside her. He just kept talking and Erik
kept answering, laughing.

The compass point stabbed through wood. She
would break the metal tip if she— Ash's hand pulled
the sharp instrument free and set it down on the table
as though she were some child who could not be trusted
playing with dangerous toys. Erik's voice got louder.
She looked up. The Viking was frowning.

Ash's voice became suddenly smooth. His hand
clamped over her arm, hard and immovable, its stark
force utterly out of place with his voice. She could not
move. His body seemed to vibrate with the force of all
that was held back.

Yet naught could be read in his face, nothing but the
gloss of handsome ease that matched his voice. He was
like the bronze shape-shifting mask, only one surface
visible at a time and a thousand different guises underneath.

She watched in disbelief as Erik was talked into something he did not want to do. She saw the moment when Erik's greed for whatever it was that the deceiver beside her had offered became too much to resist.

The Viking straightened up and turned for the door. Ash stood instantly, dragging her with him with a speed that nearly took her feet off the floor, hands clamped round her arm, her waist. She could feel the lightning beat of his heart, fast as hers. Like something shared.

"Let me go," she rasped. "Whatever you think you are doing with that creature, I will not—"

"Follow him. Now."

The mask had shifted again: no smoothness, no finely displayed ease. There was only a concentrated purpose that was absolute. Unbreakable. Her heart beat. Her whole body seemed infused with the same power that surged through him.

"You cannot make me do what I do not wish. I will not—"

"He will let you see your brother."

Heated breath choked her, then left her body in a rush. Dizziness followed on it in crushing waves, but he had hold of her, keeping her on her feet, pushing her towards the open door and the sunlight.

"But…how…"

He did not hear her. It did not impinge on that deadly concentration. He had her moving, her feet taking her towards the doorway.

"Hurry. Go straight in. I will hold Erik back but you will have no more than two minutes to explain to the boy who I am. He has to recognize me. Can you make him do that?"

"Yes, of course, I—" She shut up. Erik was waiting across the yard next to a man with keys. They stopped at the barred door. The guard unlocked it. There was blackness, blackness and the smell... She could not see. It was cold.

Edgefrith.

What had they done? She could not see him. Nothing. Her feet seemed glued, held in place. Such cold air. Dizzying. She felt the warmth of the Danish-speaking deceiver's hand at her back, the warmth of his breath touching her face.

"Go."

She stepped into the darkness, the bulk of him behind her, blocking the doorway. Erik's laughter brayed out across the courtyard like something unclean. The light behind her cut through the blackness.

"Gemma?"

THE STRANGER WAS huge.

It was the first thing that Edgefrith saw. He stood still. Gemma was clutching at his hand, still trying to give him instructions, but he could not hear what she said.

He stared at the shadowed figure in the doorway of his prison. He could not see the man's face because there was not much light. Erik did not allow it. But he could see the thick brown sweep of the man's hair and the big shoulders held very straight. The shadows made him think that he saw—

His insides lurched.

He tried not to look because then the dream would shatter the way it always did. Such things were not real. But the man strode forward. He filled the whole room just by stepping through the doorway. Edgefrith always used to step back at this point but he could not move now because then Gemma would notice—

The man kept walking, with the confident tread that had eaten up the distance across so many damp, cold floors in so many miserable rooms. For a while. The painful tightness inside him got worse in the same familiar way. Even though he knew the difference between what were dreams and what was real. Gemma had explained that—

"Speak," whispered Gemma.

He tried to force sound through his throat.

The man stepped into a meager pool of rushlight.

His face was quite different.

Edgefrith had known it would be. He did not have a father. One was dead, and the other one, the one who had almost looked like this, would never come back. Because he did not want to.

His sister nudged him and he knew he should speak but he could not remember what she had said this man's name was. He was not clever like Gemma. He did not know what to do.

But the man never hesitated. Edgefrith suddenly knew he would embrace him like Gemma had. He did not think he could bear that. Gemma was trying not to cry and he could feel all this strangeness inside him. He did not like it. He tried never to let the Vikings see what he felt. He had hidden such things all his life. He knew how.

He swallowed. Gemma said he had to pretend this man was kin.

The massive shoulders turned. He knew how it would go. His father—his *real* father—had always made a great display to cover up how much he disliked him and his mother.

He shut his eyes. But the stranger's touch was hard. Brief. No fuss. Just like the way an old companion at arms might greet another.

The tightness in his chest relaxed.

"Edgefrith." The deep voice sounded as though he said the name all the time. The man stood back.

"Well, this is one way to get out of doing your share of the work."

It was such a stupid thing to say, and the man was so calm. He was actually grinning, even with Erik Bonebreaker in the room. Edgefrith tried grinning back. The man's smile widened.

His big hand stayed on his shoulder, not obvious, not expecting anything, just as calm as his voice.

Edgefrith did not mind that. All he had to do was— The chain hidden in the straw clinked. He must have moved. He had not meant to do that, not when everything was going to be all right.

Gemma shrieked.

A shock went through the hand on his shoulder. The grip tightened, making him think the man was suddenly furious. He seemed to turn into one tight coil of muscle, the way Lyfing used to before he picked a fight. Waves of horror surged down his spine. It would all be for nothing. Erik liked having the chain there. He would use it sometimes to make him scream.

Erik had a camp full of Vikings outside the door. They would kill the man.

The hand let go of him. The wide shoulders turned.

"Gemma…" he whispered. She was kneeling in the filth that gathered on the floor looking at the damage to his leg. She did not hear him.

"Gemma, the man—"

The man was speaking, the words no more than a fast jumble in his terrified ears. If only he could remember the man's name. *"Ash."*

The man turned his head. His eyes were pure green light. Then they changed. He grinned, fast, reassuring, just like before. He turned back to speak to Erik, the grin still on his face. As though there was nothing the matter, as though it was quite ordinary to speak to Erik the savage in—

"Danish…"

The word was no more than a whisper. Only Gemma heard it. She looked up.

"Is he Dan—"

"No." But Gemma's eyes were like well-pools.

She shook her head, because they should not be whispering in case anyone heard. Her eyes fixed on the broad back in front of them. He thought she would start crying again.

But then Erik nodded at the Viking with the keys and he realized why the man called Ash knew how to speak Danish to Erik. He had bewitchment. He stood in the middle of the room, head high, feet firmly planted, shoulders squared and his eyes like green fire.

Erik's man unloosed the shackle.

GEMMA SHUT HERSELF in her room.

But even there, the flickering firelight brought shadows. Shadows that changed and shifted in confusion under her eyes. Like the changing faces of the fine bronze masks. Like the fineness of the deceiver who spoke Danish and laughed with Erik. Erik Bonebreaker, the man her supposed husband said he wanted to kill.

Erik who had kept her brother in chains. Until now.

She closed her eyes against the memory of the bruised and mangled flesh, the childishly thin ankle enclosed in a trap for a beast. Her brother had been petrified, in the pit of despair.

He had looked at Ash as though the Danish-speaking deceiver had been a *galend,* an enchanter and speaker of spells.

She did not need the cunning of a *gald-rice* herself to work out the feelings in her brother's heart.

The *galend* had set him free of his fetters. So that even though Erik still kept him confined against the completion of her work, he was not in chains. He had been given more food, light to chase away the blackness.

All because of the enchanter.

The relief that Ash had made Erik do such a thing still made her weak. But there was a dimension to that gift that her brother, the child, would not even guess at.

But she did, and there was naught she could do about it. She herself had deceived Erik and she had to see the consequences through to the end. She had no choice but to follow all the clever deceptions of her husband.

But she would not let the *galend* enchant her brother's soul away.

And neither, in the end, would he have hers.

She got to her feet. *Enchantments and spell weaving.* It was nonsense, trickery for the weak-minded. She slammed the door.

The Vikings let her beyond the gates. She was on foot and there was nowhere she could go. The whole land of Mercia belonged to them.

But she had to get outside, clear the turmoil of her thoughts, get some control back over her life. She was an artisan who understood mathematics and all the cold calculation that went into the creation of dazzling displays. She was afraid of naught.

The shadows close to the woods shifted with the rough breath of the wind, changing the quality and the density of the low sunlight and the shade. The constant movement tricked the senses. She could create that same trick with light reflected through perfectly set gemstones. She could calculate it to a hairbreadth of accuracy.

She could calculate all that and yet…nothing.

What had she done with her life? What would she do with a future she could not control?

She strode into the shadow of the trees. She had never had such thoughts. It was that creature's fault. Before he came—

Before he came, Edgefrith had been in chains and she had had no way of protecting either her brother or herself from Erik the Bonebreaker.

She stopped in the net of light and shadow cast by strong branches reaching immeasurably high, heavy, the huge buds black, yet bursting with hidden green life. Spring's power. It was an uncanny time to be out, at the changing of the light when other worlds were able to impinge on this.

If you were credulous enough to believe such things.

Her hand touched the rough bark. Ash, the oldest of trees, bridge between worlds.

He was there, in the dazzling shadow cast by his namesake. He stood quite still yet the dancing shadows streaming across the bulk of his form made it seem as though he moved and shimmered like the world-bridge, as though he had just stepped over it from some other place and time.

Why are you here?

The words could not touch the moving air between them. She was not permitted to say them.

He stood and watched her, strong as the tree she touched and as full of life. It made her heart leap with the kind of dazzled yearning that must have struck Edgefrith.

Yet her blood sang with so much more than that. She could feel its wild stirring power like the sap that rose in the bough under her hand.

That power was greater than her fear and her anger and her distrust. It seemed greater than the whole empty wasteland of her future, so that what she wanted was to run to all the virile strength that lived in the stranger. She wanted to touch its heat and its glory. Nay, she wanted him to touch her, to let his heat burn away all the aching coldness inside her.

She wanted his mouth on hers.

Magic.

She knew the darkly heated touch of his lips. She desired that. She desired all that he could give her, the savage beauty, the fascination of his body and the way it moved. She wanted all of him, each masculine detail, even to the blatant heavy fullness of his arousal touching her flesh.

She wanted everything that she had denied yesterday when he had come to her out of this same forest with the spoils of the chase. She wanted hot strength and unknown enchantment, even the harshly glimpsed bitterness of his pain and his weariness. Whatever he would give her.

She wanted him to bed her.

CHAPTER SEVEN

GEMMA STEPPED BACK.

There was no trust. No magic.

"What did you promise Erik?"

He watched her and his eyes glittered. He would betray her. She took uneven breaths.

"There is only one reason Erik would release my brother from his chains. He will expect payment." She was prepared for the denial, the lies. She would not—

"Yes. He will."

His eyes held all the bright currents of the sunlight. She could believe they held truth. The fluid, shadowed lines of his body trapped her gaze, dazzling with the reckless promise of all she desired. Wildfire. Full of danger.

Such danger. Not just to herself. She swallowed.

"What you have done for my brother is…more than I can say. Or than he can. But— My brother is naught but a child. He can defend himself from no one." Her voice choked off. She made it go on.

"You must know that I will not let harm come to him, not from Erik and not from you."

He took a step forward. Just that. He did not shout like Lyfing or bluster. But the bright edges and the deep shadows rearranged themselves. There was not the slightest rustle of displaced leaf or branch. His face swam in shadows. Man or spirit…

"You have made some promise to Erik that—"

"You know what Erik's payment will be. I have told you."

"You said you wanted to kill him."

The dark-edged form wreathed in racing shadows was very close. Its strength was utterly clear to her. She had seen each hidden, hard-edged muscle, knew the way each separate tightly drawn part fitted into a whole that struck fear in its relentlessness.

She heard the soft intake of his breath. Man. Real. She had felt the power of the life force beneath his skin. She had seen his anger. She felt it now, across half a pace of moving air and all the restless surging deepness of the forest.

His eyes were very bright. A warrior's body and a mind that turned too fast and held too many secrets to itself.

He would take.

"I know what you want." She tilted her head back until she had the glittering light of his gaze.

"Do you?"

He covered the last space between them, his body one feral mass of surging power. The dancing currents of air between them vanished. Shadows coalesced with the light. His eyes were hot.

"How do you know what I wish?" His heat tingled across her skin.

"Because of what you are. A warrior and naught else."

The rough bark behind her scraped against her palms. The ash tree. The bridge between two worlds. The link of the seen and the unseen. Appearance and truth.

He was so close. The clear lines of his face filled her vision. She could see the living flecks of green light in his hazel eyes, the dark, earthy richness of their depths.

She told herself they were predator's eyes, hard with cunning and deceit and self-interest. But she could see too much. Things that spoke to all the guarded places of her heart, places full of anger, and behind the anger, grief and loss and hurt.

The recognition of so much that was hidden flared between them, beyond the useless stumblings of words, something that spoke directly from one heart to another.

She could believe in that moment that he understood. Not because of what she had said, but because in his own way he had known all the pain and loss of betrayal. That such things had marked him as surely as they had marked her.

He touched her. His broad heavy hand found the delicate curve at the side of her neck, beneath the protection of her veil and the heavy sweep of her hair. She could have moved. If she had not seen his eyes she would have.

The hard, callused palm of a sword-fighter rested against the thin vulnerability of her skin, utterly mismatched. But it did not matter. Their flesh fused, opposites becoming one in shared human warmth.

It suddenly seemed possible under the joining power of that touch to acknowledge the hurt that raged buried inside her and not be annihilated by it. As though it could be accepted.

It could not be possible.

"Let me go." Her voice could scarce form the sounds because of the pull between them. "Let my brother go."

"You believe I seek his harm."

She stared at the brightness of him and the power.

"You do not need to seek it. Can you not know what you are? Edgefrith is afraid. He is a child, a boy who wants to be a man. He has no father, only a man who—" She tried to stamp out the image of Lyfing, but it blended over the handsome face above hers, obliterating the stranger's features, merging with them.

The touch of his hand burned her.

"A man who what?"

"Seduced my mother away from her husband. Fathered a child on her, and then abandoned her and the child. Edgefrith is my mother's bastard son."

His face was so close to hers in all its careless beauty and its pride.

"Edgefrith loved Lyfing. He looks for his features in the face of every man he meets. He sees them in you."
Just as I do.

She felt the shock go through the hand that touched her, through his body, sharp and real. But she did not care for that. The pain blinded her. Hers. Edgefrith's. Her father's.

And her mother's pain.

"Edgefrith is not my full brother." The vicious words tore at the night air, the deceptive beauty of the man's face. "My mother ran away with a handsome warrior. Someone who had nothing and gave nothing. He took her from her husband and her daughter. He was such a brave man, a real warrior. He had the strength and the power to beat my father nigh to death, and so he did."

She felt the sudden tightening of the hand against her neck. The jarring anger. It did not stop her speaking. He would know that she saw through all that he did, all that he was. He could kill her if he willed but she would say what she must.

"My mother went with that warrior. He could provide her with nothing, only what he could win by his sword or in some menial labor he despised. Yet she bore his child and followed him round in poverty. And when even that got too much for him, he left them, just as she had abandoned us."

She stopped, gasping for breath because of the ugliness of what she said, the ugliness and the pain that were inside her. But she had to say it.

"Yet even that was not the end. Now and then he would come back to her. When he was too cold or too hungry and he had nothing. He would use her to warm his bed and he would charm her. He would be kind to the son who wanted only to love him. But when the boredom set in, he would be gone, on some quest requiring his brave deeds and offering rich spoils at the end of it. What I cannot understand is— She always hoped he would come back."

Gemma shut her eyes.

He spoke, the stranger with Lyfing's face, but she did not care about that. She did not listen. All that mattered was what she would say.

"My mother died waiting for him to remember she was there. Just before the end, she came back to my father. She was desperate. There was no one to take care of her son."

She swallowed, the warmth of the stranger's hand heavy against her throat.

"I made my father take Edgefrith in. I had to beg him. It was the hardest thing he could ever have done, but he would do anything for me. I cannot imagine the pain that he felt. He never spoke of it, but in the end he loved Edgefrith. Just as strongly as he loved me."

She tried to find the right words.

"My father was not a man who spoke easily. He truly belonged only to the power of his craft. He tried to teach Edgefrith like his own son and Edgefrith tried to learn but…but there was always some part of my brother that looked elsewhere, that was always seeking for something else."

For someone like you.

"But Edgefrith did love my father. When he died, Edgefrith would not speak. He and my father were alike in that. They cannot say what is in their hearts."

She finished it.

"My brother looks for a father. Perhaps in his heart he still sees Lyfing. Because what a boy dreams of…" Her mind filled with what Edgefrith had not seen: Lyfing and the vicious triumph in his face, her father's blood on his broad-boned hands. Her own father— "A boy's dreams must be of a warrior. Unless that man is a complete savage he must despise."

She took a breath and the dark, spellbinding heat of his body filled her senses.

"Edgefrith looked at you. He looked at you and he was dazzled." The curve of his body fitted round her, obliterating all else. Such beauty and such danger. Conscious beauty like Lyfing's. It must be. She could not believe otherwise.

"You knew what you did to my brother."

Just as you know what you can do to me.

Her heart beat too fast, because of his nearness, the heavy heat of his hand, the brightness of his eyes. Even now he could make her crave his touch, the power of his body.

"You can work anyone to your will. Even a Viking will befriend you—" She broke off, suddenly, terrifyingly aware of the tightness in his hand on her flesh, the hot, bated silence of him. She was utterly alone with him, trapped between the Viking camp and the unknown vastness of the forest. He was filled with rage and he could—

He let her go.

Cold struck at her. She stared at the solid width of his back three paces away. Her breath hissed in the swirling air, a primitive sound, horrifyingly audible. He turned his head.

"There is naught to be afraid of, Gemma. I cannot steal your brother's heart from you. There is nothing in me but the savageness he would despise."

The wind whipped his bright hair across his face, hiding all expression. Nothing beyond the blackness of his voice.

And his anger. It would be there with all the savagery he had admitted to. But she could not look away from the line of his shoulders, the turn of his head.

She could not rid her mind of all she had seen in his eyes.

She felt none of the vindication she expected, only a great oppression, as though her heart would burst.

Her tight breath sobbed in her throat and he would hear it. She turned away, but she suddenly knew he was there, even though she had not heard his feet on the forest floor.

"*Gemma.*"

"I want my brother back."

It sounded like the cry of someone no older than Edgefrith. The sobs were building somewhere inside her.

She never cried.

She gasped and the cold air tore at her throat, stung

her skin. Then it was gone, obliterated by the warmth of the *galend,* the crushing strength of his arms. He held her and his heat touched the coldness. Strong.

She wanted that heat to touch her, surround her. She wanted to feel it deep inside. It was what she needed.

Such strength. He was dangerous as a Viking. Worse. A man between two worlds, belonging to neither, to no one.

"You do not understand. Edgefrith is all that I have, as I am all that he has. You cannot understand what kind of bond that makes."

"Yes, I do. I had such a bond."

"You?" It was not possible. But anything seemed possible when he touched her and she felt the power of his closeness; even the thread of understanding she had rejected.

"I did not know you have a brother." She knew nothing, not even what the burning possibility of understanding between them was. She felt the unevenness in his breath because they were so close, the sound slight and human.

"I do not. I had something more rare. A stranger who treated me as though I were one of his kin, as though I were quite worthy to be so. He called me his foster brother."

How could anyone have no kin? Or have none who would acknowledge him? Unless indeed he bore a wolf's head. Was he an outlaw, after all, her half-Viking savage?

All the questions she could not ask writhed like gnawing serpents in her brain.

"Where is your foster brother now?"

This time the reaction was greater. She felt it through his flesh, even though it was suppressed with all the savagery he laid claim to.

"He is under the earth."

"Dead? I am sorry for that." Her own father's death was there in her mind, the shock of it and the sense of loss held back because she had to survive, help Edgefrith.

Was that how it was for him? All that pressure of feeling held back because there was no place for it? She thought of the way that harsh jolt had been suppressed when she had questioned him, and she saw the truth.

"You feel such loss that—" She could not say it because her own sense of loss was too strong and she could not cope with it.

"There are some things that cannot be lost. A bond like that is one of them. That is how things are, Gemma." His voice was pitched softly, deep as the earth, gentle as his hold on her. The anger was gone. No, not gone, hidden. But he would not let it touch her. All he would let her feel was his warmth.

"You must not be afraid of your love for your brother. Such a thing is a gift, stronger than all the world's bane."

"I do not... I am not..." But was she? Was she afraid of any kind of love, any closeness to another human being? How could she explain?

"All I ever wanted was to ply my craft. My father

taught me all the knowledge of it and the skill. That skill and that knowledge filled all that I ever needed. Since I was a child, I have traveled the length of Britain with my father and…and Edgefrith." She closed her mind on the image of her mother.

Her mother and Lyfing with his boasting ways and his destructive lusts. Lyfing with his fair face and his powerful warrior's body. She could remember his beauty, even though she had been no more than a child.

It must have been like this. Her head rested against the warm solid mass of a thick shoulder, her body leaned against a lithe, tightly edged mass of muscle, full with power and taut curves and balanced lines.

Destructive. And yet she wanted it.

"That life was enough for me," she burst out, her voice striking against the rough wool beneath her face, the hard seductive beauty it hid. "I never wanted anything else. I did not ask for the kind of greed and arrogance that destroys families, that causes wars and takes children as prisoners."

She shifted in the locked strength of his arms. She had to get away from him. What if he would not let her? She gasped, but her face was buried in the hollow at the base of his throat. Her savage indrawn breath inhaled warmth, the heated earthy tang of his skin. The heat pulsed inside her in rippling waves. Her heart clenched. Longing or despair… She did not know. She knew nothing.

"I did not want to be at the mercy of feelings. I would not allow it." *Will not.*

"Hush. You cannot cut yourself off from life, or turn your back on what it brings."

"But I want to—"

"Do you? Is that how you want your world to be? So empty?"

Yes.

But her mind dizzied under the spell-craft of his eyes and his closeness and a thousand thoughts beyond her knowing. Everything jumbled in her head, Edgefrith and her father, Erik and his greed, the brilliant fascination of her craft, the safety of the cold realms of the mind, the burning man-heat under her fingers. Lyfing and his lusts. Lyfing and her mother. Ash.

Ash, only Ash. Now. With her. Her body tingled from the closeness of his. From his touch. Because of his words and the way they could reach into her head.

Because of the wealth and the heat and all the sinfully desirable beauty she had seen.

Did she want such endless emptiness as had been her world?

The heat of him moved against her, enfolded her.

"You cannot deny what it means to be alive. You would deny part of yourself."

His mouth touched hers. It was what she had craved from the first moment she had seen him standing in the forest clearing. The world jolted into focus. Her lips parted under his, drank from them. She knew what to do this time. She knew how he tasted and what he did. Black heat took her mouth, moist darkness, the firm smooth pleasure of his lips. His tongue.

Her mind slipped beyond thought at his touch. He was hot. Warmth and strength against the whipping wind and the mysterious shadows of the trees. He slid her backwards against the thick trunk of the ash tree, the wideness of it and the bulk of his body sheltering her against the restless air.

His size held her trapped, enclosing her. Yet she pushed against his weight only to get him closer. Her hands slid around his back. Thick muscle arranged in long sweeping lines, tight at the narrow line of his hips, flaring out at the heaviness of his shoulders. Her hands dug in. She felt the sharpness of his response, a wordless sound deep at the back of his throat, harsh, primitive. She had not known she could do that. Excitement flared in the pit of her stomach.

His body pressed tighter against hers, its fullness a shock, the tight thick jut of his male flesh already hardened, the feel of it primitive as the sound he had made.

His hands traced the shape of her body, finding every curve, touching it with his heat so that she sprang alive against the smooth demand of his fingers. He was so sure in what he did. The reaction of her body intensified, as though it had a will beyond her own. She watched his big scarred fingers unfasten the laces at the neck of her dress. He would see her skin. He would see of her what no man had ever seen.

The cold air brushed her aching flesh, making her shiver, but she was already shivering deep inside because of him. Heat flared in his eyes, making them utterly green, brighter than cut glass. The same flare of heat jumped to her. His gaze lowered, so that she could see only the soot-dark curve of his lashes. But the heat stayed, burning higher, even though he drew back, and for a breathless moment he held still.

So he could see her.

Her flesh tightened. He would see the flagrant intensity of her reaction, the way the sensitive peak of her breast hardened under cold and heat. He would know how strongly his touch and his closeness affected her.

That was what he wanted. The realization sent stabs of sensation through her, shooting down inside, causing aching tightness between her thighs.

The feelings, the knowledge that the sight of her aroused him so much and the openness of his response were an intimacy greater than she could bear. Her breath shortened, the shaking sound of it audible.

She had shown him her need, all the frightening feelings inside her that might be the counterpart of the desire she saw in him. He drew her towards him, turning his body to shield her from the shifting wind, bringing her against his heat.

He slid his hips against hers, the lean powerful curve of his undamaged thigh nudging between her legs. The contact jolted her. She could feel the strong full shape of his thigh between hers, the insistent movement smooth and blatantly sensual.

He kept moving closer. The solid wall of his chest would touch the flesh he had bared to his gaze. She watched it happen, the slowness of the movement deliberate, even though she could sense all the driving, harshly leashed male power of him. So that the touch of his body was something both seen and felt. The size of him. The rough wool of his tunic. The smooth-lined power beneath. The sound of his breath and the scent of his skin.

She gasped. But he held her tightly, as though he had known the shock, as though he expected and understood the hot burst of feeling, the savage unabated need inside her. Her body came to rest hard against his, resistless, everything given, as though she were a wanton.

She let him keep her so close while her body writhed. She pushed against him, the naked tightness of her breast touching him, moving until his hand palmed its fullness. As small desperate sound escaped her throat. She went still. Twenty years of caution told her to draw back. But she could not.

She stayed motionless, let his hand mold the curve of her shape, watched him, saw the scarred bronzed flesh against the whiteness of her skin. The thick pad of his thumb grazed the red swollen tip.

Her legs clamped round his, the movement bringing her soft aching flesh against his hardness. Shock blossomed at the back of her mind. But for a breathless instant she did not draw back. As though she wanted that, too. As though she wanted everything of him and it was right. Her body moved, sliding against him, need-driven, wanting.

No control.

She could not allow that. If she did, the entire skill-fully constructed edifice of her life would be destroyed, exposed for the empty shell it was.

Never—

"Nay. Let me go! I cannot. I—"

She twisted wildly in his grasp. Because she was fright-ened, demented. Mad. Mad for his touch. She— There was air between them, the blessed coldness of the wind.

She lurched away, not knowing where, anywhere, just to get away from him. From the overpowering, dan-gerous things he made her feel. Her worn shoes slipped on the wet ground, her feet snagging in gnarled tree roots.

He caught her.

She could see his huge hands on her arms, sense the size of him behind her, feel his heat.

"Let me go." She sounded wild, uncontrolled. Vi-cious.

"Gemma. Wait." The strength of his voice matched hers, surpassed it because it was paced, deliberate. The terrible fear made her arms twist against his but she could not break his grip, and it only brought his body closer so that she could feel all of it against her like a wall of stone.

"Gemma, stop this. Wait." It had the force of a com-mand, the blank invincibility of his strength. If that had been all the harshly spoken words had held, she would have fought him off even if he had killed her.

But there was something else in the very bleakness

of his voice that found a response in the raw confusion
inside her.

"Gemma."

His voice shivered against her ear. The stone wall
breathed. She could feel his warmth, the effort in his
harshly controlled breath. His hair touched her face.

"I will not hurt you."

The heavy power shifted, relaxing its hold. But she
could still feel him in each muscle, all the tightly drawn
length of his body. She was pressed against the solid
wall of his chest, the lean tautness of his hips, the hot
heavy flare of his thigh muscles.

She could sense the way he fought for each breath,
how harsh it was in the depth of his chest, feel the moist
hot edge of it against her skin. He vibrated with the
madness of unleashed desire, the way she did. She felt
the tight, unslaked hardness of his manhood, the flesh
still hot and thickened from the passions she had
aroused, by the wildness of what she had done.

She shut her eyes, felt the whisper of his breath.

"Gemma." She did not move. But her body tensed.
It was a mistake because she felt the answering tightness in his. A formless sound escaped her lips. Their
breath mingled.

"I have to go back. I have to—" She tried to think of
her room, of being there. Alone. But it seemed to belong
to another life, to a person she did not know. "I have to."

"Yes. But I will not let you go back to Offleah like

this." His hands slid down her arms to settle around her wrists. "Gemma. I will not harm you."

His body slid away from hers. There was a moment of silence when nothing moved except the restless breath of the wind and she could have broken the lightness of his hold. Mayhap. It was a chance. She did not take it. Then it was too late.

His hands moved on her body, turning her around in the circle of his arms, so that they were facing each other. Like the opponents they were. His grip tightened and she heard the sharp sound of his breath.

"That is what you believe, is it not? That I would harm you?"

Yes. The word was there, buried in her head because of Lyfing. Because of all the other things that— Her tongue had formed the word, bitter graceless accusation not plea, but then she saw his face.

Such a word could not be spoken, not ever. Not to him.

Her hands slid up his arms, fastening on the solid cords of his flesh. She forgot Lyfing. She forgot all that life had taught her in twenty struggling winters. All that mattered was taking that look out of his eyes.

"No. I do not think that. Not of you."

Instinct, all the clever thoughts of her mind, teetered on the edge of the knowledge.

"It is not so."

He must not have believed her, because he moved away. Her hands tightened on thick muscle. It was stone hard, utterly resistant. She tried to hold him as he had held her, but she could not. He had so much strength.

"Ash…"

As though the saying of his name had the power to unlock some of that blanked-off desolation, he went suddenly still under her hands. She held on, hardly breathing, knowing he had only to move one tight band of muscle and she would lose him. Knowing that right here and now she would not be able to bear that. Unable to think about why.

She watched his eyes, saw the truth, and her mind tumbled over into the unknown deepness of the new world he had shown her.

"What I was afraid of was myself."

The words shimmered between them in the wind-blown air. They were not words she knew how to say, how to admit before anyone, least of all this stranger who had cut straight through to her heart.

But he must have seen both her truth and her need. The soul-dark eyes changed. She felt the same change in the rock-hard muscle beneath her hands. She felt the brief warmth of living flesh, power against the cold. She realized how much she was shaking.

Then the war-thick muscle slid through her grip. He was pulling the cloak round her against the wind. He did not hold her. His hands straightened the heavy woollen folds with such soothing competence, as though he was someone who wanted to look after her.

She was not used to anyone wanting to look after her.

She let him do it. Then his hands touched her under-dress. She started back in the realization of the state she was in, that she would have fled the concealment of the trees just so.

The warm competent fingers paused.

"It is all right. You do not have to fear, not even when we go back."

The words were as direct and uncomplicated as his touch. She could take them at face value and accept their truth, that she would be safe. She could ask nothing else, just as he would ask nothing of her, and perhaps she could slip back into her own familiar world. Isolated. Confined.

Or she could choose to touch on what was hidden.

So many things were hidden in him, just as they were in her.

She watched the hard edge of his hand beside her half-exposed flesh. Above their heads the tree branches rustled, light and shade, ever changing. Like life.

"I was afraid because I did not know."

The words came out of nowhere. But he seemed to understand, holding his body quite still, close to hers, waiting, so that she might speak.

"I did not know what such things were like because I shut them out of my life. I had my craft and that was all that I wanted. I had not thought…I had seen that such things, such *passions,* brought only destruction."

She took a breath, her breast swelling until it almost touched his hand.

"I wanted my life to be different, well-ordered, solely my creation like the works of my skill. I wanted only that, to be left alone with my craft. I did not want to harm anyone. But then…all this came. The Vikings came and everything changed, and my world was safe no more. Everything was destroyed."

"Aye. For you and for so many."

"So many?" Her voice cracked on bitterness. "Yes, for so many. And my father—and I—would have turned our backs even on that."

She felt the tension through his skin. She raised her head. "That is how cold I am. So you see—"

"No. I do not see. That is not what I see when you are with your brother, when you feed Boda even though you are hungry yourself, when you speak of your father's death."

"But—"

"You try to pretend you are as cold and unfeeling as the beauty you create. But that is not what I see, what I feel when I touch you."

Her breath caught and her gaze was lost in green fire. He moved his hand to touch her face, sliding one finger along the line of her jaw, making her skin tingle. The solid palm molded itself to the shape of temple and jaw and cheekbone and stayed there.

But he made no other move and she realized he had meant what he said, like an honour-word, that if she wished it he would take her back and she would be safe.

The person she had been yesterday, this morning, would have accepted that. But he had freed her brother from his chains. Whatever his reasons were, he had done that. Whoever he was, Viking or Mercian, warrior or wolf's head, had no meaning compared to what she had seen in his eyes; what she still saw behind the heat of desire, stronger than that, stronger than anything.

"Then show me what I should know. If I am not cold and worthless and beyond the reach of feeling—" her hand settled over his "—teach me that."

CHAPTER EIGHT

HIS EYES BURNED. But his hand did not move under the pressure of hers.

"Nay. There is naught you can learn of me. I am not fit to teach…anything."

She could feel the strength gathered in his body, see the stark lines of his face, now clear, now bathed in the shade of the ash tree, like a shape-shifter's mask. The wind lifted his hair in dark streaming ribbons, casting shadows, revealing the power of his neck, the straight shoulder.

But she was no longer afraid of the power. Only his eyes mattered.

"Then if you will not show me, I will never know. For I will learn of none other. I trust no man."

"You cannot trust me."

Liar.

There was naught that shadows, or sense-dazzling tricks, or the tight arrogant line of his body could do. He had let her glimpse what lived inside his eyes. No mask could avail against that.

"If you trust what you say you can see in me, then I

may trust what I see in you." She raised her head. "Teach me your truth."

The brilliant eyes flared, depthless. She knew beyond reason that she was right. Her blood caught the fire. She was achingly aware of how close he was, of the sexual charge in the air. Man and woman.

Yet her heart still beat out of time. For all the heat between them, he might still refuse her and she would be lost, empty of life, forever.

She spoke into his silence, her words as fragile as a bridge between worlds.

"I am alone. I think I have always been alone, all of my life." She stared at his eyes, bright light and dark shadows. "I think if any creature who breathes could understand that, you could. Do not leave me to be alone—" Her voice choked off with all the emotions she did not know how to feel. But the understanding of all that formless confusion was there in his eyes.

His hand moved, or hers did. She could not tell how it happened, only that their flesh was joined in the simplicity that must stretch back though all the ages of time. In the complexity of human feelings that was greater than any mathematical calculation of her art.

He was pure flame, touching her and enfolding her in his heat. The heat scorched her, through the fierce gentle caress of his hands, the fluid graceful movement of his body, the sliding seductive power of his lips.

The feel of him stole her senses. He was an excitement beyond compare. His mouth covered the swollen tingling softness of hers, taking all the inadmissible passion and the dark-edged excitement. Giving it.

She realized how much he gave, that what she had thought was an empty act of greater strength and power was something else entirely.

Her arms slid round the broad plane of his back, finding the tensed muscles through the barrier of his tunic, touching their harshness, the sleek lines of him hidden underneath the coarse wool. His breath caught on a rough low sound. The muscles under her hands bunched, ridged and sharply defined under her fingers. Stark with desire.

A desire that was the fierce masculine mirror of her own.

The dark excitement mounted. The desperate urge to possess was there in all its primitive power, but with it was the burning need to return the pleasure, to know that that was possible. Her hands flattened out, stroked the long sinuous lines of his back, slid lower.

She sensed the harshly leashed tension. It was almost enough to stop her. But not so. She was in too deep, too lost in him and all the mysteries locked down in each muscle under the gliding touch of her fingers.

Her hand slid round across the rich line of the back of his undamaged thigh, feeling the moving swell of muscle, sliding higher, under the loose folds of his tunic, finding the tight, hidden curve of dense flesh. Her own breath gasped, the sound lost against the hot plundering richness of his mouth.

He moved. The power of his strength locked their bodies. The grip of his hands on her waist, on the softer female curves below, his weight, held her against him. A raw sound choked against her lips. Her heart raced and the excitement constricted her throat. But she did not let go of him.

Her hands dug into taut springing flesh, traced its strong muscular arch. She felt the hardness of him pressed against her moist aching flesh. Her fingers brushed against the hidden heaviness of his sex. The twisting mindless thrust of his body against hers made her cry out.

The sharp relentless feelings inside her flamed, overwhelming in their intensity. This time the sound she made was laced with fear. Her body shook with the raw intensity bound inside it, with the force of all the things she did not know. She had never felt so desperate, so utterly helpless.

He drew back, his hands warm and gentle on her flesh. Safe. As though his strength would protect her despite the savage wildness inside him.

"Ash…"

"It is all right."

Her hands caught at his. His eyes were black depths with green flecks of light. She was so afraid she would lose him.

She said the words her pride had never admitted since she had been old enough to be called master of her skill and her learning.

"I do not know what to do."

"Then do naught. Let my touch show you."

His breath was warm against the wind. His lips touched not her mouth but her skin, making her shiver. Not with cold, but with the heat. He eased her backwards, so that her back rested against the ash tree. She watched his dark head bend to the pale glow of her skin.

He took the tight aching peak of her breast in his mouth. A bright jolt of sensation stabbed though her. Her spine arched, pushing her body towards him and he held her, teasing pleasure out of her with lips and tongue, until the sensation flooded in tingling waves through every point of her body.

She was so dizzied with it that she did not care when his hand pushed the trailing folds of her skirt aside. She was so far gone in the taut expectation of the pleasure that she only wanted its release. Her body jerked and then stilled when his strong fingers touched the most intimate part of her.

She should not let him do that. It was too dangerous. Some part of her mind still knew it. But her flesh under his touch was hot, moist, swollen with the pounding blood in her veins. His fingers parted the soft folds. She tensed at the intimacy of what he did; but the pleasure was too great, the smooth glide of his fingers over her desire-dampened skin the most erotic sensation she could imagine.

She almost blacked out at the intensity of it. She

could not stand but he moved to hold her, his strength taking her weight, effortless, and all the time the touch of him, maddening, utterly arousing. Her body twisted, rubbing against him. Small moaning sounds escaped her lips; her skin was damp with sweat despite the cold.

She writhed in his arms like an animal. She sounded like one. She had no control. But he did not care. Truly he did not. He expected nothing of her, only this. Only the pleasure he could give, that she could take of him. A gift freely given.

Her body arched. He took its mad thrust, his touch sending her over the spiraling brilliant edge of sensation into the unknown world. Pure hot pleasure gathered and caught and shattered against his hand, his fingers sliding inside the opening of her body at the last instant so that there was no emptiness afterwards, only him in completeness and the sense of his warmth.

He held her close, sweat-damp skin against sweat-damp skin, his lips buried in her hair, the harsh tearing rhythm of their breathing shared.

He did not move, his warmth like a shield. She lay against it, her eyes closed and her body shaking. He let her do that. His gift, like his loving of her body.

Luvung. Love. The word terrified her. What he had done, he had done freely. He had asked nothing of her in return, not even now when his body pressed against hers and she could feel all the tightly leashed vitality, the unused male strength. Her future could have been made the same as her mother's. She could have done nothing about that. She would not have had the strength. She would not have had the will.

She had not understood what she had asked of him.

It was so dangerous, the power that leached from him in hot waves. She had trusted so blindly that he would not use it against her. She had trusted to a sense of honour.

A man like him did not have honour.

She watched his face turned away from her, the harsh dark-stubbled line of his jaw, the flush of heat along the high cheekbones, the brightness of the eyes half-hidden by thick lashes. The beauty of him struck her anew. Not as it had at first, like some finely drawn creation of sculpted flesh, but more deeply. Because of all that lived inside. The combination of passion and control, the power of thought and all the brilliant force of life.

His gift had been true.

Her heart clenched. She did not want to think about that. Or about what he might take when he left.

Above their heads, the ash tree moved in the wind. Its roots were deeply buried in the earth beneath her feet but its branches swayed with an energy that dazzled sense.

He would leave. And when he did, the new, half-glimpsed world would go with him.

THE BLACKNESS of the night was where he belonged, not in the lighted bower with Gemma. She slept, oblivious.

Ashbeorn paused in the pool of dark cast by the

building, one shadow in another. That was his life. It held no place for a creature made out of spun gold and melting warmth.

It had been an instant of madness born out of her beauty and the warmth she had offered without even understanding what it was.

She knew nothing.

She should not have come near him in the dark-breathing power of the woods. She should not have looked at him as though she understood when she did not.

She should not have said that she trusted him.

It was the one gift he had wanted all his life. The one thing he could never be given. Least of all by her.

He could not requite it.

He moved forwards through the darkness towards his goal, utterly silent. The seven shallow steps stood before him. Light flared above his head, smoke from burning pitch trailing in the wind.

He knew all that waited inside. It was part of him.

He closed his mind against the memory of Gemma, the whisper of her breath, the soft silk of her flesh, moving, burning. Her heat closing round his hand. The brightness of her eyes.

Her vulnerability.

He could not take on that vulnerability. He could not be responsible for it.

Why had he thought he could look into her soul?

The thoughts of her clever, educated mind, even the

harshly felt pain of her fear and her sadness had naught to do with him.

He was here for a different purpose and even if that had not been so, there could be nothing between him and a woman like Gemma.

He mounted the steps, his feet striking the flagged stones once shaped by King Burgred's men. It did not matter if people heard him, inside the hall or out.

He was perfectly aware of the separate shadow that had suddenly appeared at his back. It did not matter. It could make no difference what the boy thought, or what Gemma would think when the boy told her what he did now.

Gemma should know. She had asked for his truth.

He shoved at the massive oak door. More light spilled out, making Boda's furtive shadow draw back. He paused for an instant, giving the boy's figure time to vanish. His attempt at stealth was unhandy at best. Ashbeorn could have remedied that. If he had been a different person.

He stepped forward. The noise and the stench of bodies and spilled ale rose like a solid wall. It was no barrier to him. He strode through. The generous heat of the fire, bright light, woodsmoke laced with the tang of roasted meat closed round him. The noise of celebration. *Mondream,* the revelry of men, hall-joy.

The bright sounds, the laughter and the shouting, the cheer of good companions shut off the rawness of the night, the miserable poverty of all that lay outside the looted hall.

Someone grinned and clapped him on the back as though he were a long-lost friend. He returned the salute. The acceptance was instant, as he had known it would be. He drank the ale that was offered, letting the cool dark liquid slide in one endless stream down his throat, the dregs spill from the corners of his mouth. Droplets ran down, staining his clothing. His laughter mixed with the roar of approval.

He flung the emptied horn onto the table. The heat and the noise, the raucous companionship settled round him just as they always had.

It was the kind of welcome given to those who belonged.

"WHAT DO YOU MEAN? Where did you see him? When?"

Boda mumbled in reply. For once he seemed short on words. His eyes were sullen, his grubby rags a hunched shape of reluctance.

"The hall. With them. Erik. Last night. I saw him go in."

Gemma's throat tightened.

"Mayhap he had gone outside into the yard and someone saw him, called him in there."

She put up a hand to her aching head, straightening her veil. She wanted to drag her fingers through her hair. Scream. She could feel it building up inside her throat.

"If that was so, he could hardly refuse." It was an utterly reasonable statement.

She forced herself to look at Boda. The morning

light hurt her eyes. She wished she had slept, instead of spending the night in unquiet dreams. Dreams of him. Lost to her forever in a trackless wilderness she could not cross. Or touching her, making her body fill with the wanting of him, ache with need until she burned. And only he could bring the scorching heat of release.

"Just being at the hall means nothing of itself. It—"

"You did not see." The stubbornness in the face of her deliberate dismissal, the reluctance in every bone of Boda's body struck coldness deep inside.

It meant nothing.

The fact that Ash, the brilliant sensual stranger, had gone outside after he had left her in her room meant naught. He had…cared about her. She knew that beyond reason. Beyond even the burning knowledge of his touch. He had brought her back, made her safe, as though she were so fragile, so precious she might break. He had stayed with her until she slept.

Until he was very, very sure that she slept.

"Boda, this is a Viking camp. If you go outside you will see it is full of Danes. That is impossible to ignore. *I* cannot ignore it. I—"

"He was drinking with Erik. I saw through the window. They had to open some of the shutters because of the smoke. I watched. He did not know I was there. They were laughing."

You have made some promise to Erik…

"But—"

You cannot trust me.

She swallowed. "Could you hear what…"

"I do not speak Danish. Not like them, like *him*. But I could see. The man you say is your husband and Erik Bonebreaker were like boon companions who share everything."

Her hand, like something long forgotten, still tugged at her veil. It was shaking.

"Erik had a whore."

"OVERDRUNKEN?"

Gemma watched him, the bright spirit who had conjured magic out of her, the man of flesh and blood. His eyes were too deeply set, blackly shadowed, the bones of his face too stark, the rich skin tightly drawn, darkened with stubble.

"Yes."

Precisely cut garnets slipped through her fingers.

She would have preferred a denial.

She picked up the tweezers.

"Interesting night?"

His eyes snapped fire and then it was gone.

"Aye." He smiled. She put down the tweezers and picked up the small sharp-edged knife.

Did you share the whore with Erik like everything else?

She smiled back.

"What are you making?"

Her smile froze. He had never asked her directly, though she had seen the way his fine eyes watched all that she did while the fine brain behind them worked.

He should not know. This was her deception. Obviously there were some things Erik did not share. Beyond drinking and laughter. And whores.

"I have told you. Fine things. Adornments. I do whatever Erik the Bonebreaker wants." She paused. "You should understand that."

"Aye. So I should." There was no pause in his voice at all. He picked up a garnet. "It is a thing worth remembering."

Her heart hammered.

"Is that what I should remember of you when you are gone?"

"Aye. That and nothing else."

She looked at the brazen gall of his face. Her breath hissed. It covered a pain she was not prepared to let him guess at. She looked at the knife. At what she was doing.

"It is as well to know these things," she said, "so that one can avoid making mistakes."

If she could just adjust the setting, it would be perfect. Light reflected against the narrowed slits of her eyes. Light and shadow. The knife slipped.

"What are you doing—" His hand closed over hers. So fast. So strong. He was so very competent in all that he did.

"It is naught."

"Did you cut yourself? Let me see." His hand turned hers. She watched the supple weather-bronzed fingers, the firm curving flesh at the base of his thumb, the careful restraint of his movement. She thought of the way

that heavy, deft hand had touched her, and heat shot
through her. Her hand shook. She closed her eyes on humiliation. Fury.

"I cannot see any damage."

*No. What you do is not the kind of damage that can
be seen.*

He held her hand, much the way he had that first day
in her workshop and she had thought him kind. She did
not do anything as obvious as withdraw from his touch.
She reached out with her free hand to draw the brightness of the oil lamp close so that the light struck his face.
She picked up her heavy steel tongs and dropped them
with a clatter.

She thought his eyes narrowed. She tried another smile.

"I suspect the only thing suffering today is your head.
Whatever did you do last night after you left me?"

He let her go. It was such a small triumph. It hardly
stood against the impenetrable mask of his face.

"I went into the hall. I got drunk with Erik. Then I
slept in the rushes on the floor. Can you not tell that by
my clothes?"

He leaned towards her. His rumpled tunic smelled of
stale woodsmoke and old ale. Not just his tunic; even
the beautiful uncombed fall of his hair. It was the first
time since he had regained consciousness in her bower
that he had not washed. The rather bloodshot eyes held
no remorse, only the blankness of a mask. Nay, it was
so uncompromising that mayhap it was not the mask,
but the real man beneath.

She did not recoil. She held her place, far too close to him, to the taint of what he had done in Erik's hall when—

"You did that after you had left me."

"Yes."

She thought about the whore.

"There is naught that you would deny is there?"

She would ask him about the whore.

"There is naught that I can deny."

If she were a fool, she could imagine she caught one glimpse of the expression that had made her offer herself to him with an eagerness that must have outclassed whoever had slept with him in the straw. He turned his head, the movement graceful and full of ease. She was a fool. She would not ask the question.

No need.

The precisely cut garnet flicked into place under the skill of her hands. Perfection. She stared at it.

Precision.

"You wanted me to know what you did last night, did you not? Boda told me, but if he had not, you would have."

"Yes."

He was watching something outside, not her. She looked up. It was Boda. In the yard.

"Why? Because on the strength of— Because you thought I might make some unwelcome display of affection this morning? Because you regret what you did?"

"I regret nothing." The sudden turn of his head caught

her unawares. The bright flame in the deep-shadowed eyes was there. It was real. Her heart knew that with a certainty far deeper than thought. But his face was stone-hard.

"What I wanted you to know goes beyond that, to what I am. It is no aberration for me to be in a place like Erik's hall. It is where I belong. Whatever I do, whoever I am with, cannot change that. What I have shared with you I cannot regret. But it cannot stand against what is real."

Real.

She looked at the fine beauty of him marred by *symbelgal,* the mad wanton lust of the feast. She looked at the thread of pity in his eyes, the rough-granite hardness of his face.

She had expected this. Life had taught her to expect it. She had just lost sight of the truth in a moment of crazed bespellment under the rustling magic of the trees.

"You need not worry. I can see what is. No one has been better fitted to see that than me."

She turned away, so that she no longer had to look on that pity and that harshness.

The brilliant glitter of her work filled her aching sight. Pure lines and perfection that could be calculated to a hairbreadth. Her husband went outside to talk to Boda. Doubtless he needed the fresh air.

The tiny garnets ran through her fingertips, the bright cunningly shaped gold gleamed.

It was flawless.

The bright metal was cold against her hand.

THE MAN WHO PRETENDED to be Gemma's husband was moon-mad.

Boda tried shaking off the mud of more than a day's traveling on foot. He only succeeded in smearing it deeper into his tunic and his trousers. He sighed.

Anyone was crazed who had believed that a creature like him would be permitted to enter a West Saxon fortress. Or allowed into the presence of a king alive.

"For the king," said Boda, as though chanting a spell that had the power to open gates. Or placate a band of war-wolves who looked as though they roasted and ate children. Or fools who brought messages.

"Lords," he added humbly. How could he have let Ash talk him into this? He eyed someone's fingers on a knife hilt.

He was a fool. He had weaseled his way across the border and into a country that was in a state of virtual war and now he was going to be hanged. He had not the slightest reason to risk his neck for a wolf's head who swilled ale with Erik Bonebreaker.

The guards stared at him.

Just because someone took your friend out of chains and showed you knife tricks did not mean they were believable.

Or that they were on some kind of secret mission.

The man had made Gemma cry. Almost.

"Please."

He sounded like one of the children about to be eaten. He kept staring at the helmets and the leather jerkins adorned with the image of a golden dragon, just as Gemma's supposed husband had described them. He listened to the Wessex accent that Ash could talk when he wanted to. Imitate. Pretend.

Mostly he looked at the knife hilt. He moved very, very slowly to extract the token Ash had given him. He did not see it could do the least good.

"Careful, lad. We are not patient men—"

The knife unsheathed. Boda tried to remember the trick Ash had taught him for disarming people. He did not think it would work. Besides, there were three of them.

Four. He caught a gleam of reflected light. Movement. Another hulking West Saxon. This one in a chain mail *byrnie*. Which meant he was high-ranking and therefore even more arrogant. Dangerous.

Boda produced a twig with scratches on it.

He thought the man in the *byrnie* would kill him. He tried making a bolt for it but the guards had him. They dragged him away.

The thane in the glittering corselet stared after as though he had seen a ghost.

CHAPTER NINE

THE END WAS so close.

Gemma stared at the work laid out before her. It was almost complete, the separate parts ready to be fused together into a whole. Then it would be over. Edgefrith would be free and—

She had thought that this part would be difficult because she would have to think of a way to get rid of her supposed husband for a while to preserve the secret of what she did.

But that could hardly be necessary. He and Erik still shared. Erik would have had plenty of opportunity to discuss his commission in private.

She stared at the unearthly beauty laid out before her. The shifting shapes of the bronze masks mocked her. Appearance and reality. Light and shadow.

She pulled her work towards her. Ash was not here. He was with Edgefrith again. A boon from Erik because he had achieved such good work by the skill of his hands. When he had not been carousing and…whatever else he did.

This time, she had not been invited to her brother's cell.

The hard-edged shapes blurred under her sight. Edgefrith. Lost in his prison, looking for a savior and trusting where he would be betrayed.

She gathered the things she would need for the final soldering.

Edgefrith was a child. He had no way to defend himself. He was alone.

Alone.

Her hands stilled. She had never felt so alone in her life, or missed her father so much. She had never permitted her grief for her father. There had not been an opportunity. Erik had seen to that. The sudden flash of anger shocked her in its savageness. She drew breath.

Her father would have told her to get on with her work, that it was the only truth among the frailties of the world.

She picked up the set of tongs. She did not want her work. She wanted someone she could speak to. There was no one. Even Boda had gone, vanishing in the night like the wild creature he was. Perhaps there was nothing left for him here without Edgefrith's companionship.

She stared at bright metal and fine carving.

She wanted a person.

What she wanted burst across her brain with searing intensity. Her mind saw his face. Memory gave her the hot touch of his flesh. It was vain imagining, yet her whole body shuddered in instant response. Her skin tingled. Her ears heard the sibilant rustle of his clothing and she tightened in every muscle as though she felt the smooth thrust of his weight.

Her hand clenched round the tongs.

He was a betrayer. He had taken the peace of her body and the peace of her mind.

Eyes blinded, she flung the solid iron tongs with all the strength in her arm. They missed shattering his face by inches and hit the doorjamb. He picked them up.

"Bad morning?"

She gasped. She had not heard the door open.

He walked in, tossing the heavy tongs in his hand as though they were a child's toy.

She raised her head.

"Not as good as it could have been. How was Erik?" *And Edgefrith, my brother?*

"Happy." His eyes never flinched. "Is this for working with or throwing?"

She forced breath. "Working with. We both have to meet your friend's expectations."

"Aye."

It was impossible to break that self-possession. It was steel forged in fire. He would make her beg—

"Edgefrith was well. At least, as well as you last saw him. Better. Erik is going to allow him a few minutes out in the air each day. He asked after you."

She looked away. But not quickly enough. Not before she had seen the small flash of pity mingling with the harshness in his eyes.

Perhaps not before he read the powerless desperation in hers.

She reached for the safe anchor of her work. It would be completed, for Edgefrith's sake. She had power to do that much. Her fingers sought—

"Looking for these?"

The tongs.

The smooth length of his stride crossed the room, each footfall precisely placed, unhesitating. She did not want to look, but her gaze fastened on the movement of muscular leg and lean hip. He made the lamplight flicker.

He stopped beside her workbench. The light of the flame brought soft streaks of gold in his hair that she had never noticed. His hand round the tongs was a study in strength and subtle shaping. She did not want to see that. She did not want to have an eye and a mind trained to fasten on every nuance of beauty.

She wanted nothing of him.

He placed the tongs in her outstretched palm. She took very great care not to touch him.

"It cannot have been too bad a morning. According to Erik, I am nearly finished." *And then I will be gone.* "Is that not so?"

Eyes that missed nothing scanned the clutter on her workbench, picked out the slim, soaring shape of the stem of the sceptre, the mask faces. Then the globe wrought with the shapes of boars' heads, the fine golden flame-snake that would crown it. Beside that, lying on her bench, the slender shape of the biting beast fashioned with garnets that would be added last after the gilding. The—

"What? What is that?"

She got to her feet. Instinct sharper than thought. She touched him, sliding her hand round the solid bulk of his ribs, jamming her body against his because she thought he would fall. Or tear her worktable apart with his bare hands. He did not move, his face set, hard. Without life. Fear prickled along her spine.

"Ash!"

He did not look at her, his body one fierce line of harsh muscle. But she stayed where she was and her arms crept closer round him because her touch told her what her mind did not believe, that the need of his soul at that moment was the same as hers. Someone to share all that had to be borne.

"Ash…" The harsh muscle flexed under her touch. His head turned. His gaze fastened on her. She met it squarely, her hands sliding across the suddenly responsive line of his body.

"Ash? It is all right. I—"

"That is your work."

She did not know whether it was a question or a statement. His voice was as harsh as his body had been but a moment ago. But Erik must have spoken to him. Persisting in deception was pointless.

If only there could be truth between them….

"Yes, it is." Her hands slid across the roughness of

his tunic, the smoothly packed flesh beneath, hesitantly at first, then more boldly, growing in the confidence of what she felt, of what he must feel. "That is what I have been refashioning."

"That is the...adornment you make? And you know what it is?"

She shrugged. "It is old, barbaric, really. I suppose it would once have been some petty king's joy. It is not how one should fashion such a thing now. Yet for all that, the craftsmanship is so fine that I did not think I could match it for a start. The whole will be gilded. It is so beautiful. Look at the shapes, the fineness of the dragon here...."

She moved her hand to point out the flame-snake. But with that slight movement, all the harshly held muscle coalesced, ripping itself from her grasp with a force that spun her back against the table.

She gasped. His eyes were pinpoints of green fire.

"It is a sceptre of kings," he said. "Of the kings of Wessex. It was lost out of all knowing when Cynewulf was defeated in battle by the Mercians many years ago. The Mercians never found it. It was said the sceptre had been broken so that it would never be restored."

"I... But it is restored. The work is done. The sceptre will be soldered together, gilded. It will be as it was. Can you not see its beauty?"

"And is that what you see? Its beauty?"

Yes. The word died before the lethal anger in his eyes.

"I have restored it...."

"For Erik Bonebreaker who will give it to his master, Jarl Guthrum."

Her head snapped up. "It is my brother's life price."

He turned away.

"Do you have any idea how many other lives this… object of beauty will claim?"

"Lives? Because of its worth? Its weight is of bronze, not gold. Only the beadwork and—"

"Jarl Guthrum would not melt it down if it were made of solid gold. It is not its mere value that matters, or its beauty. It is its power."

"Power?" But she was staring at the masks, at the twisting chain of runes making up the whole *futhork* engraved down the stem. The skin at the nape of her neck prickled.

"Its power over people's minds. Even if you are not West Saxon, you must know. The sceptre was brought to Britain when people first came from Saxony. Cerdic, the first king of Wessex, used it. It was ancient even when he had it. No one knows how old it is. You can see the mysteries written on it, the faces of Woden the shape-shifter—"

She crossed herself and he paused.

"You are saying it is bespelled." She looked at the runes that had been engraved there and had doubtless been chanted over with spell words. She had touched it, oblivious. She had seen beauty outweighing danger. Always.

She stepped back, staring at the stranger in her workroom with his fine face and his forest-dark eyes and the green fire in them. Magic and hidden dangers. She thought of the way he could charm her soul. The way he ran with Erik even though he had sworn to kill him.

"A creation of dark enchantments…"

The stranger sat down. The solid line of his shoulders suddenly seemed immeasurably weary. His eyes watched her as though he recognized all that she thought, measured how much she was afraid of the deadly sceptre. Of him. What she saw was the bitterness of that recognition.

Nothing else could have made her sit down next to him, to that…object.

She caught a stirring of surprise. But not enough to change the bitterness. She watched him make the effort to speak.

"The enchantment, or the lack of it, lies in what people believe. This sceptre belongs to the royal house of Wessex. It is not just an ornament for some petty king. Before Cynewulf lost it, the sceptre had stood with Cerdic's rightful kin through every battle fought, through every struggle for survival and every drop of blood spilled."

His gaze settled on the elegant shapes rising from the debris of her worktable.

"It is a talisman. The sceptre has been there when the realm has needed guarding. People have seen the power that can guard them from harm in the masks of Woden, in the shape of the golden dragon, in the image of the boar's strength. In the runes. They would once have seen it in signs hidden and now lost to us."

"Signs of power?"

"Signs that unlock the strength in people's hearts. It was said that the sceptre was hidden somewhere on the border of Wessex, that its power could still guard the land."

Her skin went cold. "I do not know how Erik found it, or where. He had it when he came riding here from London." She stared at the repository of so much incalculable power.

At the prize that held her brother's life.

"Can you even begin to imagine what will happen when that sceptre is in Jarl Guthrum's hands? What the effect will be on a land standing alone against the might of an invasion army no other kingdom has been able to defeat?"

She could no longer see the instrument of hidden power. She could only see his eyes. The fine movement of his mouth as he spoke.

"I will show you."

THE KING of Wessex sat with the small piece of scratched wood in his hands.

Boda had thought at first that the man could not be the king because he was not wearing a crown, or a coat of chain mail, or even carrying a sword. But when he came into a room, it was impossible to look at anything else.

They all waited in silence while the king examined the token.

The richness of the chamber slowly filtered through Boda's skull. It was warm. The fire was scented. There were not only torches, but candles made of wax. The walls had tapestries. Behind the chair on which the king sat was a banner with a golden dragon. The chair was carved, the design picked out in red and blue. It had cushions. There was a table with a flask and goblets. Silver. And glass.

The king had a bodyguard beside him. The man had chain mail and a braided cloak with a golden dragon at the shoulder.

Boda wondered what it would be like to be dressed in highly polished armor with gold insignia and to have a gilt-pommeled sword slung at the hip. Of course one would also wish to be, say, ten winters older and have a few more muscles like the bodyguard. He looked like a shaggy bear that had overwintered somewhere frozen.

But all things considered, a face like that would help, too. It was handsome under the war helm, with the sort of dashing quality that Ash had. The sort of quality that made women go weak at the knees.

Girls. There were bound to be some here. An endless supply of admiring females desperate for—

"Tell me your message."

Boda started. He realized the king had been waiting. His mouth opened and shut. Nothing came out.

"You may tell me."

The king reminded him of Ash when he spoke, even though they did not look alike. That gave him courage.

"Ash said—" The man behind King Alfred shifted.

Boda glanced at him, at the half-sheathed sword suspended at his side. He swallowed.

Then he realized the king's eyes gleamed somewhere in their blue depths. It seemed possible then to believe the man was no more than twenty-four winters even though he had to be in charge of a whole kingdom. He could not imagine how one person could bear that much responsibility.

It was the moment Boda's thought-hoard no longer centered solely on his own survival.

He dropped to his knees and repeated the message Ash had made him learn word by word.

There was a silence that could strip skin off bones.

The king turned the small piece of wood over in his hands. He had heavy finger-rings of finely wrought gold. Gemma would have—

"Do you know what this means?"

Boda stared at the angular marks cut on fruiting wood. "Runes," he said cautiously.

"It is a bind rune. This—" a beringed finger pointed "—is *Aesc*, Ash. The rune bound to it is *Eh*, which is *eoh*, a warhorse. It is a sign of trust and loyalty."

The king's hand closed over the token.

"You have just told me that one of my thanes has betrayed me. That he sent the group of men patroling my borders to their deaths. That my very thoughts are conveyed to Erik Bonebreaker at Offleah and thence, doubtless, to Earl Guthrum in London. That is a heavy burden."

Boda swallowed. He had not realized.

Yes, he had. And he had come with the message, anyway. Because of Ash...

"This thane, the one you accuse, would tell me a different tale. He would tell me that the man you call Ash is the traitor. That—"

"Lord, I would believe Ash. Just because someone does not look like a thane—" or know what age they are or *who* they are "—does not mean they are to be despised, that they are not worthy of trust like any other man. That—" Boda shut up. He stared at a length of three feet of engraved steel. He realized he was standing on the balls of his feet like someone about to launch a blow and that he had just interrupted the ruler of southern England.

Born to be hanged, that was him. Or spitted with a sword.

His mouth was so dry that he thought he would choke. But the sound that broke the tension of the air was not hard-edged steel striking through his guts. It was the guards' voices at the door.

"Let him through," said King Alfred.

The guards stood back. Boda's staring eyes caught the rippling flash of chain mail in the torchlight. The bear-creature lowered the sword. It swung gently from one oversize hand.

"My lord Osmode." The king's blue-gray eyes turned to the man in the *byrnie*. Not a single thought could be wrested out of their shuttered depths.

The man bowed his head with graceful ease while

Boda rocked forgotten on his clumsy feet and stared at the thane he had accused of treason.

"WHERE ARE YOU taking me?"

Ash the stranger did not reply. Gemma watched the broad back in its faded tunic, the flawless untiring rhythm with which he walked.

They had left the horse at the edge of the trees. Bare, leafless branches snagged at her skirts. No, not bare, greening with the rising sap, bursting forth in small buds already. The sun shone. Its warmth and its light gilded the green and gray of burgeoning life renewed. She did not usually notice such things.

There was blossom starting on a blackthorn tree. The branches shivered as he passed them, the tips of leafless twigs touching his thigh, as though reaching out. White flowers shimmered against the blackness like stars.

"Wait."

She had never gone this way, or if she had, she did not remember it like this.

He turned. The sun behind him made his face impossible to see.

"I want to know where I am going."

"It is not far. Not in distance."

He stood still, his shadow thrown across the path in dense arcing blackness.

"What do you mean?"

"I mean it is another world."

Shivers ran across her skin despite the sun's warmth.

"Ash…" *The bridge between worlds.* Her heart pounded.

"Come." The shadow condensed and deepened as he turned.

She did not move.

"And if I will not?"

"In the end, it will make no difference. That world will come to you. It is so close, even now. You think you have seen it, but you have not. All you have had is one glimpse."

He moved away, rounding the bend in the path. Light caught him, then shadow. It must have dazzled even him, because his feet stumbled for an instant on the uneven path. He caught his balance, the slight dragging awkwardness of the injured leg hidden. But not from her.

She watched him disappear into the dappled shadows. The skillful movement of his body was not flawless at all.

He said he had given her his word to see this through to the end. She had said nothing. But she had given her own promise, in her own way. From the first moment.

She knew she could not trust him, but she followed.

THE RUINS GAPED, twisted and rotting in charred heaps. Night-black. An offense against the sunlight.

She would not go near them. She did not believe they were there.

"But King Burgred bought peace from the Danes."

Ash did not even stop at the sound of her voice. He

slid down the last of the slope, caught his footing, turned to help her cross the ditch that was supposed to have protected the farmstead buildings.

She must have followed, taken his hands, because she slid forward, weightless, landing hard against his chest. He caught her. Stopped the movement of her fall. Held her. Heavy bones and hidden warmth. Hot muscular heat. She did not know whether she was breathless from the fall or from touching him. But it was as though it happened to someone else.

Only the horrors in the clearing filled her mind.

"They made peace," she said again.

He set her on her feet among the cold, charred wood, letting her go. She turned round. Her skirts trailed in ashes. Dust rose in small puffs round her feet, acrid, cold as death.

"Why—" She could not get the words out. The smell of charred wood would choke her. She stared at the burned-out remains of what had once held life. *"Erik..."*

She felt how close he was behind her. His shadow mingling with the blackness.

"There are many men to feed at Offleah. At London there is an army, several thousand strong. They must live, and if they do not have what they need, they will take it."

"But King Burgred paid them."

"Not enough. They are not a force he can control and they know that." He moved, as though he could not stay still, as though he were like some damned soul driven without rest.

"But…if they do this now, what will happen in the future?"

His feet shattered wood as brittle as bones.

"They will take Burgred's throne."

She tried to swallow. "Then they will take all."

The restless feet came to a stop. Charcoal scattered.

"Not all. Not yet."

She stared at his face. The sharp bones and the deep angles intensified by the shadows. It was like looking at a stranger. But her mind made the connection. She knew. There was no other possibility.

She took a step backwards.

"You want the sceptre."

"Gemma—"

She took another step. He could not fool her. Not this time.

"You want it. *You.*" She kept walking.

"I have told you why, what it means." His steps followed, at the same pace as hers, matching them. "I have told you that—"

"That what? That I am to believe you want it for the good of the only kingdom that has not fallen to the Vikings?"

His face froze. She could describe it no other way. She had thought it frightening before. Now she felt terrified. He was not cold. There was always such heat with him. Always. Her feet faltered.

"That is exactly what I would have you believe."

She should feel better because he had stopped. There was more distance between them. If she could scramble back across the ditch before he caught her, she could flee. He was injured. She was not. If she outran him—

"What about Erik? Is he not your drinking companion? Do you share the booty from this destruction with him?" She wanted to stop talking. She wanted to run. She did not care what he thought. Only that she could be safe. And Edgefrith.

"Or will you double-cross Erik? Is that how you plan it?" demanded her voice. "Would you rather take the sceptre to Earl Guthrum yourself and get the reward? After all, they believe it is you who restored it."

"The sceptre will never reach Jarl Guthrum's hands."

She stared at his eyes.

"Why not? What a fine revenge it would make. Perhaps Guthrum will kill Erik for you if he believes Erik has failed him. You said you wanted revenge."

"Aye."

"Well, then—"

"There are other things that matter more than what I want. Just look around you. It is only one small village, but people lived out their lives here. Now they are dead, or scattered, and the whole land lies open to the same fate if we allow it. There is only one possibility for stopping this. Only one kingdom left that can halt the tide—"

"Wessex? That means more to you? You would have me believe that? You speak Danish. You consort with Erik. You are full of secrets. No one can trust you." *You told me that.*

Her heart thudded. Her feet were stumbling on the edge of the ditch. She gasped. She saw his shadow move, heard broken wood, his footfalls. So close. She could not get back up across the ditch before him. There was not time. She fled, diving left, circling. There had to be a firm path somewhere.

"Gemma! Do not go that way. There are—"

She was so quick, lighter than him and unwounded, swifter than a hawk's flight—

She saw the bodies.

HE WAS TOO LATE.

The slender figure stood at the edge of the fields. She had stopped just beyond the mark, the hedge of hawthorn that bounded the buildings. The fields spread out, tiny shoots of green already showing through the rich earth and the weeds slowly creeping. Chaos swallowing whatever order people had tried to create.

Ashbeorn came to a jarring halt, the pain stabbing through his leg scarce felt. The faces of the dead stared at the sky, dishonoured by the teeth of wolves and the beaks of ravens. Already whitening to bone. The memories seared his mind, the screaming and the bite of steel, the scent of fear and blood and the intolerable sense of rage.

Betrayal.

He forced the memories back. Only now mattered and the terrified girl.

"Gemma." He pitched his voice low. His hand caught her arm. "Come away. I would not have shown you this."

SHE SAT HUDDLED in her cloak in front of the small fire he had made to warm her despite the spring sunlight.

It was impossible to take her back to the Viking camp at Offleah yet.

He squatted down to feed the flames.

"Which side did you fight on?"

The sound of her voice startled him, but not the question. It was obvious despite the fact that their weapons had been looted that the corpses did not belong to the village. Just as it must have been obvious to her from the start that the wound to his leg had been made by a sword.

He knew her eyes watched him. He did not need to look up to see their expression. It would be the same expression of mistrust that had faced him all his life, familiar as his skin.

"The side that lost."

"Yet you are still alive."

He lost sight of the fire. There was only the blood soaking the ground, the feel of hands choking his throat.

"Yes."

"Are you Danish?"

He focused on the flames. There was no true answer to that.

"I was not born so."

"*Are you?*"

The flames ate through the wood, heat to give life. Or take it.

"Danish…" The stoutest branch collapsed under the fire's heat. Truths were always there. If you knew how to see them. "Aye. In part."

The choices spiraled out before him like visions of different futures, different pasts. The sceptre. The dead bodies. The child locked in Erik's prison. The woman.

He looked up. She was bitterly afraid. He could see it behind the blank wall of distrust. She was shaking, but her eyes watched him. She had determination beyond measuring.

"Tell me who you are."

The decision was made. She was alone. He could not leave her.

CHAPTER TEN

"MY NAME IS ASHBEORN. My father held lands at Hartwood in Surrey." An English thane. Nothing could be further from the truth.

The danger was so close around them. He could feel it. The unburied dead in the next field cried out in the silence. They had no way to speak but through him.

She had to understand what they said. Why.

He took the breath that forced the sound of his own voice into the sunlit air. The real truth began so far back.

"Years ago when the Viking army of three-hundred-and-fifty ships came to invade the southeast, my father joined them. He took me with him. I spent most of my life as a Viking. I can pass for one so easily not because I am clever at pretense, but because I am one." The truths that had been dammed up for twenty winters choked him.

There were things that could never be said into the light. Not before her. He heard the rustle of leaves as she moved. He felt her horror as though it were his.

He tried to pick out only those words that he needed.

So that she would understand what the danger truly was. So that she could protect herself from it. And the boy.

"My father's lands were wide. Both rich and fertile. Named for the stags that had lived in that country since time started."

He shut his eyes and the images came back. His own memories were those of a child, bright and unformed as dreams. His father's memories, so often recounted over too much ale, had been those of an adult. A man who had lost all that he loved because he had craved more.

"The hall at Hartwood was large, far finer than the one at Offleah. The walls were hung with tapestries and the pillars were higher. They soared into the shadows, painted in bright colors, red and blue and flecked with tiny splashes of gilding to catch the light. It was like a treasure cave fashioned out of jewels and precious metal. You would have understood its beauty."

He looked up. Her eyes were deeper than any jewels in memory or imagination. He wondered what it would have been like if he had met her at Hartwood. If he had been an English thane. If he had actually had something it was possible to offer her.

"That hall and the lands that went with it consumed all my father's thought. He was a powerful man but... The province of Surrey has been fought over for generations. It has had many overlords—Mercian, Kentish, West Saxon. My father saw only his own power. He believed it would be possible to use the Viking army to break the hold of all of them. He saw naught but his own gain."

Her eyes watched him. He had no desire to take the light out of them.

But choice and time did not exist.

"My father did not understand what the Vikings were or what they would do. The Danish army took all of Surrey but it was for the sake of plunder. The army was defeated by King Alfred's father." He took a breath. "After that defeat we overwintered on the island of Thanet where the Thames meets the sea."

"We?"

It was the first word she had said since he had begun his explanation. It was the only word she needed to say. She knew that. Her eyes were wide as they met his, quite steady. He thought their darkness was like night. Her beauty made the brighter by contrast. Its sun-gilded fineness stirred his blood even now.

He looked away.

"Aye. My father and I were with the Danes. There was nowhere else for us to go. My father could not look on the face of his king after what he had done. There is no treachery greater than betraying your liege lord. And now the consequences faced him."

"Death."

"Death? Death had already taken its price. From the people he had known in the king's household. People he would never know butchered inside their homes—" He caught himself up. Such things were not for her.

"My father stayed with the Vikings. He had no other choice. He had to prove to himself that what he had dreamed was still possible. That there was some point to all those deaths."

He leaned down to feed the fire, the healing scar on his leg pulling. The flames swallowed whatever he gave them, giving off heat that did not touch him. He was back at Thanet. At the mouth of the Severn River with the same flames licking through buildings, through flesh. At Sheppey. At Winchester in the heart of Wessex.

Where it had stopped. For both of them.

He kept his eyes on the small fire in the clearing, on this place with the bright sun striking through the trees and the feel of the earth beneath his hands and his feet. He could almost scent the flowing water of the Thames nearby, and across it lay Wessex.

He turned again to face the woman on the other side of the flames, because she must see through his eyes what was real. Only then would she know how she could be free.

"There is nothing of life with a Viking army that I do not know. Nothing I could not describe to you of what they do or how they kill people or what they take. I know because it has unfolded around me for most of my life."

The night-dark seemed no longer in her eyes but in

his own. It blinded sight and sense with the blackness and the kind of pain that could not be combated because it had no physical existence. It lived only in his mind.

"I escaped them when I was near Boda's age. I came to Wessex and I took the king's service."

"And that was what you were doing when you were wounded, back there in that field among—" He watched her white face and her dark eyes and the tightness in her throat as she tried to speak.

"Gemma, you do not have to—"

"You were fighting for the Wessex king." She got the words out. Her hands clenched in the poor stuff of her skirts. But her eyes met his. "I do believe that."

There was a pause when his brain could register nothing.

"No one in their right mind could believe otherwise," she said.

It was such a shock he could not at first follow the meaning of her words.

"Ash…" She said it, his name, and she moved forwards as though she would touch him. As though she thought that fighting with the border patrol could counter what he was, as though it could change anything.

He moved, the sharpness of the withdrawal savage in its intensity. She started as though he had struck her, but he could not help that.

"You do not understand." He took a breath through the blackness, trying to temper the whiplash savagery of his words. "I pay what I owe for the past and for the future. But it does not change what I am. I speak Danish because I was brought up as a Viking *dreng*, a Danish warrior. I know what is in Erik's head because I am like him. I can see his thoughts."

I can see through him as well as I can see through myself.

The unsayable and the unthinkable tore through him. It had the power to do that because he had permitted it. He had said to her the words that unchained the beast that had howled inside him for nigh twenty years.

He got to his feet.

"Do you want to know what is in Erik's head and the heads of all those Danes? This is not just a raiding army that will be gone next winter. What they want is—" He could not think of the English word for it. The Norse thoughts jostled in this brain. "It is *landnám*." The Danish sound crackled through the quiet Mercian air like the breaking branches in the fire.

He took a breath. "Those who go *í víking* come here to win wealth. Some choose to take their plunder and their power back to their homeland. Some, like Jarl Guthrum, choose to stay. Some, like Erik, cannot go back because they are exiles."

Like me. I know what is in Erik's heart.

"The great summer army that Guthrum brought here to join Hálfdan's warriors is no such thing. It will be permanent. They want the land itself and they will take it."

That was what he had learned in Burgred's mead

hall. That was the news he would have to take back to the hard-pressed Saxon king. Guthrum the newcomer was the threat, not Hálfdan who already looked to the north. Guthrum wanted a kingdom right here.

"The Danes already have control of Mercia and they will take its heart. After that, they will take Wessex. If they can."

He had no recollection of moving away, but the corpses were round his feet and the thin sunlight beat against his head. He stared at the whitening bones and all the loss of lives cut off. The breath heaved like a savage's in his chest and the pain was real. His words had given it the power. A power that would take life.

He looked at death's handiwork on the rich earth with the budding shoots of green life around it. It was wrong. His heart knew that with a strength beyond any thought of the mind. Life had to be protected.

Gemma.

She would be alone and she would be afraid. He should not have left her. The logical part of his brain told him he had been gone only moments. But if something were to happen to her—

He turned, and it was like turning into her arms. Because she was there, like a *fetch-wife,* like the mystical other half of himself. Her bright golden fairness gleamed, sun and shadow. He caught her shoulders and she was real, warm flesh filling his hands, striking fire out of the wildness inside him.

Her small hands fastened on his arms. She did not

move away from him but stayed, less than a breath away, her body like a whisper of warmth against the tightness of his flesh. Her eyes met his, the way they always did. Her lips were parted, their fullness moist, their touch a thing remembered in his bones. Her softness and her sun-warmed scent were the stuff of madness, calling the heat of a predator out of the tumult of his blood. Because that was what he was—mad, a savage.

She was shaking.

He loosened the terrible strength in his hands. "Gemma...I am sorry. I have made you so afraid and brought you grief. I wish there had been another truth I could have given you." He took a breath through the harshness inside him, watching her face and the rippling play of emotions in her eyes.

"But if I have no other truth, believe this much. I will not leave you. If I take the sceptre from Erik, it will be for Wessex. And it will be when you and your brother are safe."

"I know that." He was stepping away from her when she spoke. Her voice was low, the words simple, as though they were something so obvious they did not need to be formed.

"Gemma..."

"I have come to help you."

Her hands became entangled in the folds of his sleeves, trapping movement, so that he stumbled, the weakened leg hampering him. He caught his balance,

him, boneless. Her slight weight dragged against him as though she could not stand.

He could not let her go, even though her touch made the pain inside him grow deeper, like something that would maim. He took her body against him, sliding one arm behind her knees so that she came resistless into his hold.

She put her arms round him.

The gesture was small, confiding. She turned her face into the coarse folds of his tunic. Her eyes closed. He held her head so that she could not see.

She let him touch her and say the meaningless words that belonged to a comfort he could not give.

He took her back to the fire and set her down, dragging her cloak round her. The pain made his fingers clumsy, stealing sense the way it did with battle wounds. He settled the heavy folds of wool, refastening the brooch at her throat.

She let him do all that as though she trusted him. It was what he had wanted all his life, someone to trust in him.

He had wanted what he should never have been given.

The pain closed over him with a power that would take all.

He thrust it aside.

He had to get her back.

THE MAN SHOULD have been dead. *Dead.*

Osmode stared at the combined might of the West

Saxon *Witan.* He walked down the length of the great tap-estried hall at Kingston. Through the assembly of those favoured thanes, ealdormen and bishops who advised the king, who in these days were also his war-council.

He turned his back on them to face the dais. His spine was stiff. With contempt, not fear. Never that. He was going to make fools out of those wisest of men. He had to safeguard his position from the threat of Ashbe-orn. He would.

The king himself sat on the high seat. They had carried his banner into the hall. It hung behind him like a sweep of fire in the torchlight.

Behind the high seat was one of those whom the king graced with his favour, this one not even Saxon, but a Briton. Off to one side stood the Mercian peasant. The boy who had brought the message from the med-dlesome bastard who should be dead. Had been dead. Osmode's hands flexed.

He forced himself to kneel.

"Speak." The voice resounded across the high-roofed chamber. The silence that followed assaulted the ears.

"Lord." He wanted to speak strongly. His mouth was dry. "Lord—"

"I want the truth." Alfred's face was intent, so still, his eyes clear, fixed on Osmode. As though they were the only two people in the crowded chamber. As though they could speak of things as they truly were and the future might be made different, a matter of hope.

Osmode hated that. It was an illusion. There was no

hope. The fool of a king had seen to that himself. He should have bowed to the Vikings when he had the chance. Instead he had chosen resistance.

Doomed idiot. Osmode was not stupid enough to risk life and limb for what was already lost.

He began.

"Lord, everyone knows the man Ashbeorn is at the Danes' encampment, at Offleah."

"Aye."

The king of dangerous illusions had a way of saying something that pointed in no direction at all. Osmode floundered on into the emptiness of the ensuing silence. If he but knew what was happening at the Viking camp....

"Lord, there is a pack of wolves at Offleah. They raid and pillage where they will, even into Wessex. The men of Hálfdan and Guthrum test our strength." *Let my messenger get through to Erik and you will find out what strength means.*

Osmode looked up. No one had accused him. No one knew what the truth was. There had been nothing in the creature Ashbeorn's message to tell them. And if there had been, who would this hard-pressed king believe? A half-wild half-Danish upstart sprung from traitors? Or an Englishman with a blameless record, a veteran warrior?

"When I spoke of this before, Lord, you wished to wait." Osmode's gaze was cool, direct. He had the right to advise as well as any man here. He had only to keep his nerve. His mail-clad figure was faultless. He kept the power tempered by deference. Trustworthiness. This most foolish of kings needed guidance, direction.

"Lord, the time to wait is past. The choice is gone." He lowered his head. He thought the Mercian youth beside the dais stirred. It could not matter. The boy was a peasant, wilder than Ashbeorn. He knew nothing.

"Lord, these are harsh tidings, but you must believe them. I speak only for your protection, for your advantage. You cannot trust Ashbeorn. He will go back to what he knows, to where his heart lies. With the Danes. It is me you must believe."

THEY WENT BACK.

Gemma's awareness of him was a thing beyond mortal senses. It filled her completely. The sunlight had no existence beyond the sheen of his hair, the sleek glimmer of his body on the path. The touch of leaf and branch was not there. Only the smooth heavy warmth of his skin. The breeze stilled beside the fancied whisper of his breath.

Far beyond that was the more intimate touch of his mind. All that he had said, all that he had shown her.

But he had not told her everything. There were still secrets locked in his heart.

She wanted to touch all that was hidden. She had to. The need burned her like madness.

Wood spirits could take your soul. She had been taught that since childhood. They snatched people away, lured them with their beauty and their power into the forest's deep where they showed their captives things both great and terrible. So that they took people's thoughts until there was nothing left in them but the longing to go back.

She had never quite believed such tales. Just as she had never believed in the wild craving of man-love.

She did not believe it now. Could not.

It would kill her.

The spring sun gilded his shoulders, glowed nut-brown fire out of his hair before they plunged into the dark dip that held Offleah.

It was so much colder on the valley floor. She had never noticed that before. She almost ran the last steps towards the shelter of her rickety bower. It was dark inside, empty. But for the darker shadow that was him.

She could not stop shaking. She was terrified that he would see it.

She slipped into the inner room. But her hands fumbled with the door latch, the scrape of wood and metal scoring the empty silence.

"You are cold."

"No."

But he might as well not have heard her. Spirits did not answer to a mortal's beck and call.

He fed the brazier in her room, creating warmth and light out of the frozen dark. She watched the movement of his hands. He never had the slightest trouble kindling fire, unlike her, even though the power of fire's heat was part of her trade.

The light and the warmth spread towards the bed

where she sat. She thought of the way he had made fire beside the ruined village and the field full of the dead. Full of the corpses of people that he had known.

She thought of what he had said.

She thought of all that had been revealed and all that had been hidden in his eyes.

He stood.

"The fire will warm you. Why do you not rest? There is naught else that need be done today." There was a small pause in the cold air. "You will not be disturbed. I will not be here."

She lowered her head, her hand moving to the fastening of her shoe as though she would ready herself to rest. He would go. He would walk through the door and she would be alone in the room that was hers. He would give her that much. She knew it.

She could bolt the door when he was gone, and all, somehow, might be as it had been. *She* might be as she had been.

He turned away, all the secrets still locked in his head. All the magic and the terror.

All the pain.

"I do not want you to go."

He stopped, silhouetted between the slowly spreading fire-warmth of her chamber and the cold light of the room beyond.

He turned round.

"You would not wish me to stay."

His stance was light-footed, his body held with an

ease that was trained. His shoulders filled the doorway like a pool of blackness. There was no attempt to conceal the power. It was…flaunted. He had not consciously done that before.

She lifted her head.

"Why should I not wish it?"

He took the first step back into the room. She folded her hands neatly in her lap.

"Do you think you can make me afraid?"

His feet made no sound at all on the floor. Her heart thudded. She thought he must know that despite her mask of indifference.

Masks.

The question that had burned in her mind since she had seen the dead bodies and held him in her arms came out.

"Why will you not let yourself grieve for those who died?"

He never paused. The reply was in Danish. The only comprehensible words were *arni gáfu,* feasting the eagles with the slain. He wanted revenge. The harsh sounds shivered into silence. It might have been Erik standing just so in her bedroom. Erik the Dane.

"How old were you when your father took you to be with the Viking army?"

The carefully balanced body became still, all its fineness and its power held into one taut line.

"Why would you ask such a thing?"

Her hands balled themselves into fists despite every

ounce of will that she had. But she kept her head high, kept watching him.

"How old?"

"I do not know."

She thought of her own life and how everything had been so smoothly calculated and ordered. Even after her mother had gone, her father had made it so. Order. Safety. The power of knowledge.

"Can you guess?"

"I can remember…enough. I cannot have been much less than four winters. I doubt more than six."

The heavy shoulders shifted slightly, the shadows intensifying, showing the straight lines of a warrior's strength, a Viking's strength. A man in his prime.

"I know not."

The power of knowledge. It had been her pride. But it had been a knowledge of things, of calculations.

How could anyone truly know what was in another person's head?

You could work anything out if you tried. Even magical beings with soul wounds.

He moved. Towards her or away—

"Why?" she shouted over the small fathomless distance that separated them. "If you were a child, without power over what was done, why do you feel responsible for a choice you did not have? Why do you believe it was your fault?"

The movement of his body was not as controlled as

it should have been. The shadows shifted. The growing brilliance of the fire he had lit for her showed her his eyes.

The distance between them was obliterated.

CHAPTER ELEVEN

ASHBEORN HELD her small shaking form in the dark. It was the last thing he wanted to do but she had seen what she should not and there was no going back. She clung to him as though such a connection were possible between a golden creature like her and what he was.

She had to know.

He stared at the blackness. There was light in the room from the fire but he could not see it. When the blackness shifted, it was only to let in the memories. Memories that had their own light, clear and sharp edged. The blackness of them was hidden in their heart.

"I was with the Viking army for ten winters. Perhaps more. We did not count such things. They were not important. Only the present mattered. The past was gone beyond recall and the future never extended beyond the next hope of gain."

She shifted, sending the ache of awareness deep inside him. But he knew it was the beginning of the unstoppable movement away from him.

"I could say that I was a captive, with no more choice than all those people who had been enslaved and who passed through the army's hands as a prize of war."

"You would say the truth." Her soft curving warmth still lay against him as though she believed that. As though she pitied him. He stared at the memories.

"That does not even begin to encompass the truth. It was my life, being with the Vikings. All else belongs to a world that was lost, mine and my father's, no more real than a dream. How to be a Viking was all I knew."

The darkness seemed so thick, it could be felt, like a weight pressing against his ribs, stealing breath.

"It would be a fine thing to say that I hated every moment there, that I longed always to be free. It is true and yet not so."

He heard the catch in her breath, felt it through the vulnerable flesh pressed against his.

"It is not an easy thing to explain." His voice sounded controlled, filled with a detachment that had nothing to do with the panicked bewilderment of the small child ripped from its home, with the burning anger and resentment of the boy. The bitter decisions of the man.

"I was there and the vast sprawling life of the Viking army unfolded round me. I was part of it and I was not. My father still pretended he was the English thane, different from them, better. We both knew it was a lie."

His hands closed over hers. They were fisted into his tunic.

"I clung to the lie as much as him. I told myself I was an English thane's son long after I had forgotten what it meant. I told myself I was somehow different, that I did not belong to a band of thieves and marauders. But that was not wholly true. There were times when I did belong. Times when the hall-joy was mine, when nothing else existed in the world."

The bones of her clever fingers were fragile under his hands. He began to untangle them from his clothing.

"That is how it was, whether we were here in Britain, or across the sea, or wherever there was plunder."

Her fingers would not come free, as though she still wanted to hold on to him. But there was no point in trying to do that. He was very careful, because her small hands held all her skill.

"That was how I lived. Until the great army attacked Winchester. It finished then and my father ended his life."

Her fingers came undone.

He knew that only by the intensely heightened sense of touch. The darkness robbed sight. He wished he could see her. He wished he could say anything but the words that would come out of his mouth.

"The army sacked the town."

"You—you were there." Her voice was a slight thread, a thing scarce to be heard. But he could feel her horror through his skin. "With..." The small sound stopped.

"You can say it. With the Danes. I was there to fight against the present King Alfred's brother. If fighting you could call it. It was a descent into hell."

Her hands lay against his, their lightness and their unsteadiness like a bird's wing. Like something so vulnerable, he wanted to take her in his arms and hold her crushed against his own body until the trembling stopped and the warmth flowed through her, through them both.

But he knew he would not stop there. His wanting for her was something complete. It burned his blood and tore at the bonds of his mind.

He was no refuge for her. A creature of no belonging, with only the scars of the past inside, stretched perilously tight. He moved away, the last possible contact between them severed—

"That was where you had to be, with your father."

The scars broke.

The impossible dilemma lay open and bleeding in the dark.

"It was kin loyalty," she said. Her voice was clear, as controlled and detached as his own had been. "And you may deny the fact that you were an ordinary captive. But that is how it was. At times, even a hostage must fight for those who hold him."

She spoke as though it were possible to have truth and honour. He knew it was not, just as his father had known.

"I did not want to leave him."

He did not believe the words had taken form. He had never said them, not to Swithun who had been closer than blood-kin, not even to the king he now served and whose brother he had wronged.

"He wanted me with him. I had not fought before. He thought it was time. Even though I was young enough that I could only make a fool out of myself. But I was well-grown and he began his drunken boasts of what I would do. So many of them drank before battle. It seems to make things easier but it does not. It is a trap for fools, or an excuse for—" He got up.

There was nothing fit that he could say to her. His steps crossed and recrossed the small compass of her chamber but it was not the hard-packed earth beneath him, only the morass there was no escape from.

"Whatever it is you must say it. Whatever your father did—"

"Nay, he did not behave like— He was not so lost. He—"

How could he say it?

"Perhaps somehow he knew that he would not survive," she said. "Perhaps he was *fæg*. Fated." Her voice was soft. She provided the acceptable cloak for such terrible desperation.

But she was too clever not to guess what lay underneath. Just as he had guessed.

Fæg.

"Perhaps he did not wish to survive. Nothing had fallen out the way he had intended. He was an oath-breaker fighting his king. What if he felt he could not go on and so he had brought his son to be blooded in battle?"

In his mind, he stared at the green fields beside Winchester. At death cutting off life.

"His last words were all of regaining what we had lost. He expected that of me—to go on."

"What did you do?"

It was so much better that she said that. He could not have stood it if she had offered pity or the empty words of exculpation that masked contempt.

"I did not do what he asked. I could not. It was not the fighting. I could make some sorry attempt to wrap that up in what passed for honour if I wished. It was the rest. The… It was not human what happened in that town."

He could not say another word to her of that. He stopped beside the shuttered window. Outside was the evening light and the vastness of the forest.

"It was Alfred's brother who stopped it. His army drove us back and we fled, without even the spoils. Some made it back in safety but not many."

"You would not have gone with them."

It was an odd statement, as though it arose out of whatever was in her head as much as out of what he had said.

"Could you… Was it possible then to go to Alfred's brother and…"

"You cannot imagine what had been done."

"But not by you. It was not you who did such things."

She sounded so sure. Yet she had no reason to know that. He had thought that she feared him and what he might do. He had expected that; part of him had almost willed it to happen to protect her from him. Or to protect himself.

The morass got worse. And the pain inside. He could not move.

"I had fought against the king. I was part of a raiding army, a creature in clothes worse than this who could scarce remember how to speak English. It was not fitting—" The last four words were the only ones that mattered out of all the logical reasons. He took a breath that scored his throat.

"I could not have done that."

He could not think how to explain it to her. He did not have the words, even the thoughts to express the blank certainty inside.

Thin wisps of the night air found their way through the badly fitting shutters of her window. Their coldness touched his skin. The sharp tang of the forest came to him, vast and full of life that held no pity, but also no betrayal.

"How did you live?"

She was watching him from the shadowed bed. He could feel the intensity of her gaze on his skin. He forced the truth past the pain inside his chest.

"Like a wolf's head. Like the wolf itself."

"You lived in the forest. That is where you learned to hunt. That is why you walk in such silence, as though you are part of the woods. But— But you would have been alone."

He thought she moved. He turned his head and met her eyes.

"You were alone and then you found the man you called your foster brother."

The pain shattered into blackness.

SHE TOUCHED HIM.

Gemma did not know how she dared to do it when it was not what he wished. When he had moved away from her because of that. When she had nothing that could deal with such pain.

But she could not leave him.

"Tell me what happened."

She thought he would not. That he would recoil because of her touch and all would be lost. But whatever had to be said, he would say. She felt the swell of his breath against her hand.

"Swithun took me in. His family did. It is not a thing that is easy to believe. I was like a brute beast living in the forest. I was a thief. It was winter and so I stole what I needed to survive from them. They caught me out in my theft."

The warm body under her hand shifted with his breath.

"I did not want lies. So I told them, in my stiff and unused English, exactly who I was. I was fifteen or thereabouts. It was the only form of pride I had left."

She could see his eyes, night-dark and green. She could stare into them but they did not see her. They were focused utterly on that other world of nightmare, and she did not know how to break through. She could sense the harshly controlled power that held back everything that he felt.

She could not bear that ruthless sense of restraint when all that had happened to him had been so wrong, so viciously unfair and so damaging.

She did not know how he could have come through all that, how he could still live and breathe and give such warmth, to herself, to Edgefrith who had been helpless.

It was all so wrong. The cruelty of it irredeemable. She could not speak. She did not dare to move one muscle where she rested against him because then he might realize the full and brutal measure of her anger.

But she could not let him go in case he thought she would abandon him.

"But what did Swithun's family do when they knew? Did they—"

"Did they turn me back out into the snow? When they finally came to believe what I had said? No. They kept me there. It was Christian charity. I had forgotten what people were supposed to do for that."

Her fingers dug into his tunic.

"They gave me what I had always wanted, what I had dreamed about each night, lying in the straw with the warmth of the fire and the reek of ale and the Danish voices shouting. They tried to give me an English thane's education with Swithun."

And it was too late. Too late for this. Her hand spread out over the wild impassioned beating of his heart.

"They made sure I knew how to behave, how to speak and what to do in a church. I had little time, but I learned what I could. I can even read, more or less. They would have taken me to court a year later but I would not go. At that time…" There was a small pause, a hesitation in breath that was felt only because she held him. "At that time the court was at Winchester."

His pain was something she felt through the hot touch of her body to his, through the pores of her skin. Through her mind. The raw closeness of it terrified her. It was devastating, beyond her experience.

"It must have felt as though you were still alone. Even among all those people."

"Apart from Swithun. You understand what it means to have the ties of blood kin. In my eyes that is how he was to me. Even though I had not one half of his worth."

"You have." The words cut the dark air, without pause for reckoning, bursting straight out of her shuttered rage. The blank sheet of muscle moved, power sliding under her hand. She tried to hold it.

"When I found you, you were near to death from your wounds. You should have died. But you walked, crawled, I do not know how, but you were miles from that battlefield. You did not go back to the safety of Wessex. You moved towards what can only be danger for you, farther into Danish land, towards this place."

Small pieces of what he had said and what he had not said began to find their places deep in her mind.

"You did not wish me to help you even though death stared at you and touched the coldness of your skin." She straightened her spine.

"You would not endanger some stray woman who happened across your path and you would hold to your purpose despite pain and loss. Those are not the actions of a self-seeking barbarian."

She stared at him.

"When you came here you chose to help me. You chose to help Edgefrith. He is no responsibility of yours, yet what happened to him struck through you."

She saw the response in his eyes. Her heart read it, despite the stone face and the fierce stillness of his body.

"As for Erik, your first words were true when you learned he was at Offleah. You believe his payment should be death. He has done something that merits only that."

"It was my brother whom he killed."

"Swithun?" She swore. "It was not his body lying out there in the fields unburied—"

"Death in battle? No. He was not granted that, though he fought. He was one of those captured in the battle at Wilton just after Alfred was crowned. When the settlement was made and the Vikings withdrew from Wessex, the prisoners were to be returned."

"They did not send Swithun?"

"Yes, they did." His eyes watched the soft firelit darkness of her chamber and she knew he could not see it. "At least what they sent was—" He stopped. The restraint was unbreakable. It was doubtless for her sake. It was worse than if he had spoken.

"You must tell me." She felt powerless, mad with rage and powerless because she could not help him.

People should not suffer the way he did, the way his brother had.

"He was not alive." It was all he would say. She thought the powerlessness would kill her.

"But why would—"

"Why would anyone make such a mistake with what was supposed to be a simple matter of trade?" The wide shoulders shrugged, muscles bunching under her fingers. "Victories require celebrating. Such celebrations are not…controlled." She watched his eyes and the living play of emotion and memory.

"I know how such things are." The memories in his eyes sharpened. "The prisoners should have been left alone because they were valuable. I do not doubt that those would have been Jarl Guthrum's orders. He is not a fool. But the prisoners were not left alone. And so Swithun intervened. He would not accept what was not right. And so he died."

"They killed him…."

"They?"

Her stomach lurched.

"Erik," she said. "It was Erik who killed him." Her mind raced, finding the consequence. "Then it is true. You have no business with Erik except vengeance and—" *You will take it.* The next words, obvious, inevitable, the words she would have said to any other man stuck in her throat.

Oaths.

The scattered threads of truth began to weave in her head.

"You could have avenged Swithun and you have not. You have some other purpose." She felt the power under her hand, burning, ruthlessly controlled. The threads knotted, finding their pattern like fate's web.

"You will hold to that purpose. Nothing will sway you from it, not your strength, not every instinct of your blood or a Viking *dreng*'s training. You will not betray that obligation. Despite every savage lesson you claim to have taken inside yourself, you stay true."

There was only one loyalty that could equal the duty a man owed to his kindred: loyalty to his king. There was one king who held that loyalty greater. Because what he wanted was not vengeance.

He wanted the restoration of what was right.

So did Ash.

The realization caught her like a blow and her mind recoiled. Yet the truth was there in his eyes. The traces of things she should have seen and guessed from the start. Things the shadows of her own memories, the shadow of Lyfing the warrior, had hidden from her.

"You have a different loyalty. You will hold to your promise."

"That is not a thing that is said of me."

She shook her head. Truths had their own life. Ash's had been there all the time and she had not understood it.

"Then it should be. You can make me believe you wished to come to a Viking encampment. You can make me believe that you are at home in a Viking hall. You can even make me believe that you understand a creature like Erik Bonebreaker to perfection. What you cannot make me believe is that you would act like him."

She stared at the stone face. Her hands rested on the dangerously tightened lines of a body carefully shaped for power, a Viking warrior's body, a *dreng*'s. Its strength so precisely balanced, almost healed.

What was not healed was on the inside.

The knowledge tore at her heart. She could see why people wanted to spend their lives putting things right. She could not bear the wrongness of this but she could not change it. The sense of inadequacy cut through her.

She had spent her life on the cold and intellectual calculation of her craft. She had never faced what he had. She did not have the knowledge to heal. She did not even have one fraction of his generous warmth.

But she had what he did not: faith.

It was the only gift she could offer.

"You do not have to tell me why you are here. I do not need to know. It can make no difference. It would have made no difference when I found you."

She watched his eyes. Only his eyes.

"I helped you because I wanted you to live. I had no purpose beyond that when I stopped in the forest, when I touched you. So many thoughts went through my head. You were unknown to me. You were stronger than me, and if I took you in to care for you, I knew the wound would not hold you for long. I knew you must be a warrior, even then. I feared I would anger Erik if I brought you back. None of it mattered."

The very air in the room went still as though she could not breathe it. All the vaunted skill of her mind could not help her here. There was only her heart. That heart beat, with a force as wild and savage as his. She forced the next step.

"The only thing that mattered to me was you."

Her heart made the leap into a world that was utterly unfamiliar to her, where there was no skill and no artifice existed.

"It is still so."

"You do not know what you are saying."

The harshness of his voice could have flayed skin, but his eyes burned.

She could not reach him with her words, not completely. The hurts in him went too deep.

But if she could make him believe. If she could step into the realm he lived in, the realm of the unsaid, where deeds expressed thought, and the force of life, brilliant or terrible, was felt so deeply.

Perhaps she could show him all that it was not possible to say through words. Perhaps she would be able to reach all the wild heated burden of his heart.

She was touching him. The power between their bodies was known to both of them, vibrating on the edge of awareness through all that had been said, through every word and every look and every small movement made in this room.

She moved against him, her hands spread out, open-palmed against the wall of his chest. She had touched him so before, while she had spoken, but this was subtly different. Deliberately so.

Light flared in his eyes, light and heat, and she could not breathe at all. Her hands rested against him and the sexual charge between them was open.

The fire caught her, the wildfire that had first sparked life into her in the breathless air of the forest. The bright-edged feelings ran across her skin, making it tingle with the same shocking awareness of him.

Nay, it was a thousand times stronger standing here with him in this room. She had learned his sensuality. She had tasted its strength and she knew the desperate response it brought in her. She had learned about him.

If she did this, she would have no control. Neither of them would stop as they had before. The need and the wild force were too strong.

Her heart thundered and she knew if she took the next step, the person she had been would no longer exist.

The choice was hers. For all his claim to savageness, he would never force her to something she did not wish.

She knew that with the truth of mind and heart, and the knowledge gave her courage.

She would do anything if it would take away one tenth of the raw pain in his eyes.

She would do anything for the sense of connection she had felt for him from the first moment. Human warmth and understanding—that was his gift though he could not see it.

"I knew not what I said before. But I do now. I know what I think and what I feel. What I need. I need you."

She touched him.

"I do not want to be alone."

Her hand moved across the tight-held tension of his chest, the rough movement of his breath, until she could feel the wild harsh beat of his heart. That was what she would have. If he would let her. If he would not turn away.

His arms closed round her and the magic was there. No more words were possible. None she could say. Perhaps none he could believe.

He had been as alone as her, homeless and driven, imprisoned in his thoughts and his nightmare memories. As isolated as she had been with the mantle of her calling and the great fear she had never acknowledged, that loving meant being betrayed.

He was not meant to be alone.

The anger choked at her, anger for all the things that should not have happened, all the things that could never be put right. Her hands closed on the hard planes of his body, fastening on the dense mass of fiercely held muscle, turning the slightness of her own form into his so that they touched completely, nothing held back.

That was what she would touch—all of him, the boundless strength and the vital grace, the harsh tension locked into each separate muscle and the fast beating of his heart.

His heat enfolded her, heat and power to drive out the pain.

He held her quite still for one timeless moment and the warmth of him pierced her heart. Her mind knew the loss that would be waiting for her when he left.

He could not stay.

Her body moved against his. She heard the unsteadiness in his breath, felt the secret moist intimacy of it against her skin. Her flesh burned. The heat burst into flame.

CHAPTER TWELVE

THERE WAS NO AWARENESS beyond his touch, no existence. Nothing mattered except the endless twining movement of their bodies, the smooth, fierce caress of his hands, the heat of his mouth on hers. His taste, clean as the forest air and earth-deep, hotly male. There was naught beyond that consuming touch of hands and lips, the roughened sound of his breath, the whisper of clothing.

He carried her to the bed, swinging her off the ground the way he had on the hillside battleground. As though she weighed nothing and the full measure of her strength and her being had no meaning against his.

Her body melted into his arms because she could not stand. Her senses dizzied with his closeness, with what he did, with the overwhelming awareness of his power.

Her awareness of him. Ash. Of all that lived in his heart.

Her clothes were already half off as she sank against the mattress. His fingers undid the girdle at her waist. The bunched material of her tunic and her undergown pulled tighter against her flesh, the slightest pressure sending waves of anticipation across tingling, sensitized skin.

He had such care.

She had felt the tension packed in each powerful sinew, the terrible harsh completeness of his need, but he held back, as though he thought she were fragile, something that needed to be treasured. She stared at the size of his hands against the curve of her waist, the deft movement of his scarred fingers.

Awareness beyond the ordinary reach of the mind told her what even her heightened senses could not. That he felt this moment as deeply as she, beyond mere physical need, with a deepness that could not be calculated.

Her heart leaped. Her small fingers, marked with their own scars, tangled with his. She saw his eyes, and the desire and the clear brightness of them made her blood race. The wild beating of her heart in her chest was strong as pain.

No one had ever looked at her so, as though she could be desired beyond the price of life.

He undressed her.

All she had to do was turn her body with the careful, relentless, utterly arousing movement of his hands. And when he had finished, the desire was still there, brighter. It burned her skin, scorched inside, straight to the core of her body, bringing the moist, aching heat to an insistent, stabbing sharpness. So that her senses could have spilled over into waves of blossoming pleasure. The way it had been in the forest when he had touched her. Just from the heat in his gaze.

She moved restlessly, her body thrumming, yearning for the one touch that would send her into the mindless bliss of release.

His hand touched her naked skin, sliding from the curve of her hip to the full, aching swell of her breast. She watched his fingers shape her flesh, his palm settling over the delicate roundness. Hot tingling sensation surged through her so that she pressed herself against him, small sounds of need coming out of her shaking lips, her body urging him until his fingers sought the tightened peak.

She gasped, her whole body a tight urgent thread of wanting. He would see how she shuddered, how desperate she was to take the pleasure he gave. To take. That was all she had ever done with him.

She twisted away, gasping, her breath coming out in small harsh sounds and her ribs heaving.

"Gemma—"

She looked up and saw shock.

"This is not what you wish."

"Not what I wish?" The wide open darkness of his eyes brought the words out of Gemma's mouth. "It is what I wish more than anything. You do not know how much. You think you are the savage who does not recognize limits. It is not you, it is me. You do not know how much I want you. Ash—"

She saw his eyes darken, saw the match of her own hunger and something else, something that tore at her heart.

"Can you not see? I am so greedy for you that I

cannot hold back. I want you so much that if you touch me again now, I will be lost."

She was shaking. She did not know how to say what she felt.

"But I will not only take. You have given so much to me."

"Gemma—"

He caught her arm, drew her slowly towards him. The touch of his hand on her flesh, the touch of his gaze brought heat.

"Then cannot you see? This is what I want. To see the look in your eyes when I touch you, to feel that wanting through the heat of your skin."

His hand moved to the curve of her waist, the swell of her hips. Her breath shuddered.

"Give me that much of yourself, Gemma. And take that much from me. I would give you that gift because I have no other."

Her heart caught as his hands touched her skin, the same way he had touched her before, with a care that did not hide the need. She could feel it through that touch of skin to skin, just as he did. Her own need for him and her desire flared without control.

Her hand lighted on his, mirroring its shape against her skin, pressing the heat of their flesh closer.

"It is you I want. None other." Her voice wavered on the tightness of tears she could not shed.

Her heart beat with such force he must hear it. Her blood raced. Her body moved against the skill of his hand. His fingers found her slick wetness, the scorching aching folds of her flesh. He knew how to touch her, his body so close. Her own body tightened, the heat inside breaking like waves.

His touch, at once familiar and shockingly new on her fully naked skin, sent the pleasure spiraling out of control. She moved against him and restraint was not possible. The limits faded.

His fingers carressed her slick wetness, the scorching swollen folds of her flesh.

Her body writhed. She thought she shouted at him. There was nothing but him and the way he held her. His touch. Only him.

The intensity and the shattering release were just as they had been in the forest when he had touched her so. She closed her eyes and held his body and took the harsh sound of his breath as her own. She held him so and tried to pretend that this was the first time and not the last, that it was possible in this world to give and receive something as true and elemental as love.

But the pain that waited on the other side of her terrible need caught her heart. It was so strong it would take the life from her.

She could not let it. Not yet. She forced her eyes open on the darkness. There was firelight and the fierce living warmth that held her with such gentleness. The warm spicy scent of his skin. The faint, strained sound of his breath. The trailing threads of his deep-brown hair mingled with hers.

Surely it was possible to give.

She moved, though her limbs had no strength and her breath hurt. She slid round, leaning low over the width of his body, pressing the heavy shoulders back into the mattress. Her loosened hair caressed the skin of his throat. Her unclothed flesh gleamed pale and luminous in the half light. She felt the dangerous tension in the heated wall of muscle beneath her.

Her fingers found the buckle of his belt, felt the sharp tightening of the smooth muscle of his abdomen.

The shadows shifted. Shadows. Always. She would not allow them. Not here. Not now.

"What I want knows no limit."

She slid her hand higher across his chest to forestall the breath with which he would speak.

"I know what you will say, that there is no future for this." The words echoed through the dark. Just as their consequence, unsaid, echoed through her head. *You will leave me. I will be alone just as my mother was, because I wanted too much.*

It did not matter. This was Ash. The harshness of his breath was under her hand. His eyes held hers, light and shadow, and underneath, the clearness and the strength.

"You would protect me from yourself as you would protect me from Erik's malice."

Her own breath came as harshly as his, because the next words were vital. Her hands moved over his body. Such hard-locked power, and even the lethal strength of that body was naught against the strength of his mind.

But she knew what he would give. He had let her see it because he had thought her afraid.

She was not afraid. Not in the way he thought. Her only fear was of not being able to help him.

Yet even so, her heart stumbled over the next words.

"The only way you can help me is to be with me. Now. Just for this time." She held her breath.

Please.

The word scored through her head. She would say it if she had to. If it would move all the fierce resolution of his mind and all the hidden pain. If it would make him let her love him with her body so that the terrible knot of that pain might be released, burned away. If only for now.

Her hand slid lower. Her heart beat more wildly than his. She kept her gaze on his face. His eyes were dark in the fire glow, their black centers widely dilated. Her fingers found the sharp edge of the belt buckle.

She pulled at it, her hands awkward. She clenched her jaw, the stupid tears so near the surface stinging at her eyes. Her fingers fumbled. *Let me be given the grace to do this much at least. I cannot leave him yet. It is not just my need, but his.*

"Gemma." He moved. He would not give her even this chance. The worn leather caught against her hand. Familiar— The words came to her out of the smoky warmth of her chamber, out of the sharp tang of the forest flowing in through the half-open window.

"So you think I need help with this, as well? As you

would help me with all things—" The courage she needed would be more than she had.

"I need no help." Her voice came out with the coolness she used on those who dared question a maiden who was also a master smith. Her hands rested on the tautened line of his belly. "I have done this to you before."

"Before—"

"Indeed." Her gaze held his, the challenge suddenly wild and edged with awareness. Her bare skin tingled. The heat rose inside her. She let him see it. That was what he wanted, so he said. The thought made her burn.

"I had you at my mercy. I brought you here from the forest and you could not know what I did." She smiled.

"What did you do?"

Her mind filled with the vision of his naked body on her floor, covered with mud and bruises. His beauty and the sense of his strength had cut through her then, as they did now.

"I dispensed with so much that was unnecessary." She forced the smile through her voice with all the power of the courage she did not have. He would not see the tears inside her heart. Not ever.

"I knew what I was doing." Her smile stayed and the prize was there, in the softness of his eyes when he looked at her and the touch of his hand on her hair.

She took the dangerous step.

"I saw that which was hidden. I found it was what I wanted, just as it is now." The coolness of her voice gave nothing. But he must guess the true meaning of her words. That she wanted him despite all that he had revealed about who he was. Because of it.

He would see. Such a subtle mind, and a quick understanding. Always.

Except that he did not know how to trust his own trueness.

She turned her face into the curve of his palm. So steady. So warm.

"I touched you as I should not have done then."

"Gemma—"

There was all that she wished in his voice. The same kindness that was in his hand, the sort of understanding that brought acceptance. She struggled for the words, his nearness all around her, making her senses swim.

"What I did was wrong. But that could not stop me. Because there was something between us from the first moment that had its own life. There was a truth that was beyond right or wrong. I trusted it."

She felt the sharp reaction through his body. Denial. She knew it. But the next words tumbled out, anyway. Unstoppable.

"Is it not possible to trust that now?"

Her hands tightened. The scratched leather strap, not cold and rain-swollen as it had been then, but warmed through from his heat, snagged under her fingers. She could not free it. He had to help her. She did not know whether he would.

"Please." This time the word was spoken, no more than a breath he would not hear. But he did.

The strong warmth of his fingers tangled with hers. So that they worked together, seemingly indivisible, the double thread of the need acknowledged at last, hers and his. The clothes vanished and the wealth of his body spilled into her hands as it had before. But filled with living warmth and power.

The fierce, liquid strength with which he moved, the caress of his hands, his heat against her bare skin were more than her heart could bear. She would die of such closeness.

Her hands rose to his shoulders and buried themselves in the soft, tangled mass of his hair. His lips caught hers and she dragged his head closer, opening her mouth to the heated devouring touch of his. He had to know how much she wanted him. That this heated loving, all of it, was what she desired.

His bared skin touched her. The darkness of the chamber, the glow of the firelight and the sharp, fecund scent of the distant forest merged into brightness behind her closed eyes. The feel of his body against hers was the most exciting thing she had known, heavy and rich, full of masculine urgency, cloaked in a tender restraint that increased the bated intensity a thousandfold.

Her skin tingled and her flesh ached with the wanting all over again. Her body twisted round his, opening itself to him with an instinct that went beyond her knowing, driven by her need but also by the desire she could feel in him. She wanted that beyond anything. She wanted him to feel in return the gift he had given her.

She moved with abandon, reveling in the fiercely held tension she felt through each tight male muscle, sensing the way his blood burned. Her body knew all of him, heated touch and harshened breath, the pulsing hardness of his arousal. Her hands slid down to the subtle curve at the base of his spine, hesitated. There was thick muscle even there. There was a strength that was limitless, yet she could feel the tension in it. Her fingers tightened, drawing him closer against her hips.

She heard the catch in his breath, felt it with her lips, took it with the warmth of her mouth. His body tightened against hers, the movement flagrant in its pleasure, darkly intimate. The uninhibitedness of that movement made her mind dizzy and her own breath catch on the wild promise of touching him, the gift of closeness.

The damaged, thickly muscled thigh slid between hers. So many scars, inside and out. Her body opened to his urging, surrounded him, feeling his heat, the tight hardness, the sudden shocking touch of his hand.

Her body, despite all the power of her will, was stretched taut in the anticipation of what he would do next. She shuddered against the unexpected, fiercely erotic exploration of his fingers. That touch on her moist sensitized flesh was relentless, yet skillfully smooth. Maddening.

Her heated flesh seemed to melt round the sensual movement of his hand. Her body pressed against his strong lines. The tenseness inside her gathered, tighter, urged by his movement and the heat of him, until it dissolved into wild intimate pleasure, as uninhibited and erotic as his touch. The pleasure broke in waves, possessing all of her, mind and aching body.

She clung to him in the firelit dark, fingers digging into his flesh so that she must have hurt him.

"Gemma…" The deep, harsh thread of his voice seemed part of the darkness round them, the darkness that had taken his past and would take their future. She knew what that single word held. Touch and sight fastened on the shadows of his form, the fire's gilding and the blackness.

"Let me be with you." Her voice pushed the dark aside.

She held him. Her body moved with his, accepting the fierce strength of his need, his desire, inciting it, because this was what she would take of him, and give to. All that he was.

Her hands caressed heat, skin dampened with desire, tight curves of muscle, wanting and giving.

The tingling aftermath of pleasure still rocked through her, so that when she felt the touch of his fingers making her ready, that was part of the pleasure. Her arms closed tight round him, skin to skin, the first thrust of his body felt through flesh made soft and eager by the wild sweetness of desire.

The shock pierced through her like the hardness of his flesh. She gasped, her breath feathering across the heat of his skin. Her body achingly aware of harshly contained power and the intensity of need.

The slowness of his movements let her moist flesh mold round him, opening to take the size and the hardness of him and the scorching heat, building the wild unslaked desire for his fullness.

The longing tore at her and her body writhed, hips pushing higher towards sleek heat and sweat-slicked muscle. She felt the harshness of the reaction in him, the thinness of control. His heart beat savagely and the muscles were corded hardness under her hand.

She guessed all that was in him. She had been allowed her own glimpses of hell. She could not allow such restraint. The savageness of need was in her heart, too. Past pain and present need. Grief and loss and regret. Aloneness that ate through the soul.

"Ash." Her voice could scarcely make a sound against the darkness tinged with fire. "You cannot know how much I need you."

He heard her because he was so close. Her body lifted towards him, meeting the powerful thrust of his. Pain sparked, tearing at her, like the pain in her heart. She felt him still, but she moved against him, need driven, mad with it.

There were no words for the desperation in her heart but he understood as though he were the other side of herself. The strength of his body and his spirit took hers, melding with it, the fusion an elemental pulsing force. The pain was engulfed in the power of their closeness. It obliterated all. Nothing said, nothing held back. The power limitless. The release complete.

THE DARKNESS HAD a fire-gilded edge. The flame color tinted her smooth skin and made lights out of her hair. She lay curled up, knee to shoulder like a child.

Ashbeorn's chest heaved, the force released in mind and body still dangerous. He could not move. Could scarce draw breath. What he felt for her was beyond his reckoning. He had known that from the moment he had woken with her in this bed.

The intensity of what his body craved was greater than could be controlled. His chest burned and he could not get breath. Desire. Naught to do with the *witchcræft* in her gaze and her thoughts and what she said.

She had spoken out of pity.

He hated pity, because of the contempt that always lay behind it. Yet she had used such words—

He could not think on them. They had the power to touch things in him that should not be woken. To make him think things that were not possible, that had no existence.

No future.

Not for her, not for a high-class woman who loved beauty and learning and the fineness of a world free of taint. All the things he did not have and could not give.

He wanted to touch the curved body lying next to him.

Her own beauty and her fineness and her warmth were burned into mind and skin and sense.

It was the fineness that stopped him.

Her chamber was soundless except for the harshness

of his breathing and the softer sound of hers where she lay so close. Not touching.

He could feel the aloneness creeping back through the shadows touching his heated skin. Soft-footed and cold enough to kill. He was used to that kind of isolation. But she was not meant for it.

She had believed she could defeat it. She believed so many things.

She had believed in him.

She did not have anyone else.

He turned towards her, forcing movement through his body. She looked small and defenseless. For all her cleverness and her skills, she had no experience of what they had shared. He would have hurt her.

He could not bear the thought of that.

Suppose she was afraid— The nightmare of what he was hung around him like the shadows.

"Gemma." His voice struck through the dark with too much force. She looked up. In the half light her eyes seemed sheened with tears. The nightmare clawed at his skin, achingly familiar. Chillingly new when reflected in her eyes.

"I am sorry."

The tears were there, gleaming on her skin. She did not sob. There was just the slow glide of tears. He did not know what to do.

He was not entirely civilized. He had known that. Only she had not.

"Gemma." He touched her. The familiar power of the

nightmare beat at him. But he could not allow its power, not yet. His hand closed over her wrist. Her hand twisted. The rejection should have been expected. He was not her comfort. He let go in case she thought he would coerce her. But her fingers caught at his, small nails digging into his flesh.

He stopped.

"Gemma? I am sorry that I—"

"I am not sorry," said her small clear voice. "Not at all." The glitter in her eyes was defiance. "Whatever the future brings."

Her skin felt cold against his heat. His palm opened and her fingers settled against his flesh. "Nothing can make me sorry for this moment."

"No." The word could cut through darkness. She had seen what he had not been able to. Truth. Stronger than right or wrong.

He drew her against his warmth and she came into his arms willingly, as though the trust was still there. And the truth.

He held her as she was meant to be held, with all the care he wished he could give. And when her body warmed through with the heat of his, her mouth sought his with the same willingness. Desire's match.

The hot throbbing hardness of his flesh flared instantly, deep and need-driven. But the care was threaded through it, like something natural and right. Her body melted under his touch. Her skin heated against his lips, its softness burning at every curve and hollow until he found what he sought. The hidden intimate folds of her flesh pulsed against the touch of mouth and tongue, the jolts of arousal hard through his own flesh.

Her heat scorched, melding with his, the shuddering completeness of her pleasure the prize that could make his blood race. She clung to him with all her strength, wanting his passion as he wanted hers. Truth. It bathed everything. The slowness with which he entered her, the heated welcome of her body, the exquisite care of each thrust. The burning passion inside his heart.

The limits were not there. He could not see them. Not for the past or for the future.

"IT IS NOT TRUE."

Boda would have shouted it if he could have got his voice to work properly. It would have made no difference. No one would have listened. Or heard him. The swell of voices round the great hall at Kingston was like summer thunder.

The traitor Osmode knelt with his hand across his heart while all the other thanes spoke at once.

The king did not silence them.

"But what he is saying is not true." He lunged forward, but the overlarge bear-creature who guarded the king had hold of him.

"Let me go—"

The great paws jerked him back.

"Peace, lad," said the king's guard. His voice, deep and strangely accented, seemed unconcerned, as though something were actually going according to plan. "The thane will speak. No one asked you."

"But that's just the point," howled Boda. People never did listen to him. It was the bane of his life.

Across the hall, Osmode's barrel chest swelled. Alfred let him speak on. It was like being stuck in one of those stories where only the fool knows the answer that would help the king and he cannot tell it.

"The king is wrong."

"That was a brave remark. But not one I would repeat if I were you."

Boda's ears caught the small sound of rasping metal. Nothing so obvious as the three-foot sword. Just a knife. He could feel its point between his shoulders. He swallowed.

He was a stranger in this hall, here on sufferance among all these thanes who commanded men and fought battles. Who knew far more about Danish earls and statecraft and serving kings than a grubby Mercian peasant did.

Osmode's eyes beseeched his lord's.

"The Viking army covets the riches of Wessex. They look for the opportunity to take. They test our defenses. That is why there are so many men on the border at Offleah. They seek chances. When they find them, they will use them."

Osmode the thane paused, as though waiting for the reaction. It came in the unquiet ripple round the hall. He glanced down in deference before his sovereign, but Boda could sense the growing confidence, the assurance of a trusted man.

"Lord, I fear Ashbeorn has given the Vikings the chance they seek. All know of your generosity towards him despite his father's treachery to your house, to this land—"

Boda started. The rippling sound round the hall got louder.

"But…" *Ash had not told him that.* The point of the knife could be felt through the wool across his back.

He tried to remember what to do. The only trick he knew, taught by someone who had treacherous kin.

He tried to work out how long he would have. Even on the chance he was strong enough. Whether there would be time to speak.

And what he would say.

"You took him deep into your counsel," declared Osmode, warming to the task, relaxing into the king's continued silence.

"But he has repaid your trust in false coin. All know that you place a man's loyalty to his lord above all things. This man has broken his vows."

Boda's muscles seemed to shape themselves without the exercise of will.

"The ties to those among whom he was raised are too strong. Askrborn—" the Danish syllables split the restless air "—has chosen that kinship over loyalty to Wessex, to you—"

It worked. Because the bear creature was surprised and did not believe he could do such a thing.

"Liar," screamed Boda into the few seconds he had. "Ash's word is true." The words hit the painted rafters and the thatched roof even while the king's hall in Wessex faded into that other hall in Mercia and Ash drinking. Speaking Danish with Erik— He got a hand free to point at Osmode. "That man will trick you. He is the traitor."

Osmode yelled back at him.

One of them lied. Boda was no longer sure who.

The most extraordinary thing was that the bear-creature let him say so much before efficiently elbowing him in the throat. The world burst into pain. The *seax* blade was before his eyes. He strained to see the face of the king through a sea of retching agony.

But the crowned king was not looking at him. Or even at Osmode. Alfred watched the fractured mess that had been made out of his *Witan*.

The king had hawk's eyes.

HE SLEPT in her bed.

The way Gemma had always imagined it from that first night when she had crawled under the covers and pretended his unconscious body was hers.

He was there when she woke.

The first sensation was of his warmth. Then his weight against the straw mattress and the size of his body. Then the soft sound of his breathing.

She lay and listened to the sound. The warmth seeped right through her. She was afraid to move in case the spell broke and the man in her bed was not real. She wanted to look at him, but she kept her eyes closed against the dawn.

Daybreak was a time of magic, when spirits walked with humans. Before full daylight drove them away. She moved her hand with infinite slowness across the three inches of space that separated her from magic. Her fingers touched flesh. Just a tiny, small square of its lushness.

Her fingertips brushed across warmth, rough-smooth with body hair. The heated curve of his inner thigh. Real. Her heart leaped with memory.

The light in the room slowly got brighter. Outside was the world. He would vanish into it, the heated lover of her dreams.

He would go. Even though she loved him.

The realization of what she felt struck through her with a clarity that stole her breath. She bit down against the choking pain in her throat.

She would not make a sound. If she did, she would wake him and even this moment would be gone.

Her heart beat and her mind suddenly filled with the thought of her mother. The stricken look in her eyes when she had known Lyfing would not come back. New understanding burned through her veins.

Her mother had given her heart to someone she should not. It had not been wantonness or caprice. It had been a passion with the strength to kill her. She could see that now in all its implacable cruelty. The only key that made sense of the disaster of four lives fell into her hand.

Her eyes scorched with tears. Nothing made up for

what had happened to her father, but she understood. The tears slid out—for her father, for Edgefrith and, for the first time, for her mother.

Their pain merged with her own. She let it out while she kept silent, while the magic stranger's warmth still enfolded her and she touched his skin. And the memory of shared passion and pain and understanding guarded her heart.

The light was very bright when she moved. So much had to be done. Today above all days.

He slept. Still. With the kind of exhausted completeness of those who have been wounded in mind and body. There were deep-blue shadows under his eyes and the dark spiking growth of stubble across the line of his jaw.

Yet the light would wake him soon. She watched his face lost in the dream world. He had so many burdens for all his strength, and she had added more.

She wished he could sleep on and find the complete healing he needed. So simple. Utterly impossible. She wished with a fierceness she had hidden for years that the Vikings had never come here. That people could live without death and destruction and impossible choices being thrust upon them.

She got up. She had to finish the sceptre. She had to give it to him and then he would be free.

CHAPTER THIRTEEN

"HE MUST NOT—"

"Did you croak? Or was that the frogs in the pond?"

Boda glared. It hurt to swallow. It hurt to breathe. Particularly it hurt to speak. Jokes were out of the question.

"Offleah," croaked Boda. "The king." His voice swooped like a green boy's.

"Offleah? Homesick, are you? Then you can come with us."

"What—" The rest was lost as he was hauled to his feet. The bear-creature had gone. He was now in the charge of an apparition. There was no better word for it. It glittered almost as much as the king. It might have looked like some kind of warlike saint if it had not been quite so lethal.

"Why are—" There were people out in the courtyard. Horses. Men. "What are they doing? Where are they going?"

"Uf ræde."

"Raiding?" His voice surged into a high-pitched squeak.

Finely arched brows rose. "Can you not ride?"

Boda briefly imagined rearranging the thanely sneer so that it appeared somewhere else on the apparition's gilded person. The apparition smiled.

"Should I tie you into the saddle?"

"I can—" He saw the king. "No! Not him. He cannot mean to ride to Offleah. Erik will kill him."

"You think my cousin so easy to kill? Better than Erik Bonebreaker have tried it."

"Cousin?" But he saw the likeness. It should have hit him in the face. He stared at close-linked mail, at heavy, gold arm rings, at the long slashing line of a scabbard chased with silver and gilt. He glared at glittering smoke-gray eyes. This man could hang a creature like him. With one gesture of his finely gloved hand.

"You do not understand," said Boda, choosing each word as though it were a nail in his coffin. "You should."

It was quite possible to bellow at someone in a whisper if you tried.

"Erik will be waiting for the lord, your cousin," he yelled in his ruined voice. "He will be waiting for you. For all of us. He will know already exactly what we do. Osmode will have sent to tell him."

"Will he so? Who would have thought that?"

Boda's bruised throat gave out. Across the yard, Alfred moved. Body armor rippled. The steel links of his chain mail were riveted with bronze. The gleaming double lustre was like sunlight through cloud.

Osmode the thane stood at his shoulder, like a loyal

retainer, like someone who had the right. He was almost as fine as the gold-decorated *Atheling* who now confronted him.

Much finer than Ash with his patched clothes no better than Boda's. Ash with his Danish words. Ash drinking with Erik, sending messages to the ruler of Wessex.

But Ash was true. He had to be, because it had to be possible for the despised and the placeless in this world to be worth something.

"It is a trap." *Stubbornness, will be your undoing, Boda,* Gemma had once said. He saw the king vault into the saddle. His strong body caught sunlight like flashing lightning, every eye drawn to its brilliant fire. He was smiling.

"You will lead your own cousin into a trap."

"Lead? Not me. I shall be in the rear. So will you. Osmode is the one riding in front. He offered to go on ahead of the troop and scout for us, prepare the way. He was so keen, the king did not want to disappoint such a loyal servant. Shall we go?"

IT WAS EASY enough to find her.

Ashbeorn paused. Gemma had come to where her heart was. She sat in the familiar surroundings, head bent over her work. Her work chamber glowed, like a dragon's treasure-hoard.

It was where she belonged. He had seen it from the first moment he had stepped into her world.

The workshop had driven him mad at first.

He was uneasy at being within walls. Yet the orderliness of the room held a strange peace, strong as a lure. He had told himself that he hated its bright glitter and the firelight mixing with the sun, and the sense of concentrated purpose.

All the time he had known that this was where she belonged and he never could.

He wondered what it would be like to have learned a craft such as hers, instead of belated grammar and rhetoric, and how to kill people.

He had only been taught one aspect with any thoroughness.

She did not see him at first, so intent in her world. His fingers touched a discarded clay mold on the bench by the door. He could no longer look at her. Something inside would break if he did, like the clay in his hands.

He could not allow that. One thing he had learned. He could not afford feelings.

There was only one thing that would help her.

"Gemma."

Her face was as remote as that of a goddess. Then she looked up.

The possibility of avoiding feeling shattered. Her eyes were so unguarded, not remote at all, but full of liquid brightness. The consciousness of all that had happened between them in the silent hours of the night, the commerce of man and woman, burned. It scored through his flesh, bringing the same heat and the same hunger.

She said nothing. Her eyes held his and the hunger

was there, reflected like light in a mirror, the other half of his flesh.

Of his mind.

The possibility of that reached beyond anything he had known—that her thoughts might seek his with the same fire. Even now, when she knew what he was.

The possibility hung, stretched like the gold thread she wove. Then the brightness of the sunlit room changed. Shadows raced and the shifting air currents raised the hairs on his skin. Her head turned. She saw who had followed him.

The life drained out of her eyes. Gone. The only thing left was the pain.

The drive to move, to speak what was in his head, burned him. He stood still.

The shadows settled into the shapes of truth and he leaned his shoulder against the doorpost of her brilliant room. He watched her gaze fix on Erik the murderer standing at his back.

"Finished." It was his own voice that carved the Norse word into the silence.

Erik bared his teeth, his avaricious gaze sweeping over the richness of the chamber.

Gemma.

"Finished," said the murderer.

Her shoulders squared, waiting. But when he said nothing, her gaze flickered from Erik to him as though under compulsion, drawn, seeking a response that he did not give. The response that the man who had taken her maidenhead and shared her bed owed her.

He rested one hand casually on Erik's shoulder and spoke to him in the familiar language of his childhood. Her gaze stayed on them both, cool as summer rain. But he had seen the dart of fear. It churned his gut. He turned away while the part of his mind that was his alone screamed with the words he wanted to say.

You will have your brother back from Erik. I will make something that is good come of this. You will have your life again to do as you will. I will not leave you—

His hand tightened on Erik's heavy-muscled flesh. His eyes sought the finely-balanced shape of the sceptre.

The words in his head were a lie. He would leave her.

Erik stepped forwards under the invitation of his hand, laughing at the coarse jests that flowed from his mouth with the ease of long familiarity.

Gemma stood in front of the worktable.

The words dried up. Erik looked.

The sceptre lay on the workbench. Its sleek lines and its fire were hidden under a cloak of dull gray. He knew what it was. The amalgam of mercury used before the gilding. Yet even under the covering that would be driven off with fire, the power of the sceptre could be felt like a living force.

He had to convince Erik that what he gazed on was not real.

"Out of the way," said Erik in English.

Gemma halted, poised, the determination obvious in each line. If she tried to resist Erik— The muscles in his body tightened.

"Erik has come for my work."

Their eyes locked.

In the split instant before Erik could move, he caught her arm. Her weight was little more than half of his. Her body swung into him without control. The length of her landed hard against chest and hips and legs. She could not disguise the rapid beat of her heart and the uneven sharpness of her breath. He felt it, like a distorted reflection of their bedding. It tasted of fear and anger.

If she but knew, she would taste the same mixture in him.

He smiled.

"It seems my wife is lazy this morning," he said. "Her best work is in the night, not the light of day."

Erik's laughter came as he intended it, full and sharp with the release of tension.

The smoke-blue eyes in the half-veiled face watched him.

"Erik has come for my work." He pitched his voice lower but it lost not one iota of its compulsion. Her gaze stayed on his.

"It is not finished." The harsh breath she took swelled the full vulnerable curve of her breast against the wall of his body. His hand engulfed the fragile bones of her wrist. He should move back. Let her breathe at least. He did not.

"It is not finished," she repeated. "Not…not yet."

Her voice stumbled but her gaze held the blank harshness of his as though she could somehow see through it to the hidden part of his mind that belonged to him. Or to her.

"Not yet." Her flesh pressed against his. Her voice was a whisper that Erik, greedy hands splayed on the table among the fineness of her work, would not hear.

The breath seared his own chest.

"Yes. It is as good as finished now." There was no part of his mind that belonged to him. Nothing he could give. She had to know that. "It will be finished before tomorrow."

The words came out of the emptiness she had seen in the dark heat of her bedchamber, out of the marred creature she had given herself to for one night and who in the light of day could not requite what she had done.

He let her go. She must have seen the truth beyond words, or she was still afraid of him. She slid away, like a candle flame before the dark, leaving him to Erik and the deception that was his *cræft*.

Erik's eyes narrowed.

"It looks like this model, but gold? You are sure it is finished but for…" Ash watched the familiar sign against enchantment. "If I could but see it—"

The Norse words stopped, cracking on temper. On the unease of a man who had to deliver what he had promised his master. Tomorrow. Reparation for Jarl Guthrum's ill favour caused by the death of so many helpless hostages who could have been exchanged for *geld*, money.

"The work is done. You will see—" The words slid off his tongue. The start of the deception planned in the

dark beside the soft, living flesh and the rich unconscious warmth of the woman beside him.

"The rest is beyond my hands. It is said the masks
must lie unseen in the dark for a day and a night, and
the runes must be touched first by the dawn's light else
they lose their power."

He watched Erik's face. The arrogance of a *hersir*
mingled with the superstition of a mortal man who must
live on luck because he faces death so often.

"You may look now if you wish. The choice is
yours."

Erik's gaze stabbed at his. But all he saw was the mirror of his own thoughts, working at a level deeper than
reason. Luck and risk.

"Nay," said Erik. "Dawn is soon enough." Reluctance dripped from every word. The luck stretched tight.
"But there will be no more delay. Tomorrow I will be
gone from here. I meet Jarl Guthrum and the sceptre
will be his. If it is not, it will be you who explains to
the Jarl."

Ashbeorn bent his head in acknowledgment.

One night. One night and this would be over. Yet even
as the thought formed in his mind, the shadows crowded
in, like death shades at the hunt. Every instinct honed in
the primitive contest of the chase, in battle, sharpened.

"One night," said Erik who murdered the helpless.
"No more—"

"Of course."

The shadows dragged at Ash, even though they had
no reason. One night was all he would need to free the

child, to get Gemma and her brother on the road to Kingston and the crossing into Wessex.

He had that much time. The king would have his message by now. Alfred would know. He would tarry at Kingston. He would keep Osmode there, under guard if necessary. He would wait.

Behind him, the woman moved, as though she, too, felt the unknown disturbance in the air. As though she would put more distance between herself and him. That was what she would want. He could not hold her trust.

Trust.

The doubt stabbed like sudden hail through the air.

He could not hold trust from anyone. He was not an English thane like Osmode. Who would a king truly believe?

Yet Ash had sworn—

He watched Erik. Danish words rose to his tongue. "The gold will be—"

The door of Gemma's work chamber smashed against the wall. Light reflected off meshed links of steel.

"Erik—" The oath that followed was English. Descriptive. The next word was his name. *Askrborn.* Then, "Betrayer. He is Alfred's man. Did my message not get through?"

Ash looked over the distance of three paces to the man who had tried to strangle him.

"Osmode."

Erik stared. "What message?" His face was a study

of volatile confusion. His hand reached instinctively for the hilt of the *long-sax* at his hip.

Gemma gasped. Ash did not look at her. He did not need to. He knew what the expression on her face would be. The same expression that had followed him all his life.

He smiled at Osmode.

"Your sense of timing is a matter for wonder, as ever. Shall we go outside?"

The luck and the possibilities shattered.

Askrborn THE BETRAYER, Alfred's man, wanted her to stay inside with the sceptre.

Gemma's hand clutched at the rough timber door frame at her back.

Askrborn had glanced at her from the doorway for one fractured instant of time, and she had understood what he would say. It had been simple, as obvious to her as drawing breath. Half a glance from his hazel eyes and she could read it.

She pushed herself away from the wall.

She could read the glance of a man she did not even know existed.

She crossed the room towards her worktable, her legs unsteady. Her whole body was still raw with awareness from the power of his touch. *Ash*. Her mind ached as harshly as the body that still craved him, still shivered with the power of what he had done in the darkness of her bedchamber. Of what he had given. No one had given her such a gift of closeness: of both body and mind.

She had believed she had touched on his heart. Now she did not know whether that man existed, what he planned, what he would do or who he was.

Truth and betrayal.

She glanced at the sceptre beside her hand, its brilliant heart and the fineness of its shape hidden under the mask of lightless gray. Yet the true fire was still there underneath. Nothing anyone did could alter that.

A person could not change their heart, though they might change their name or their speech, or who the world thought they were. Not if their heart held truth.

Truth and the power of oaths.

The wind ruffled her hair. Its coolness made her shiver. Yet under the coolness lay the hint of spring.

THE FIRST THING Gemma saw in Erik's yard was not Askrborn or the mail-clad man called Osmode. It was Edgefrith. Now allowed out for his few minutes air each day by the grace of the unknown man.

"Gemma!"

He caught sight of her and would have run across the yard, but his guards hauled him back. She flinched, shaking her head at him, thinking he might be safer even in Erik's cell than here. But though he stood quiet, the guards did not take him back.

Doubtless whatever would transpire out here was

far more interesting than guarding the jail of a helpless boy.

Erik was standing over something on the ground.
Her heart lurched without reason. She walked towards
the small tight pack of men gathering around the thing
on the muddy ground. She made no pretense to hide in
the deep shadows of the buildings but they did not notice her. Their intensity sent ice crawling down her spine.

At Erik's feet she could see a bundle of blood-splattered cloth. It moved. Just as Osmode's foot lashed out,
she cried out.

It unbalanced him. The blow glanced aside. Every
head turned to look at her. She saw Erik's face.

At the vicious movement of his hand someone
grabbed her, twisting her arm so that the sweat sprang
on her flesh and she wanted to scream.

"No. Leave her."

Only one voice had that sound though its shape
seemed changed, thick with the accent not of Denmark,
but of Wessex, somewhere in the southeast. He got up
as far as his knees.

Blood seeped from a swelling cut above one eye that
must have nearly blinded him. She did not know what
other injuries he had. All she could see was the fury, the
edge of betrayal when he looked at her. She did not understand. How could he think she would have cowered
inside and left him to suffer this alone?

Her eyes tried to tell him, but what she would have
said so clearly without words shattered against the wall
of blankness behind his slitted eyes.

Erik turned back and as the blood-splattered shoulders in the torn tunic squared to meet what would come, she knew. She should have stayed with the West Saxon sceptre. That was the only thing he wanted. Not his life that hung in the balance in Erik the Bonebreaker's muddied yard.

He wanted what lay beyond.

"Do you plead for your traitorous slut?"

He could do nothing. The pain in her arm, lessened only slightly as her guard settled his grip, told her. The viciousness, the fury laced with eagerness in Erik's face told her. Yet the narrowed gaze held Erik's. The man reduced to crawling on the ground waited, as though some other outcome were possible.

Erik flexed his large and meaty hands. The circle of warriors shifted and she saw not with her own eyes but with the bright hazel eyes streaked with blood and memory fixed on Erik. Erik, who killed prisoners as helpless as herself and Edgefrith. Erik, who should be stopped by those who sought what was right.

"The wench did what I told her." The blank wall of his gaze never wavered. The fear was in her own heart, crippling.

He would not accept what was not right. And so he died.

She knew what he would do. By coming out into the yard she had pushed him into trying to protect her.

Do not—

"Do you truly think—" said Askrborn "—that I would have given her a choice?"

Erik's hands clenched and unclenched. She knew he believed what was said. It cut straight to how he would think. But she also knew what Erik was. She could not understand why he did not move, the inexplicable hesitation that underlay the wild fury.

"Why do you wait?" yelled the Saxon called Osmode. "That creature has betrayed you. Will you allow any man to do that and live? Or are you not a man yourself? Just a coward? How much time do you think you have?"

Erik's neck crimsoned. She watched the fire of wrath and bloodlust and damaged pride suffuse his face. Every gaze, including her own, moved to the mail-clad Saxon. She read anger as strong as Erik's. And behind it something else. The tang of fear. Her mind made the leap of recognition. *How much time do you think you have?* That was what underlay Erik's hesitation to vent the full force of his cruelty. Fear.

Ash knew it. He knew something she did not. She watched the way his eyes assessed Erik.

"No one calls me coward," yelled Erik. "No man living can hold me from what I wish to do. No one. There is not a man on earth who has the power to stay my hand—"

Erik's heavy body turned. She felt the breath scream in her throat, the tightening of her muscles, the wild primitive urge to break the grip of the warrior holding her, even if it cost her life.

She saw Erik's hand move.

Ash spoke. Danish words, sharp and incomprehensible, cut the tingling air, their speed and their assurance accurate as a spear's thrust. The only words she could understand were *Jarl Guthrum.*

Erik lashed out. The suddenness of the fury unleashed shocked her. But not Ash. She saw the fast twist of his body to deflect the full force of the blow. Still it struck. Sickness jarred through her own flesh. She wrenched herself forwards against her captor's hold. He tightened his grip but she no longer felt the pain. Her arm was numb. She thought she made some sound, her body arching forward, her eyes straining to see. But the lethal rain of blows from feet and weapons did not happen.

Erik held them back, yelling in Danish. The baffled anger and bloodlust in himself, in the rest of the pack of men, burned through the air like the stench of death.

"They are going to kill him."

She looked round.

"Edgefrith—" She did not know how he had managed to make his way to her but then she saw in the eyes of his guards the same intentness on the scene of life and death playing out in Erik's yard, the pack instinct to be part of it.

"No! I— I do not know. Edgefrith…" It was like looking at a stranger's face, not her young brother's. She could see fear, but also a strength of conviction that might have belonged to a man, to a warrior.

"Erik will have to kill him. It is a matter of honour."

"Edgefrith…"

"I thought he would not be like—" The name of an

absent father was cut off. Perhaps also the name of another father who was dead. A small, frightened boy looked out of the man's eyes.

"I did not want him to die, as well."

The fingertips of her left hand brushed his sleeve. It was all she could do. No greater touch, no words were possible.

Erik reached out, his ringed hand fastening on a torn tunic. The men in the packed circle shifted, the sudden unease as palpable as the intensity had been. Gemma held her breath. Erik spoke. She saw Osmode step forward, heard the scream of obscenity. It was answered.

"Kill him," yelled Osmode. "The man is a traitor."

"Yes. So he is. Like you. There is more than one traitor who can be of use to me." The English words hung in the air. She felt the shock of them in Edgefrith's rigid body close to hers.

Osmode's jaw dropped. She could see the answering smile on Erik's face that did not reach the thwarted viciousness of his eyes.

"This man has fought on our side already. He speaks our language. He has already given me information about your English king. Things you never told me. He will give more."

Coldness blossomed over Gemma's skin in waves.

"You say you have brought Alfred across the Mercian border that I may take him in battle before Jarl Guthrum comes on the morrow. That is good enough. But this man will bait the trap."

"This—" Osmode's face changed from incredulity

to a kind of triumph. "Is that so?" His breath hissed through the charged air. His booted feet moved round the figure on the ground, scuffing the trodden earth, stopping behind. Where his victim could not see.

"Is this how King Alfred's favoured is fallen? To become what I am? Nay, less. For my choice was free, not that of a craven made to save his skin."

Gemma saw the feet move.

"No…"

"It is all right." Edgefrith's voice cut across hers, the words clear in the light, no longer hushed. The flat conviction in his childish voice, the deadness in it, shocked.

"Erik will protect him."

She watched the Viking stoop.

"You do not understand." Her voice choked. Erik's hand tightened viciously over the other man's flesh. But all he did was haul the bloodied figure to its feet.

"Erik cannot kill him," said her brother. "He is dead already if he has no honour. People cannot live without honour. He has betrayed everything."

She tried to see Ash's face, but even though his head turned she could not hold his eyes.

"I understand full well." Edgefrith twisted away as though the contact she had sought from Ash could burn him. Behind the anger, his gaze was bewildered, sheened with unshed tears.

"Edgefrith—" but her guard was dragging her away. There was nothing she could hold on to. Only Ash standing in the yard. Alone. The Vikings milling round him. Erik spoke, the rapid fire of words low, angry. Urgent.

Ash had something Erik needed.

He had given it.

She watched the wide shoulders, the graceful tilt of the bloodied head before Osmode's scorn and Erik's urgency.

Before Edgefrith's eyes.

"Ash…" No one heard it, not the Vikings, not the West Saxon, not Edgefrith. Least of all, the man himself.

The guard dragged her into the workroom just as the courtyard behind her erupted into noise and the churning of hoofs.

He slammed the door behind them.

CHAPTER FOURTEEN

"WHAT IS IT?" Gemma yelled for the third time at an unyielding back. "What is happening?"

She wished she had taken the trouble to learn Danish instead of despising it. She wished she were six feet tall and armed. She lunged past the guard's shoulder for the window.

He caught her, throwing her back as though she were a sack of flour.

She slammed into the ground. Pain stabbed through her head as it struck the edge of the wall bench.

SOMEONE WAS SHAKING her.

She opened her eyes. It was the guard. His matted beard jutted into her face. Breath stinking of stale beer nearly choked her. She gasped, retching, fear and sickness scoring her throat. Her skull was splitting.

"Get up."

She could not. She could not focus enough. She tried to move. The room tilted.

"Get up."

The voice, harsh, disembodied, came from some-where else. She got as far as her knees. She wanted to throw up.

"I said move. I have not the time for you. Hurry. It is as well I got here sooner than I planned."

Her workroom was full of people. She could see their feet, hear their voices, while she crawled round on the floor like a brute beast. She had to get to her feet. The effort brought a gasp, answered by laughter and the coarse gibing of voices she could not understand. The pain and the humiliation were something that could not be borne. She thought of Ash beaten into the mud of the courtyard. Hurt worse than her. In more danger. Ash...

She suddenly distinguished his voice amongst the others.

"Ash—"

Someone pulled her to her feet. She thought her heart would burst with gladness. He was there. She clutched at his sleeve, at heavy, gold arm rings.

She looked up.

"That is better. Stand up." She stared into an impas-sive face, red bearded, well-groomed, harsh. Eyes the color of the North Sea. As bleak and cold. Intelligent.

"Are you sure she will do it?" He spoke English. Well. Someone who took the trouble to master what he needed.

"She will do it."

Ash.

Her heart began to pound against the fragile cage of her ribs. He was standing beside her worktable. With Erik and the man called Osmode and her filthy guard. He was not looking at her. His profile was cleaned of blood. Only bruising and the red mark of crushed skin marring the perfect line of his brow. His hands sifted among the tools and the clay molds and the vials of powdered gold.

"The wench is stronger than she looks," said Ash. "I can vouch for that." The laughter of men coursed round the room. From Erik. From the other Englishman. Even from the guard who could have understood only the tone, not the words.

Ash did not look at her eyes.

She could not look at his. At anyone's directly. The pain was too great.

"The wench will do as you wish, Jarl."

Jarl. It was not possible to fight some things. Not for anyone. Whatever he might have hoped, or intended, or tried to do.

The earl's thin mouth smiled. One of his teeth was missing from fighting.

Guthrum. The name that had terrorized three king-doms found its shape.

"She knows how to do what she must." For the first time Ash looked at her, a contact with the power to cut through bone. The hazel eyes held her, more surely than the heavy hands of the Viking earl.

No. She did not know where the word came from. It

was only inside the aching morass of her head. But it was there. It—

"Then fetch me the child," said Guthrum.

He let go of her. No one watched what she did. The guard left the door open and sunlight flooded into the room. She could have fled. Mayhap.

Fetch me the child.

Only she and Ash stared at each other. They did not look away, because each knew what it was to be trapped by a force that could not be overcome. The inevitability seemed a bond that fettered like steel and cut like a blade that would separate them forever.

She did not move and she did not look away. Not until shadows filled the doorway of her chamber, one harsh with power and one insubstantial as a spirit.

The last of her heart's blood seemed to flow from her veins.

Guthrum broke off the rapid fire of his speech to Erik.

"Good," he said, his skillfully unaccented English directed at Osmode and at her. "It is past time."

She saw the consuming terror in Edgefrith's eyes and almost stronger than that, the terrible, confused anger with which he looked at Ash. The handsome, battered face gave nothing back, but neither did it look away. Then her view was cut off as the lithe-muscled bulk of the earl moved.

"Listen, wench. I am sending you and this child back to the English king of Wessex. I wish him to know that I hold the sceptre of his ancestors, that I have its magic, that it is mine to keep and use as I will. When it pleases me. You, who have refashioned its power, will tell him that."

The shock froze her veins. The price of her freedom and Edgefrith's rested on her table beside the earl's hand. Refashioned by her. The power in its subtle shapes waiting, gathered in the runes chanted over it in the hour of its creation. Power in the hand of the man who wielded it.

"No." It was not her voice shouting through the spiraling horror.

"Edgefrith—"

"No! I will not do such a thing." The thin body twisted in its jailer's grip, trying to strike. "You cannot force me in this, Gemma."

Erik turned round. Edgefrith did not look at him. Or at her now. He was utterly focused on Ash.

"Nor can you force me, you coward. You *nithing.* You treacherous—"

Ash hit him.

It was so fast, Gemma's senses could not take it in. He used only the flat of his hand but he was so strong that was enough.

Enough— She watched the bright red mark suffuse Edgefrith's face. She watched what was in his eyes.

Guthrum straightened. "I have no time for this. If you will not do as I say, boy, your life ends now. And your sister's."

Her brother's eyes no longer held the look of a child. "The choice is quick."

"He will go. So will she." It was not her guard's hand, or the earl's that pulled her forward. Not even Erik's.

Ash.

"No…" The word was not even a whisper of breath and she did not know what she denied. But he heard it. She knew with that sense that was attuned only to him. It made no difference. It could not. His grip tightened, dragging her after him without effort. She looked at the scarred hand that had struck her brother. A warrior's strength won in the end. Always. Her mind knew that.

Not her heart.

She shut her eyes. Earl Guthrum's voice followed out of the dark, reeling off instructions in his precisely worded English. That she would go with her brother. That neither she nor the boy should think it possible to escape. That his men would follow. That the slightest deviation in her path would end her life at an arrow's range.

"It will be fitting," said the earl, "for that most Christian of kings. He shall see I am no barbarian. I shall send him a woman and a boy." The thin mouth smiled. "They shall rob him of his power. You will do it. Then I will take him, when he sees he is trapped and helpless."

Unless she ended her life at an arrow's range. There was no future left for her. But for a child. A child who had been forced to grow a man's heart.

People cannot live without honour.

She could smell death.

Warrior's strength swung her round to face the table. The sceptre.

"Take it."

The scarred hand caught hers. He was holding something. She could feel it. A small shape, hard ridges, smoothness, clear lines. The backward-looking beast made of garnet. His hand pressed the small ornament into her palm, then dragged her hand towards the sceptre, the cloaked gray shape of power.

"Pick it up."

Her heart missed a beat. Thundered on.

"Take it," said Guthrum, the preciseness of his voice snapping on impatience. "Alfred will have crossed the ford by now. Pick up the model of the sceptre. You will take it to him. I would have him see that token. I would have him know the truth of what I hold in secret. He will see my power."

The heat of Ash's palm fused with hers, the hard cold shape of the ornament forced against her hand. Her fingers closed over it. Hovered above the rough gray lines that concealed magic.

The dizziness in her head would kill her. She would faint. She could not help it. She would swoon and the earl would see and—

"Alfred will know how to requite this gift you have made."

She had not yet heard the earl's laughter. Now she did.

Ash's hand covered her closed fist, forced it down onto the sceptre of Wessex. She touched the token of his death. If she took the true sceptre, Guthrum would kill him once the deception was discovered.

Their fingers tangled.

She held his life.

He is dead already if he has no honour. The childish voice with the man's words mocked her.

Death for her lover having achieved what he wished.

Death without it.

No one could put such a choice on her.

Her throat tightened. No one should ever have forced a boy younger than Edgefrith into a Danish army all those years ago, damaging not a life, but a soul. Kings should not have to send the most loyal of their men to such a place again, a place like this.

People should not have to see endless death; not just the extinguishing of life, but of its meaning.

She straightened her shoulders just as Ash had done before Erik's malice.

You could not kill love. Not even if you killed life.

Her fingers molded round his. A small woman's hand should not have fitted so perfectly against that larger warrior's hand. It did.

Their gazes did not join. Not in front of Guthrum. They did not need to.

He could trust her.

She trusted him.

She picked up the sceptre that meant his death.

DUMPED AND ABANDONED. Again. Boda spat into the greening earth.

The leather-clad archers hidden by the trees took no notice.

He cursed.

He had thought, even draggling at the tail of the raiding party like so much unwanted baggage, that there would have been a chance.

Even half a chance.

That somehow, at some time before they burst into the hell-pit at Offleah, he might have managed to reach the vanguard where the king rode in his burnished armor, like a blazing target for Erik Bonebreaker to bring down in blood and screaming death.

They had no idea. Not the fine king, not the so clever, cynical war-god who was supposed to be in charge of Boda-the-unnecessary.

The wind stirred the budding branches. Boda shivered. He was less than two miles from Offleah. Stuck with a band of lackwits playing with bows and arrows.

He had no idea where Alfred was.

Perhaps he could shoot someone. The highly polished yew of the bow stave was hard in his hand. Easy. They all had their backs to him. Then he could run.

The string slipped beneath his sweating fingers. Suppose he caused death? He eyed the brawny back of the fair-haired war-god in front of him.

They deserved it for being lackwits.

Chain mail and beneath it, someone's flesh. Maybe he could shoot an unprotected leg. The sweat gathered at his neck. He—

"Will you put that thing down? I am trying to concentrate."

The bowstring snapped back on his hand causing a suppressed howl. A dozen large men turned to glare at him, including the brilliant thane whose concentration he had interrupted.

"Well if you cannot see—" began Boda round the stinging fingers he had jammed in his mouth.

"Shut him up."

The muddy ground hit him. Someone's knee was in his back. He tried raising his eyes. The war-god tapped one impatient foot in front of his nose. He twisted his neck.

"Lord." There was something about the way thanes managed to glare. "I did not intend to kill you." He spat out a mouthful of last year's sere grass. "I only meant to—"

"Incapacitate me? That should relieve my mind?" A dark blond eyebrow climbed.

"Lord...I would not willingly have caused you harm—" That sounded really convincing, caught with a notched bow in his sweaty hand. "I—I only wanted to get away. I did not see how else..."

"*Nothing* else sprang to mind?" He thought the man's lips twitched. Nay. It was not possible

"I did not intend to kill you," he repeated sullenly.

"Just as well."

The man was trying not to laugh. Thanes. No one else had such arrogance, and this one an *atheling*, a king's kinsman.

The king. Boda raised his face higher. He looked at the notched arrows in a half circle round him. At the many narrowed eyes that spoke death.

He swallowed mud. The arrows did not move.

But there would never be another chance. Never.

"It was not you I wanted." *Arrogant lack-witted thane.* "I wanted to get to the king. I wanted to tell him—"

A ringed hand silenced him.

He heard it. Hoofbeats. Dozens.

"Lord! You do not understand—"

The knee lifted off his back. It made no difference. He could not move because his spine felt as though it was broken in six places. He had no bow.

"Wait—"

They left him.

"You do not understand. The king is in danger. I have to tell him about Ash, about—"

He chased after them.

"About Erik..."

THEY RODE BETWEEN two guards: one for her and one for Edgefrith.

Gemma glanced at the face of the man who had knocked her to the ground. He noticed her staring at him and smiled. He could afford to, out of the memory of that moment and because he knew she would do what she was told.

The matter of concern was Edgefrith. His face was white. His skin now showed no mark from the blow he had received. The damage was on the inside. His eyes burned.

Her escort had explained, in great detail, what would happen if Edgefrith proved difficult.

Edgefrith did not speak. She could not speak to him.

She fixed her gaze ahead, along the endless, winding line of the mud track. She could see nothing. It was like moving in a nightmare with no beginning and no ending. Ahead, somewhere, was the king of Wessex. Behind her, hidden from sight, were Earl Guthrum and Erik.

And Ash.

She could not think about that. About Ash. About passion beyond limits and need so savage it held the edge of death. About all the vital force in his eyes, the heated glide of his skin against hers, the dark whisper of his breath, the bated strength.

The kind of strength that would choose its own ending.

Her hand tightened on the sceptre. She thought its hidden power would burn through the coarse gray concealment she had fashioned. Its power seemed terrible now. It demanded too much.

Blood.

She heard them. The thunder of hooves made the ground shake. Then she saw. Light glinted on gold and iron harness fittings, on the sharp points of spears held aloft.

But mostly it glittered from a man in armor made of pure steel and glowing bronze that sparked incandescent in the sun. The fineness and the grace of him drawing every eye, the sheer power making the heart surge. Behind him was a banner woven in gold.

Edgefrith made a strangled sound.

"No." She said it. Even if the guard killed her for it. Edgefrith turned, the tortured blackness of his eyes drawn between her and the glittering figure of the West Saxon king.

Do not. Please trust me in this. The words were only in her head, unsayable.

The troop wheeled, clods of earth flying from hoofs, the wind catching cloaks. A warrior peeled off, flying towards them, straight as an arrow.

Gemma spurred forwards to meet him, dragging her startled guard, making Edgefrith follow. She heard a shout, felt the sharp pull on the reins. She would not stop until she had to. Stupid to think a few more yards could make a difference to the glittering figure in the mass of men, but she would do it. An arrow's flight more distance from Guthrum and Erik.

The warrior met them. He was huge, like a great shaggy bear, eyes deep as night under the war helm. She saw the way his eyes widened at what she held, the way his face changed at Earl Guthrum's message.

"We must get to the king. Now." It was her voice that spat the words, across the voices of the men. She could feel Erik at her back. She thought she could hear them. *"Now."*

"It is a trap," yelled Edgefrith. "They are behind us, Guthrum and Erik. They will—" She moved, striking Edgefrith's horse, urging her own mount forward, hitting out with the only weapon she had, the sceptre. It struck her guard's face. Her reins tore free. She spurred forward. Too late.

Too late.

She could see the gleam of the sword raised at Edgefrith, then nothing, her sight blocked by the great bulk of the West Saxon warrior.

"No…" Her scream was drowned in the thunder of hoofs behind them, shaking the ground and filling her ears. An arrow's flight. The group of three before her split apart. Edgefrith was safe. She could see him. The Viking fell. The Saxon warrior turned, yelling, his eyes on something behind her.

She turned, saw the flash of metal just as the sweating horse loomed beside her. Terror burst in her brain and she moved. She saw the Saxon lunge. Her mind told her he was too far away even as he struck, but her guard collapsed, the red-bearded face a blank mask of surprise.

The Saxon grabbed her reins.

"You killed him." Her brain could not seize the reality.

"Mayhap he was already dead. As you should have been."

Only as he wheeled their horses round did she see the throwing spear in the Viking's back. In his *back*. It could have come only from the ranks of Guthrum's men cresting the rise. From *Guthrum's* men.

He was there. With them. Riding in their midst. He had cast the spear and that action had betrayed him. And saved her life.

Ash.

"They will kill him—" She wanted to turn, to go back. But it was impossible. The Saxon's horse shouldered hers, pushing her forward. She had the sceptre. Edgefrith was flying ahead.

"Hurry. We spoil their aim." She heard the terrifying, deadly hiss of arrows. *An arrow's flight.* Not from Guthrum's troop but from the English. The open space erupted into screaming chaos. Edgefrith and the readiness of the Saxon troop had thrown Guthrum's plans. But it would be mere seconds before the arrow fire was returned.

She would not reach Ash in the Danish ranks, not even if by some miracle he still lived. He had known how this would be, how the end would come. They both had.

She held the sceptre and spurred her mount, bent flat over the horse's back. The ranks of the Saxons parted to let them through. It looked like chaos, but perhaps it was order. It must be. Mayhap all battles were so. Someone screamed. She saw what Ash had faced all his life.

The horses slowed.

"I must find the king. Now."

The great figure of the Saxon warrior turned. "So eager, lady, to show him what Guthrum holds?"

"No. What I hold. The sceptre is real."

BODA WONDERED whether he would be killed for saying, *"I told you so."* On the whole, he thought he would. He looked out of the shadows.

"Saint Chad!"

"Do you ever shut up?"

"No." Boda hung at the edge of the trees with everyone else. Staring.

He reminded himself that he had spent his entire life dreaming of seeing a battle.

Mayhap he should have dreamed of something else.

"But Erik does not have that many men."

"Earl Guthrum does," said the war-god.

"Guthrum?"

"Aye." Laughter assaulted his ears. Despite the carnage. Despite the fact that he had been right all along and had tried to tell them. Idiots.

"Guthrum is—"

"I know who Earl Guthrum is."

"Then—"

"If you remember," said Boda, signing his own death warrant, "I told you this would happen, and you walked straight into it. Look at the king. He shines like a target. This battle—"

"Skirmish," corrected the thane. "The Danes are supposed to see the king. That is the whole point. They will press forwards to try to take him. At the right moment, we fall on the enemy's rear. They will run. To the victor, the spoils. Here, take this." It was a spear.

"We?" said Boda. "Spoils?"

The thane rolled expressive eyes. "Then stay in the trees, child, and wait till it is over."

Of course he could not. But— "They are fighting each other. Look."

"They are Vikings. What do you expect?"

It was Erik. His opponent took a blow on his shield that would have felled an ox. He kept standing. But there was someone at his back. A circle that—

Ash did not have chain mail like Erik's opponent. Ash had rags. Ash was quite probably Danish. *They are Vikings. What do you expect?*

"Saint Chad's bones—"

He crashed through the trees and ran.

THEY HAD LEFT him to Erik. Temporarily. Erik had to save face or die. But whatever the outcome, win or lose, they would fall on him like wolves.

At least, they had not entirely left him to Erik. He leaped aside as someone tried to trip him. If he strayed too far towards the onlookers, they struck. Only the chain mail *byrnie* had saved him.

There was no doubt of the ending. But Gemma was safe. Gemma and the boy. He had seen the West Saxon shield wall close round them. It was the only thing that mattered.

Someone hit him in the back, taking his balance. He twisted, bruised muscle jarring, Erik's blade slashing at the same instant. The fire-hardened links of the warrior's battle net held.

But he would not take a warrior's death.

What had happened in the courtyard at Offleah had only been the slightest taste.

Hatred and impatience stifled the air. It was hard to breathe. The world narrowed to the focus of Erik's malice, the pain-filled movement of his body, the shifting circle of betrayed men around him pressing closer, hampering him.

If he lost his footing, he was dead. A beast's death, helpless and savage. He dodged a blow from behind, aimed at disabling his right shoulder, only the shadow of it seen. Erik lunged into the momentary advantage, eager. Too eager.

Ash's blade struck, drawing blood. But the blow was deflected from its killing power by his own loss of balance. It was only enough to torment.

Erik roared.

Ash sprang forwards while Erik was blind with fury. But someone caught him a blow he did not see. It was followed by others, a rain of splintering, disabling pain. He fell, rolling as Erik's blade stabbed inches from his throat.

Erik roared again, this time in the anticipation of triumph.

He tried to regain his feet, forcing his body to act as

though there were no damage. He would have failed Swithun if Erik lived. He could feel his brother's shade at his shoulder, see the white face of Edgefrith, filled with the fear and hate and betrayal that should not have been known to a child. He would have failed them and all who came after.

He twisted as the boots and the spear butts struck, using the broken shield, fighting to gain a footing in the mud. The blows were so many. Pain burst through him.

"Kill him," screamed Erik. Across the blood lust of his voice another yelled the name of a Mercian saint and then something that only a person brought up among ditch thieves would say.

It could not be.

Erik glanced round. Boda, holding a spear with the expertise of a petrified three-year-old, crashed over the rise. Erik turned.

Ash got to his feet. The sword was gone from a hand that was probably broken. There was only the edge of the shattered shield. He launched it and his whole weight at Erik just as the hill filled itself with West Saxons under a hail of hissing arrows.

"Is he dead?"

Ash looked at the wide dark eyes and shifted himself off the heavy flesh that had once tortured Swithun and kept a child in chains.

"Yes. What the devil do you think you are doing here?"

The eyes did not blink.

"Did I kill him?"

He glanced at the hilt protruding beneath the corpse. It was the Viking's own *long-sax*. "He—" and then he saw it. The broken shaft of the spear Boda had been waving like a small boy playing games. The steel tip was crushed under Erik's weight. He looked at Boda on his hands and knees in the mud and knew which answer he wanted.

"Yes."

Boda blinked and nodded briefly, a man's gesture.

"I know I could not have done it without you hitting him but…I am glad I killed him."

Ash looked away at the bloodied desperation of the battlefield, at the men who shared Boda's terror and who sought courage. "Aye. I owe you thanks. It was a warrior's deed."

"Do you think so?" The anxious lift in Boda's voice was so familiar. "They all thought I was useless. So they would not listen to what I said."

Ashbeorn made his limbs move as the voice went on.

"I admit I wanted to show them and I did, but when it happened— When it came to it I did not think of that. I just could not bear the thought of Erik killing you. Not when you had done so much that was right."

It was the pain and the dizziness that made him believe he heard that. The dizziness was intense. He did not think he could stand. He had to concentrate on that. On getting Boda the high-hearted idiot out of here.

"Wait." A hand caught him. Highly polished mail glittered. He looked up into the face of the king's cousin.

"What is happening—" The question burst out of him, even though he had seen with his own eyes where she had gone.

"I know not. We could not decide whether you were dead or Danish."

"Not me. The king."

"Enjoying himself enormously waving a sceptre. Look."

Ash turned. It was like watching the tide in sunlight wash over the highest cliffs. At its head a streak of flaming gold, not bearing a mortal weapon but something else.

He saw Osmode charge straight for that brilliant figure, hacking his way with the desperation of the damned through all who stood between. But before Ashbeorn could draw breath, the headlong rush was blocked.

Osmode fell, the death he would have given turned on himself. The shades of all the dead men in the field must have been behind the blow. The king never faltered, moving like light.

"So. That is the end. I think we should get out of my cousin's way. He is not in a mood to tarry. Come. Guthrum will withdraw before the onslaught. He is too canny a fighter not to. We will take the field but we cannot hold it. Guthrum knows that. Alfred will have to fall back to Kingston. We must go."

Cool eyes so like the king's swept over Boda, over the dead Viking. Over him. "Can you ride?"

"Of course. I am not…"
The other man's face told him what he looked like.
Dead or Danish.
Not much to choose.
Boda took his other arm.

CHAPTER FIFTEEN

THEY DID NOT STOP at Kingston.

Gemma watched the gathering dark. The cold cut through her clothes. Her body ached. The horses had swept over the ford, past the high bulk of the king's hall. Onwards, across the flat lands, into the endless rolling slopes of Wessex.

She watched the small figure beside her. She thought he would fall from the saddle in weariness. She had tried her best to explain to Edgefrith what had happened. Why. He had looked at her and nodded and said that he understood. He had even let her fuss over him to a certain point. But he would not speak.

She turned and stared blindly ahead.

She knew Ash was alive.

That was all she knew. He had not come near her, and she had not been able to find him in the press of men. The king's bodyguard would not let her out of their sight. In answer to her less than polite questioning, they would say only that he rode with the king's cousin. And some strange peasant from Mercia.

West Saxons never changed. Arrogant lackwits all of them.

They called him Ashbeorn. The *lord* Ashbeorn.

She did not even know who he was.

He had killed Erik. He and the Mercian peasant had done it between them.

Erik was dead.

They stopped. Someone helped her dismount. There were lights, torches hissing with burning pitch in the wind, the great shadowed bulk of a timbered hall. She caught the fugitive glimpse of many colors, soaring thatch. The courtyard was paved with great hewn stones. A royal estate.

The courtyard was full. She clutched at Edgefrith's arm. So many people, such a press of horseflesh and shouting sweating men: loud or quiet, exultant, battle-weary, hurt.

Wounded.

She started walking, dragging Edgefrith with her, threading her way through the press, pushing. She heard curses. The bodyguard plunged after her. The crowd thickened so she could not move.

It was like a waking nightmare where she could not reach her goal. Every step was made of lead, blocked. She thought she saw the king but the bright figure on the steps turned and it was a different face, beside him a shorter figure clothed an incongruous mess of rags among so many soldiers.

"Boda—" The shaggy head turned. Edgefrith's eyes lit up just for a moment.

Then she saw him.

"GEMMA," YELLED BODA.

Ash turned around. She was there. She looked exhausted. Like someone who had endured more than should be given.

But she was safe.

Erik Bonebreaker was dead. She was in the protection of the West Saxon king. The dangerous power of the sceptre was gone from her hands.

She should not look so…lost and afraid. Like something hunted. He shoved forward, past Boda's restraining arm, past the crowd of men. Into the light of the torches.

She gasped. The soft, breathless sound carried over the top of the swirling noise. She might as well have screamed.

All that had been in the face of the king's cousin was reflected in hers, magnified a thousandfold. Worse than that, the hunted look in her eyes intensified with each step he took.

The boy, Edgefrith, threw an arm protectively round his sister. Ash did not know what lay in his eyes. The child would not look at him.

The press of the crowd swirled round them, one of Alfred's bodyguards belatedly pushing through, taking her arm. She was safe. It was not him she should turn to. It never had been.

He stepped back.

There was so much to be done. To be explained. He turned towards where he knew the doorway was. But he was so blind he could not see it. The torchlight danced with shadows over the steps.

His shoulder brushed the massive oaken door frame.

The atmosphere changed.

"Ash." Boda was clutching at his arm again, as though he thought he could not stand.

"Ash, you have to find the physician. Someone has to see to your hand at least, and the saints know what else."

"There will be others hurt worse than me."

"Name one," muttered Boda behind him. "We left the wounded at Kingston," he said more loudly. "All except a few minor hurts. And you."

Half his mind noted the determination. The proprietorial use of *we,* as though Boda were already Alfred's sworn man.

Alfred.

The king would be inside.

"Ash."

Boda's grip tightened on a spot where someone had kicked out in an attempt to break the elbow. Pain shot up his arm. He grabbed the wooden pillar in an effort to steady himself. The weathered oak vibrated under his hand. He swallowed pain and the uncanny feeling of dislocation.

"Ash, the *Witan* will be in there. Bishops. The king. You cannot go in there like that."

Dead or Danish.

He turned his head. "Do you think there is anyone in the king's court who does not know who and what I am?"

Boda, who had crossed the threshold from youth to man in one bloody instant, held his gaze.

"Yes. I do think that. Probably nigh on half of them. Even me for part of the time." The man's gaze never flinched. "That is why the king did not explain it to them. He wanted Erik out of Offleah and he wanted the raids stopped. He wanted people to see the truth for themselves.

"You made them see."

There was a pause during which the unreality in his head grew and the heavy timber thrummed under his hand like something living.

Boda stepped back, loosing the death-grip on his arm.

"I will go with you whatever it is that you decide, Lord." The unruly, messy head bowed, as though he were the thane he was not.

His hand slid over the darkened oak and he realized what the flickering torchlight had not shown him before. It was carved. The design picked out in faded paint that should have been restored years ago. The colors were hard to discern. Blue, surely, and madder red. The design sprang to life. Serpents, double-headed and entwined. Serpents that guarded thresholds.

Above was the image of a hart in its pride.

He went inside and the beauty hit him. Not the faded colors and the tapestries in need of repair, but all the glow of newness. The bright spark of fresh paint strong as jewels, the clean sweet scent of the herbs strewn among the rushes, the light and the lofty shadows that held an eternity as vast and untouched as a child's dreams.

It looked as though it were real. The endless length, the soaring beams, the raised dais where— He saw the king. With his cousin and the rest of the *Witan*. Boda's bishops. The bodyguards and...the faces of the men who had sworn as he had on that desperate day of the crowning at Wimborne. An oath that transcended everything.

The past, both pasts: English and Danish, collided with the present, intertwined as surely as the enchanted serpents at the threshold.

He walked the length of the hall that had never been his. There must have been people there who made way for him. He could not see them. His boots struck the wooden floor with a sound that was both real and unreal, present and past. He let them flow over him. They were his familiar shades.

But kings had to deal with futures.

The one thing he did not have. It shimmered beyond his reaching. Like the hall. Like Gemma's wounded face.

He would not think of that. He could not.

He knelt before the West Saxon king who held Surrey. The movement sent pain through each damaged muscle, robbing sense so that consciousness swam. So that he could not focus on the king's words.

There was so much he had to say, to explain to the West Saxons. So much that had to be made clear about Erik and Guthrum. So much that had to be said in public so that the king's judgment was not maligned. So much to be said to Alfred later, in private. So that he knew once and for all.

The words would not come. He knew what should be said. All the experience of his life told him. But the words would not form. The spell of the forgotten hall spoke louder. Not to him, but to some person he might have been if he had stayed. Some English thane.

He tried to focus his mind but his sight had darkened, blotting everything out. The breathless heat and the noise of the hall took thought, took everything like the roaring of a sea storm. It was the sort of noise people made at a victory feast when they cheered.

He tried to move, to get away from the noise, but it was too late. The darkness held him. Like the power of the hall, like the English voices shouting. Like the first sight of Gemma's face against the forest branches. Too late. He must have touched something with his damaged hand because the shards of pain took his breath.

"WHAT WILL HAPPEN?"

He thought at first he was still in the hall because the voice was Boda's. Boda who must have stuck to him like a leech. But the shadows against his closed eyes were different. Not the hall. He knew every flickering light in that hall after dusk.

"What do you think will happen?" The second voice was brusque, impatient, half-familiar. But the logical thought necessary for the placement of it was beyond him.

"But…will he live?" asked Boda the persistent. "I mean, will—" The voice stopped. It was distraught, frightened. Emotions he could not match floating behind the heaviness of his closed eyelids.

"Of course. My patients do not die. Nothing is broken beyond the hand. If you cannot be useful, stand back and give the woman some room. She has more stomach than you. If you would hand me that bowl, lady."

The physician-priest. Boda should be pleased. He was lying…somewhere. His body no more than a leaden mass of earth-tied damaged flesh and crusted blood and dried sweat. His mind floated far above the *banloca*, the cage of bones that bound people to the restrictions of the earth.

There was a blur of movement above the leaden flesh, the splash of water. Scent. Faint and clean. Like spring and the sun.

Gemma.

It could not be. It was only fever dreams. Unreal imaginings of drugged senses. They would have taken the time to stupefy him with poppy or smoke. That was why his mind floated for this moment with a freedom that was not given to creatures of flesh and blood.

The physician touched his hand.

When he woke again it was much later. Yet the voices were still there, still talking in their separate world.

"But can such a thing be true?"

Water splashed again. Cloth touched his arm with a practiced deftness. The priest.

The woman was weeping. He could not bear that. He had to do something. But nothing in the leaden, abused mess of his body would move.

"Of course it is true. What would you think?" Boda's voice, still boylike enough to relish revenge, mimicked the priest's earlier impatience. "I should know. I was there. In the hall with the *Witan*. The king gave him this estate back, and another one farther south. All his family ever used to own."

The words struck through him, loaded with a significance his spiraling thoughts could not grapple with. All he could focus on was the woman's crying. It was a shape of despair, lightless and alone.

"It is true. The lady knows it." Boda's voice turned away. "If you know it is true, why do you still weep? I do not understand."

But Ashbeorn did. Even a king's gift could not change what mattered. He moved. But the priest caught his arm.

The darkness hit him, blank as a wall of stone. He could not get around it. It was as black as the woman's tears.

THE WEST SAXON WAS a creature made of gold. If Gemma had been asked to fashion a king out of all the riches of her craft she would have created him. Something that had the power to dazzle thought.

She had his favour, the chance to work her craft unhindered for all of her days under the protection of his house.

But he had offered her more than that. He had offered a gift.

A fair one.

Her feet struck the floor of the hall. She thought sparks should have kindled the musty covering of rushes. On one side of her was Alfred's cousin, on the other side the East Anglian who had ridden out from the Wessex host to receive Guthrum's message.

She tried smiling. It was not etiquette to throw king's gifts back in their faces. Even fair and generous kings had their pride.

So did she.

At least she told herself it was pride, not just the pain of her heart disintegrating.

Her escort followed her out of the hall. She only managed to get rid of them at the door to the room where Ash lay. Ashbeorn.

They wanted to come in. They were worried. The East Anglian out of instinct, the king's cousin out of the subtle labyrinth of a mind she did not quite care to fathom.

But she could not bear any witnesses to this, to the ending she had foreseen from the first moment. Besides, it was she who would leave soon enough. These men owned the future. The thane lying inside the chamber belonged with them.

She stood in the doorway. She could not see him at first. Then he moved, and the light showed her.

The Lord Ashbeorn, owner of this estate of Hartwood, former owner of another farther south, did not rest in the great canopied bed. He knelt before the hearth.

Deep shadows and small points of firelight played over fine skin and densely packed muscle. Light and warmth. The shadows dispersed and regathered, wreathing like the smoke ascending to the darkness of the thatch.

He watched the flames. It was impossible to turn away from the sight of him. Each muscle, each fiercely drawn line, held an intensity that ensnared sense. The power in him was raw. He might have been a creature of legend, from some terrifying land of the past that merged into enchanters' tales.

He seemed so utterly self-possessed, even though she knew the precise moment he became aware of her. It did not make him speak. The intensity, absorbed and impenetrable, did not lessen one iota. A hunter in his cave.

A savage.

His hand held a goblet fashioned out of plied strands of glass, green over blue, immeasurably fine. The fire in the hearth was scented with apple wood and dried herbs. At his back was a tapestry of many colors. His feet bruised meadowsweet.

"I will not take your gift."

He turned his head.

"It is the king's gift."

She would not meet his eyes. Such a thing would kill her.

"Do you think I am a fool? That I do not know your

family had lands farther south, as well as Hartwood? That those are the lands your king would give me?"

"All of my father's lands were forfeit. All were in the king's gift." His voice was as controlled, as blatantly laced with power as his body.

"*Liar.*" The word came out with the same rawness and the savage power that was enclosed behind his terrible self-possession. "The king gave me his patronage, to ply my craft for his house, wherever I wished," she shouted. "And then he decided to restore this estate to you and give the rest of your family's lands to me. I am supposed to believe that?"

She thought her heart would burst because of all that was hidden in it.

"Why would you have arranged such a thing?" Her voice cracked with power, but the contained strength in him matched it. That intensity suddenly, shockingly became focused on her.

"You wish to know why I did it? It is because I did not believe you would accept anything from me. Yet I thought you might accept the king's gift."

"But that is not—" She swallowed through the rising tightness in her throat. "I did not expect reward from you." Her heart beat so hard, the pain of it greater than her strength. "I did nothing for payment."

She had believed that he had understood, in that moment in her workroom when both their hands had touched the true sceptre under Erik's eyes. She thought he had seen what was in her heart, a truth and a fire that had matched his.

"I will not take it. I do not need—"

"Do you know what I wanted you to have?" He stood up. There were clothes beside him, carefully folded on the chair he had disdained to sit on. He would reach for them, for the cloak at least. She tried not to look at his skin.

He turned round, fully. The movement was deliberate, like a gesture of power. She could have thought it the obvious kind of power. She could have thought that if she had not known him.

"What I wanted you to have is all that I lost. All those things for the want of which I became the savage that I am."

He took a step towards her so that the light caught his body. So that she could see every last pitiless mark of what Erik's men had done to him.

"I would not have such savagery touch you. I wanted you to have a place of peace because that is what you love. I wanted you to have somewhere you could go, somewhere that you could take Edgefrith. A place you could be safe from—"

His words cut off. Not because he would not speak of the heaviness of the price he had chosen to pay, but because of the unbreakable determination of what he felt. The same intensity she had seen in each damaged muscle lived in his mind.

Courage.

"I wanted your safety from the first moment I saw you, with that creature Erik poised at your door. It is still what I want. You must know that." Her heart seemed to tighten, the oppression of what she felt impossible to bear.

"I wanted you to have somewhere to go back to, even if you traveled with the court because of your work. I wanted—"

She saw the stark, bitterly savage movement of his chest, as though the highly charged air of the room took his breath. As though the last words had to be forced. Out of the deepness of all that he was.

"I wanted you to have that which I do not. I wanted you and that lost, terrified child to have a home."

He moved. Fire-gilded skin and power.

"Ash—"

It was not even his proper name. It would have no power to stop him.

ASHBEORN GOT as far as the window by the force of what was in his head, his body shambling like a cripple's. He could not undo the shutters with one hand. He stared at their blankness. All the bright warmth of the room behind him.

A home.

What he had wanted for Gemma. What he had wanted all his life and which his heart was now too black to accept. The warmth and the colors and the memories at his back mocked him. So strong. Stronger than pretense or any disguise. It was not the damage to his body that could not be healed. It was the damage inside.

Gemma had known that.

He had nothing to give.

He heard her footsteps. She would go. It was best if she did. Best for her.

He knew she was safe with the king's protection.

Yet there was only her and the boy. She did not like being alone. Only he understood the truth that lay behind her mask of self-sufficiency.

He turned.

She was watching him, eyes dark with all the things he had wanted to conquer, to wipe out for her by the gift.

"Ash." She touched his arm, just above the red welts where someone had tried to break it. She was crying.

"Gemma—I did not want to make you weep."

"I am not weeping." She stared at him, her eyes wide. "It is only that I did not understand what you wished to do."

"Gemma..." She seemed not to feel the glassy sheen of tears on her face.

"How could I not have understood?"

"Hush. It matters not. I never told you. I cannot— I am not used to saying such things. It is because I have never—I have never had anyone to say them to before. Only you."

"And I have been so cold to you."

He caught her hand. For a moment she resisted, but he could not let her go, not with such a look in her eyes. He held her, as gently as he could. Wanting her to feel all those words still unsaid, the ones that were utterly beyond him to give light to.

The silence was complete. Even the crackling of the fire eluded his senses. Pain clawed at him as time stretched out. Still he could not let go.

And then, gently, her hand uncurled under the warmth of his.

He would have held her so forever. He slid his fingers round hers, drawing her hand up to the gleaming planes of her face, so that her fingers mingled with the tears.

He heard the warm, startled intake of her breath against his hand. It burned his skin so that he wanted to catch that small vulnerable sound, that faint warmth, against the greater heat of his mouth. To take her breath inside him, with all her sorrow.

Instead he forced his lips to smile.

"See? You weep because you have such a cold heart and no pity." The last word caught at the tightness of his throat because that was what she must feel behind her horror, pity for the physical damage. And perhaps, because of her tenderness, pity for the dishonour.

She frowned, her lips curling.

"Aye. It is not pity you deserve. I can see that." Her almond-shaped eyes tilted at the corners and the tears spilled out. "It is only that—" Her voice choked.

"It is all right."

He had not meant to take her in his arms because her nearness meant too much to him, more than she would want, and the hot ache of the savageness still beat in his chest. But she leaned towards him, as though drawn. Her head landed on his chest. His arms closed on the fragile line of her body, and her warmth was there, touching the naked, burning heat of his own body, absorbed into it. She was shaking.

She leaned against him as though she could not stand, and he was afraid of the driving force of what he felt. He drew her unresisting body back, away from the shutters and all that lay beyond them, back into the quiet warmth of the room.

She sat on the very edge of his bed, her spine stiff with tension, as though she would break. He moved away, in case he touched her again. The black need inside him was beyond control. She was not looking at him, her gaze lowered to the level of the bed. He picked up the embroidered cloak, swinging it over the savage heat of his skin.

"Gemma."

She did not turn.

As he watched, she reached out to touch the twisted covers that marked the place where he had lain. Her outstretched hand, her whole arm, was shaking. Her palm landed on the mattress, moved over the faint indentation, tracing the outline of his body, real or imagined. Slowly. As though he were still there.

He took a step forward. She must have heard, but she did not look at him. He stared at the trembling, utterly determined movement of her hand.

"I thought—" She stopped, her tear-streaked face a mask of fierce concentration, as though she could not find the words she sought. Or as though the words in her head were too terrible to speak.

"What? What is it, Gemma? Say it."

If she could just say whatever it was that haunted her mind, he could—

"I thought you were going to die."

"You thought… Nay, but I did not." He caught the restless hand, frightened by its movement. He tried for the teasing tone that had brought a response in her before. "It would take more than that to kill me. You were out of luck there."

The small movement tugged at the corners of her mouth again but this time the light did not touch her eyes.

"You could have died, each time. In the yard at Offleah with Erik and his men. If Earl Guthrum found what you had done with the sceptre and—"

"It did not happen. It would—"

"Boda told me what happened on the battlefield…." Boda, the child warrior, had much to learn. Her hand pulled against his. "You would have died. Even a few minutes later, you would have died."

She looked up, and this time the light words died on his lips. The truth was there. If the West Saxons had not ambushed Erik's men, even, perhaps, if Boda had not been so impulsive, he would be dead. She knew that.

He sat down, trying to keep hold of her hand.

"Gemma, it is over. Done. And doubtless now the tale grows in Boda's telling. But you should never have had to see such things, or think of them." He briefly considered stringing Boda up from the gallows at the crossroads. The corpse would probably have carried on talking afterwards.

"You must not…" He could not even think what to say to take that look out of her eyes. He—he realized where her gaze rested. She kept staring at the swelling and the distorted red welts on his arm.

He let her go, grabbing at the edge of the cloak, fumbling at the folds of the material, cursing the awkwardness of all that he did.

"Nay, do not." Her hand tangled with his, catching the cloak, twisting it away. He stopped.

Her fingers were locked on the embroidered edge of the heavy wool. She did not draw back.

"You were right that I should see this." Each word came out clearly despite her tears.

"Was I?" He watched the tightness of his hand beside hers against the dark wool, the sharp rise and fall of his chest, the glimpses of marred flesh, as though they belonged to someone else.

"I wish to God you had not seen what you have, or heard it, or had to think what you have thought."

"I do not wish it."

Her fingers did not move. The knuckles were white. White as his own. It was not someone else's pain. It was his, the humiliation as complete and deep as it had been the last time he had left this room.

"This is not fitting for you." His words came out with the same careful precision as hers.

"What you did, or what Erik did? Erik's men?"

"Erik's men? In their eyes I had betrayed them." The breath scored his throat. Their hands almost touched. "I did betray them."

"Do you think there was another decision you could have made?"

"No." That much was so clear. He thought of Swithun, of the West Saxon king and the burned-out village and the dead men in the field. Of the terrified child, Edgefrith. Of her.

"There is no other decision I would ever have made."

"I knew it was so. I knew it when I came into the yard to find you when I should not have, and you took the blame for what had been done. I knew it when you came into my workroom with your deal already set with Guthrum. Even though everything in my head told me it was a betrayal, my heart did not believe it."

Her gaze sought his. "You must have known that in the end."

Her eyes, shimmering with unshed tears, were as direct as a warrior's. That unspoken moment when their hands had met and touched the sceptre took shape in his mind. He had known then that she thought as he did, that her courage was there like the counterpart to his, the same determination and the same mind.

Her hand moved, touched him. The cloak fell away and she saw all there was. He watched her eyes note everything, all that had been done, each mark left by the hands and the feet and the weapons of the men he had betrayed.

She said nothing. They did not need words, just as

they had not under Erik's gaze. Her body leaned forwards until they touched. There were still tears.

His arms closed round her, despite the bruising and the shattered hand, and she met him. He had meant only to hold her, but her lips touched his mouth and her body moved with his, fusing with it completely. Heat flared and the need beat inside him, the rawness not diminished by the pain, but inflamed by it, the desire for her locked in each taut muscle, in the hot, savage surge of his blood.

She must have sensed that, despite the fact that each movement of his body was made with such exquisite slowness, because of the pain. Because she was fragile. Because he had heard and seen her weep.

She knew. Nothing could hide the primitive completeness of his desire and yet she touched him. Her soft flesh and her small bones and her delicate touch were his, the gift beyond comprehension, belonging equally to now and to that moment when their thoughts had joined.

CHAPTER SIXTEEN

THE TOUCH OF HIS MOUTH, the bright, enticing heat of his passion stole Gemma's senses. Nothing but him could drive away the nightmares of all that had happened, the blank empty wastes of the future stretching ahead.

Her lips slid across his, the way his desire had taught her. She sought his heat, the moist dark cavern of his mouth. Oblivion. It was there, in the fierce turn of his head, the slow sensual glide of his parted lips. She followed him, spellbound, drawn into the magic, wanting, seeking more, all of her being centered on the kiss, the feel of him, desperate.

Do not ever let me go.

The words were in her head, unspoken. In the hotly erotic need of her mouth. She was afraid to touch his body. Because of the bruising everywhere and all the damage and the pain. But he seemed not to care. His body pressed against hers, pushing her back into the softness of the mattress.

His tongue entered her mouth, hot and fast, and she took him in, the blatant inducement of her lips urging him deeper, because if he filled her so with his heat and the power of his desire, she did not have to think, only feel. Only know the miracle that he was there.

There with her. Living. Her hands touched his shoulders, plunged into his hair, drawing him closer, seeking the elegant curve of his neck, his head. The kiss measured eternity. Her senses dizzied with it. But she could feel his body. The craving for him built. He knew that. It would be as plain to him as day. He knew her.

His undamaged hand skimmed her side, tracing her shape, outside the barrier of her dress, the warmth and the power of palm and fingers sensed, but not enough. Not nearly enough. She writhed. His mouth slid from hers.

"*Ash…*" The word was choked out of her, the name that was no longer his. She tried to bite it back, to stop the rest of the words and the feelings locked in her head from coming out. He would hear that she was terrified—

If he looked up, he would see her face.

"I am sorry. I did not—"

His gaze caught hers. The rumpled sweep of his hair could not hide the bruises on his face. But his eyes were so steady. The same memories and the same black horrors were in his mind. Shared. Some of the words came out. Not all, because she could not put that burden on him.

"I cannot get what happened out of my mind except— When you touch me so…" Her gaze lost itself in the fathomless depths of his.

I love you so much. I need you at this moment, now and forever.

She could not say such words. Never. But it did not matter. His mouth brushed the heated skin of her throat, finding the rise of her collarbone above the neckline of her tunic.

"Then let me touch you."

His body nudged her back against the bolster. She watched the dark sweep of his hair against her shoulder, caught the gleam of his skin. The cloak was gone. She could see all of him, the stark feral line of his naked body over hers. Her throat went dry and she could see not the damage and the marring, but the power. The beauty of each taut line and the fluid strength.

His mouth fastened again on her skin and her body tightened, sliding higher against the pillows. His hand followed her movement. She felt its weight and its warmth, saw it trace her ribs, seeking the curve of her breast. His hand molded over her shape and her back arched. The softness of her breast brought full against his palm and the clever moving circle of his fingers.

She gasped, tightening under his touch, even through her clothing. He made the longing inside her ache and burn for him. Sharp jabs of sensation stabbed through her lower belly. His touch quickened so that she writhed. His body caught the movement of hers, sliding with her.

The movement must have caused pain but she saw only the strength in each tightly packed muscle, the arching line of back and chest, the densely flexed compactness of his thigh, the swollen latent fullness of his sex.

The sight and the feel of his naked maleness against her fully clothed body would send her mad. She was like a creature possessed, without thought or restraint, only desire. She tried to hold herself back, because he could not want the crude, ugly desperation that lived in her.

She made a faint sound. He looked up. She did not want to meet the graceful turn of his head because of the heat and the desperateness in her eyes. His gaze locked with hers and he read it, all that she could not hold back or beat into a semblance of civilized control.

It did not matter. The same heat was in him. She watched it burn in the smoldering darkness of his eyes. She watched the raw intensity of her feelings revealed in him and she could not look away.

He slid down her body. His naked skin gleamed in the shadowed curtained space of the bed. He moved lightly, but he let her feel him, a solid, rippling sheet of heated flesh. It was a predator's grace.

She could see through the brightness of his gaze all that he felt, sense the focused intent of what he would do.

Her breath caught. Her heart beat fast. He touched her clothing, sliding the pooling wash of her skirts high across her legs. The paleness of her own flesh gleamed alongside his, exposed to the half-light and the shadows. And all the time her gaze was trapped in his. Fire.

His hand touched her thigh, smoothed down it. Hot chills of anticipation scored through her flesh. She ached in the most secret part of herself, the part that craved the wild addictive release he had shown her. Heat touched her face, her skin, the hidden intimate folds of her body. The need was tearing, absolute. She saw its primitive bright-dark image in his eyes.

He lowered his head.

His lips followed the sensitized trail left by his fingers on her inner thigh. Her throat tightened. His mouth hovered a thread above moist curls. She could feel the warmth of his breath.

She watched the curve of his head, the spilled abundance of his hair against her skin, the arch of his neck. The feral, bright-shadowed length of his body.

Her need of him was bone-deep. Unquenchable. She could not bear the thought of the future.

"Touch me. Make me forget."

Her body spasmed at the first touch of his mouth. He held her with his good arm, her body locked against the moist heat of him, against the wild skilful invasion of mouth and lips and tongue. He took her fast and that was what she wanted, the uncontrolled heady mindlessness of it.

It was what he gave. The world narrowed to that hot merciless skill, that heat. To him. Her hips pushed against him, shameless, and he took her need and her madness with his mouth and his touch, taking her desperation inside himself until her world shattered in bright sharp-edged release and they were falling, together, the touch of his body with her, as though it would be so always.

He was still there when her senses swam up out of the dark.

"Ash..." She tried to tell herself that that was not his name. It no longer belonged to him. But her mind could focus on nothing else.

She felt his hand move gently beneath her crushed skirts, across the heated skin of her thigh.

"Ash?"

"Hush." The edge of his breath shivered across the burning flesh he had so recently touched. The disordered bedclothes rustled. The dark whisper of living breath touched closer. Hotter.

"But—" The words, question or protest, were annihilated under the touch of his mouth. She gasped, her body jerking, but the touch was softer this time, as though he knew. As though he understood that she was so fragile from the power they had shared that she could break from his touch.

He was gentle in what he did, slow and tender. So careful that she felt each small wave of pleasure through her aching skin, every shifting nuance of touch and movement, the slightest change of pressure, the smoothness and the beguiling warmth.

She would not have believed that the need could still be there. But it was. Just as driven for all its fragility, light as gossamer and binding as linked steel. Her need flared, ignited by him, for him. Only him. Her body moved for him. The warmth of his mouth became heat, heat that would burn her. But it was held back, so that the longing mounted and the pleasure rippled outwards in rhythmic waves, slowly, so that their sense-melting completeness could be felt in every heated, responsive inch of her body.

She gasped, one endless, voiceless moan of longing. She thought the intensity of the pleasure would kill her. Nay it was not the pleasure, it was the care. It was the deliberate gentleness that caught at her breath and made the banked tears slide out from under her closed lids.

Her fingers reached down to touch his hair, his shoulders. Her body arched against him in the darkness behind her eyes. Flesh and heart and mind tightened into one aching thread of pleasure. His mouth moved. Just one slight whisper of movement and the restraint broke.

The pleasure was deeper, a thousand times more piercing than before. And she knew that her need of him would never abate even if she never saw him again. Its strength was too deep inside her, greater than body or thought.

When the web of dazzling shadows left her, he held her still. She could feel his warmth and his presence and that was the greatest blessing of all.

His head rested against her thigh. He did not move. There was silence in the luxurious curtained fastness of the bed. Naught but soft shadows and the warm weight of his head. The silent unquestioning intimacy of that tore at her heart.

She touched him. His breath came hard in the bruised wall of his chest. The wildness of passion mixed with the pain that must be there.

She wanted to give the same deep loving to him as

he had given her. She was afraid of what would happen
if she did. So many things strained against the thin walls
of her heart, so much that she could never say. The
words wanted to burst forth as though they had a will
of their own.

*I love you. If you would have me, I would never let
you go.*

Perhaps she could have said that to Ash, the creature
of the forest who, like her, had had nothing. Naught but
the matchless, heady gift of himself. But she could not
say it to Ashbeorn who was high in the king's favour.

She reached out her shaking fingers. The silken
warmth of his hair spilled over her hands. She felt the
touch of his mouth on her skin, the molten heat that possessed all of her. Her breath caught and she was lost in
the snare of him, in the longing.

She slid round in the bed, her movements lithe and
easy where his were made at such cost. She felt the tension and the hard-held power of him.

"Let me touch you as you have touched me."

Her hands moved over the heat of his skin. She held
her breath. But her touch was allowed. The warmth of
his body welcomed her, complete and unreserved, as
though nothing could ever divide them. Her heart would
die of the pain. It was all there, all that she wanted, the
wild pulsing need and beneath it the lure of such closeness. The gift of it beyond comprehension, or aught that
she could requite.

She touched him as she wished. The hardness and the

hot silken skin and the harsh pulsing of his blood. She heard the rough sound deep in his throat cut off. Her hand stilled, terrified he would reject her.

"Please."

She did not know whether she spoke aloud or whether the word was in some hidden recess of her mind, intense and primitive as the sound he had made. But his frightening strength rolled back, taking her with him, taking her touch and the terrible depth of her need, giving her access to his body, letting her feel the response in him to her touch.

Her shaking fingers caressed his shape, feeling him move against her.

"Gemma…"

The soft whisper in the shadows shivered across her skin. She watched him, the restless movement of his body, the flat, tightened muscle of his abdomen, the sharp rise and fall of his chest. The bruising and the swollen red marks. She would not think of that. She watched his face, the absorbed tenseness and the bright glitter of his eyes behind half-closed lids. He would see her staring—

She glanced away, but the heated touch of his hand drew her back, so that she watched him again. Could he see the same intenseness in her own eyes?

He must. The unbroken hand pulled her closer, so that she was kneeling over him. The intimacy of what she did bringing the blood-heat to her face, across her skin. But he did not pause. His eyes and the touch of his hand urged her closer until she knew what he would do.

She gasped, staring at his eyes. But all that their wide darkness held was the acknowledgment of shared need, its power and its inevitability. And the heat that tempted and drew her onward, like someone spellbound.

The clever fingers touched her. Her flesh was so sensitized to him that the slightness of that touch was enough to make her gasp again. Shudders wracked her and the heat increased.

Her response to him was more than she could control, but it did not matter. The deepness of his eyes took it all.

She let his fingers slide across her slick skin, dipping inside her, making her ready. She felt the urgency in him tighten, sensed the ruthless power that held it back.

"Ash—" It was not a word, not his name true or false, but a harsh sound of need. His hand slid away, covered hers where it held him. She watched as his fingers meshed with her own over his burning hardness, guiding the power of his flesh into hers.

The deep invasion of her flesh made her body move, the first reaction instinctive, unstoppable. She heard the roughened sound in his throat, felt the power of the reaction in him. The rawness and the pure intensity of it struck through her and with it the desperate need to give, to return whatever she could of the burning cleansing passion, the fierce intensity and the bright searing edge of release.

Her body moved against his, tentatively at first because she was so ignorant. But then faster and harder, matching the urging of the taut ridged muscle beneath her, inside her. She watched his face, the sudden brightness in his eyes, the mirror in male form of the fierce desire that had taken her, wild, overwhelming. The pleasuring of it and the wildness of it would drive her mad.

He must know that. He must see it. His hand caressed the tight line of her thigh molded against his, the screamingly delicate flesh of her belly, the curve of her breast. She cried out, wordless, the sound caught and reflected in his eyes, such brightness as would kill her. Then his body moved, with a strength that injured flesh could not possess, rolling with her against the softness of the mattress, joined for one breathless moment and then sliding away, leaving her.

She reached out for him, blind, seeking his warmth. She touched the hot hard flesh slickened with her own juices and his. She pressed closer, holding him, taking the driven, mindless thrust of his body, the raw sound deep in his chest, feeling the harshness of release as the hot gush of his seed burst against her hand.

THE RELEASE HAD a power beyond madness. Power strong enough to sweep away all the horrors in Ashbeorn's mind, until there was only light, shattering and complete. Measureless.

And yet the pain followed. So soon. Intense enough to rob sense. So that he did not know for one blinded moment whether she was still there. He could not feel her warmth in the darkness or hear her voice.

There was only the unfinished pain felt through mind and body, through the appalling mess of broken bone. He reached out with the hand that still worked. He thought he heard her breath, short and ragged. If she wept—

He touched the warmth of her flesh. It molded against his hand, firm as though she trusted him. And he knew that the need of her was not slaked by what he had done. It burned deep inside him, with its own life. It would be so always.

"Gemma…"

Her hand curled round his, locked with it. She was so close. He should have known that. He tried to move away because the future crowded the unlooked-for vulnerability of his mind. But the effort was more than he had bargained for and the pain shot through his hand, forcing out a small sound he no longer had the power to hold back.

"Ash?"

The question hung between them. But he heard the guilt loaded into the shortened name that only she ever used. He could not bear that.

"It is naught." He could not so much as move to prove it. There was nothing beyond his voice to reassure her. He controlled it. "Or mayhap you were right all along and I am about to die."

"I am always right." The accustomed coolness in her tone told him she had picked up the wryness in his voice. The sharp hesitation that had come before her words had been voiceless. "I thought you would have realized that by now."

"I shall keep it in mind."

He stared at the deepening shadows of the bed and tried not to think about her courage. He did not know what he could say to her. None of the words and the questions that pressed on his heart. She was not his, even though their bodies touched and her breath whispered over his skin.

He tried to force thought out of the weariness and pain mixed with the bone-deep intensity of passion. The future had to be dealt with: the future and the inescapable ties of the past.

He focused his gaze on the light and the shadows beyond the bed.

"This chamber was always mine."

The small startled movement of her body brushed his skin. He forced speech.

"When I was a child younger than—" he could not say the name of the frightened boy "—younger than your brother, and I woke to the morning light in this bed, I did not need to open my eyes to know what was around me. It was all there." The words struck through his blood like cutting ice.

"Everything—the warmth of the chamber, and beyond it the great hall. The barns and the haylofts where I hid, the horses I rode, the fields full of grain and cattle and sheep, the forest game, the weirs full of fish. It all had life if only it was cared for. Even when my father and I chose to leave it, the land still fed and clothed the people who stayed. Such things endure."

He took a breath. The soft curve of her body followed his, molding against him as though they were one. He sought the words.

"I do not know what it is like to have a skill such as yours or such learning. I will never know. Yet—"

"That is not—"

"No." His voice snapped, cutting off what she would say, but he could not stop it. It was too difficult to get the words out. "A home that will support life's needs has a value even for someone who has a calling, like you. And how—how much more so for a boy growing into a man who struggles to learn such things."

He stopped, thinking of the lost frightened soul of the boy who, for all his fine heart, had not his sister's quick cleverness, who might never make a goldsmith if he tried all his life.

"Land can give a sense of worth and a purpose. Everyone needs that. A man needs such a basis who must one day provide for others."

She must know what he would say. He could not get the words out more clearly. He did not know how to go about explaining what was in his heart. He could not think of Edgefrith because of what he had done. Because the child's pain and bewilderment were too close to what he had once felt.

"Gemma—"

"I should have seen what your home means to you."

The statement took him by surprise. Because he was not thinking of that. Because—

"I should have known. You tried to tell me before. Not just now, but at Offleah. I did not understand."

She had missed utterly what he wanted to say. She had—

"It is a thane's home," said Gemma.

The other half of the truth he owed her took shape.

"It is so beautiful," she said. "It would take little to restore its fineness."

He stared at the faded room, the brilliance still visible beneath the dust and neglect. It would be possible for someone with Gemma's skill for beauty to restore it. He could do it himself in lesser measure, as he must. It was not the strong timbers and the rich furnishings and the grace that had altered. It was him.

"Aye," he said. "It is a thane's home. But I am not a thane."

He felt the shudder that went through her flesh where he touched it, heard the sharp intake of her breath. Her silence.

Then she said, "Is that what you believe?"

"Yes." He did not know how else to answer, how to tell her what must be said. The shadows flickered. The edge of the wall hanging caught his eye.

"Did you see the tapestry when you came into the room?"

"Yes." He sensed the uncertainty in her body. Then she said, "It is beautiful."

She worked to create beauty. She would understand through that.

"Aye. I thought it so. I thought it perfect—the bright colors of the huntsmen's clothes, the fine hounds, the white stag with the golden antlers, the burnished spear points. Sometimes it is almost like that when the king hunts. Like a brilliant show. I have been with him."

They were so close that the softness of her hair coiled across his marred skin like the gold threads she spun. Its gossamer weight shifted with the harshness of his breath.

"But I did not always hunt like that." Her pale skin gleamed in the shadowed light, unreal, utterly fragile. "I used to use stones, or sticks sharpened with flint." He felt the flutter of her breath. "I used my hands." His words cut the scented, fire-warmed air. "There was naught to choose between me and the beasts I hunted."

Her body, curled up against him, went rigid.

"I cannot change that." He tried to move, to give her the space and the freedom she would wish. The pain crippled movement.

"Did you hate him?"

The force of her words stopped him.

"Did you actually hate your father?"

She had turned and he could see the pale heart shape of her face.

Yes. I had to hate him out of loyalty to those he betrayed. Out of loyalty to all that he destroyed.

Truth.

Yet not the whole truth. Nowhere near the unfathomable complexity of that.

"When I was a child, my father would sit on the edge of this bed and talk to me for hours when I should have been sleeping. It did not matter what he said. He was just there. He would talk to me about crops and cattle as though I were the reeve of his estate. He would speak to me about all the injustices of the overlords of Surrey as though I were a political conspirator. He would tell me stories that would please a small boy."

He waited for the shades of disgust to settle on the clear lines of her face. Her gaze never left him. The very fineness of her body held tense as steel. She did not move.

It seemed possible for the first time to say the words, to try and explain. To let the bright memories that lived in this room take their place alongside the later horrors that had overwhelmed everything.

"I was all that my father had, though I did not think of that at the time. My mother was so long dead of the fever that I do not remember her." He took a breath, watching Gemma in the shadows. "He loved her. I never understood what that meant, to love someone so much and to lose them."

The world narrowed to the small curve of her shoulder, the gleaming threads of her hair in the darkness. Naught else had existence. The deep effort of her breath was something sensed in his own flesh.

"It is grievous to lose love," she said.

The shadows round them closed in, taking the light, sliding across skin like something sensate. He stirred restlessly.

"Perhaps it is not possible to survive such a loss."

The meaning of that waited ahead of him. He kept his thoughts on his father's bitterness, on her own parents and the mess of her upbringing. On all the losses she had suffered. Her future had to be different. He had to give her that, something fresh and new, not tainted.

"My father was driven by so many things—ambition and pride and bitter grief. And by the way he loved." It was the first time he had acknowledged that, the tie of love that had endured through everything that had been destroyed.

"So many things made up the path my father followed." He took a stinging breath. "I chose my own path."

The darkness and the close air of the shuttered room would choke him. He forced breath through the ache in his body and the weariness, through the pain that was no longer just physical.

"My future lay with the Wessex king, with all that he is trying to achieve. And now it also lies with this place."

He could not think of being alone in the warm sumptuous wasteland of the room, with the ghosts and the dead spirits that filled the brightness, and the shadows held in by the tapestried walls. Could not think of the beauty of the hall and the endless miles of fields beyond. All of it changed and yet intimately familiar. The past and the future intertwined like the designs in gold that sprang from Gemma's trained fingers.

He knew what was real.

"This is my future, but it also holds my past. Whatever I do or whatever I choose, I will not be free of that. Can you understand that?"

"I understand that if you had not been who you are, English, Danish, outcast and thane, I would be dead and so would Edgefrith—"

"I did not—"

"And I do not know how many others would be facing death if you had not found Erik and the sceptre." Her voice struck across his like an opponent's sword. She leaned closer, the light glistening on skin still damp from their shared loving.

"How many more would die, if you had not been Viking enough to learn Earl Guthrum's plans?"

Her words struck so clearly, cutting off what he would say. He had never spoken of such things to her but he should have known she would see, all of it.

Yet some things she did not see.

"You know my loyalty is to Alfred. But nothing changes what I am."

"Do you think I do not understand that? That Edgefrith does not? He knows that the information you gave Erik for his safety, the information you promised Guthrum, was false. He knows you betrayed nothing. Just as I do."

Her fierceness caught him off balance. Her eyes glittered, the smoothness of her body taut in the dark with the intensity of what she felt.

He did not wish to harm that.

"Can you think that my brother does not understand about you, that I do not?"

"Yes. That is what I do think." He did not need to see the change in her eyes, the sudden withdrawal of her body. It was like turning a sword on himself.

"But you saved my life." The words hissed at him through the shadowed light. "And Edgefrith's. First at Offleah. Then on the battlefield when you threw the spear in front of them all, knowing they would turn on you then and there. I know that. Edgefrith does—"

"Edgefrith cannot trust me." He had not meant his voice to be so harsh. But he could not control it because of what he felt and the shock blossomed over her face.

"No…that is not true."

"I have done what you warned me against, what you knew in your heart would happen. You told me what your brother dreamed of—a lost father, a warrior. You told me what he longed for and what he thought he saw in me." The pain gathered, waiting for the words. "What did Lyfing look like?"

Her gaze stayed on his and yet not so. Her eyes were darkened with memory, seeing him and not seeing him.

"Was he dark? Fair? Short or tall?"

She said nothing.

"Tall, then," he said. "Neither dark nor fair. Strong, I would say."

"Very. Both strong and tall, with rich brown hair, and so fair of face, one could not see what was behind it."

His breath caught in the aching restriction of his chest.

"So fair and so strong," she said, "that no one could turn away from him."

Edgefrith looked at you and was dazzled.

The accusation she had made in the forest hung in the lighted chamber, seeking him out with the accuracy of a skilled bowshot.

"I walked into your brother's cell and I made Erik free him of his chains. I made a vulnerable boy see the father he had lost. I made him feel gratitude and trust, and then I destroyed that. He saw in Erik's yard what no child should see. When his courage made him protest, I hit him."

"But—"

"Gemma, I struck down your own brother, a terrified child."

"You saved his life." Her gaze struggled with his. But he caught the faint tremor in her voice. He could almost feel the cold slide of it across her skin. "He understands."

"Does he? Is that what he says?"

"I—" Her voice stopped before the precipice.

"Gemma, he can no longer look on me."

As you can not. Not now.

He watched her averted head.

"I would not wish such things on you."

Make me forget.

It was all she had asked of him. All she had said. So much he had tried to give her with his body; what she wanted, the release of desperate passions, not the kind of joining that could have bound her to him, that might have produced a child.

The rest of the gift lay not in him but in the price of her future.

He watched the gleam of her skin, the rare perfection of her beauty revealed in light and hidden in shadows.

It is grievous to lose love. Perhaps it is not possible to survive....

"Take the lands I offered, for I have naught else to give. Or if you cannot, then at least accept the king's gift of the patronage that is due to your skill."

He watched the steadiness of her eyes. Naught else existed. The mind-dark and the aching brightness of the room closed in.

"Take a different future from mine." He forced out the only word that was left.

"Please."

Her gaze never faltered, never left his.

"Yes."

CHAPTER SEVENTEEN

SUCH A SMALL WORD.

Yes.

Gemma's voice reverberated in the silence of his sumptuous bed, his warm, bright, light-streaked bower.

The gift he offered was matchless. It was what he wanted—nay *needed*—to give her. It was only she who desired forever, who would, could contemplate trapping the future of a king's thane, and risking all that lay beneath the wall of Edgefrith's silence to get what she craved.

She watched his eyes, caught the first glint of surprise in their hazel depths because he still believed she would refuse what he asked of her. She caught the fierceness of relief, the terrible power of it.

"I need to thank—"

"No." The sharp sound, cold as black ice cut through her words. She made some sound, but his voice stopped her again.

"I know that it is good land. It will support you—you and the boy."

Edgefrith.

She could no longer see Ash's eyes. Only his averted head. "I—"

"You will not want for anything."

She watched the rich fall of his hair, silk smoothness roughened by her own hands, the sleek lines of arm and shoulder and compressed thigh.

"No. I shall lack nothing."

Only my heart's desire. Only you.

The temptation to say that, to let out the blind desperation of her need, was more than she could bear. Except that she had no right and he would not want it. He was lost to her.

She had known it when he had sent her the gift, when she had seen him here in the room that was his. When she had tried to show him in this bed what she felt for him through the desperation of her touch, and he had withdrawn from her. Even then. Because he would not place any further risk on her future. He wanted her to be safe. He would make sure she was.

She had only one gift for him.

"So it is done. Over. We both have our...place." She could not use the word he had used—*home*. Not when she must live there without him. She had never wanted a home, never felt the lack of it. But she did now. With a pain and a hunger that seemed eternal.

"Aye, we both have our place."

He did not look round, but she knew. The other half of her gift lay in her hand if she knew how to give it.

"I refused your gift to me because you did me too

much honour, not too little." Light shifted over densely packed muscle. She spoke on, her words hurrying loud into the silence.

"I did not understand what you gave." Shadows formed and fled over naked skin. "But you understood. Because you understand this place and all that it means, past and future. Your home." Her breath skipped. "This is a true king's gift."

She found she was speaking straight into his eyes. The words came to her, jumbled, out of the air. But she spoke them, hoping he would understand the thoughts behind them.

"They came to see you while you slept. Did they tell you that? The king came, himself. And his cousin. And the dark-haired Celt and the East Anglian. They spoke to me. The one who is the king's cousin told me about you, about how you came to the court at last with Swithun because the king needed every man. He told me about the battles you have fought. About the pledge you made to King Alfred at Wimborne."

"He told you about—"

"The warriors of the dragon, those who are oath-sworn."

She did not care about his shock or his anger. She could see straight through them. She could see, guess, part of what was hidden.

"He told me that the private oath you had pledged to Alfred, and to the golden banner of Wessex, meant more than life or self or the common oaths sworn by men to kings. That you would undertake any service he asked, whatever it involved and whatever the cost. That none of you would rest until the Viking threat was overcome."

He glanced away.

"I could not break that. Whatever anyone thought. You have to know how it was."

She saw the struggle to say what was nearest to his heart.

"Alfred was crowned just as the host of which Guthrum is part, what men called the summer army, came. They joined the troops already massed at Reading. There was only one land left for them to conquer."

She watched the undamaged hand tighten.

"Alfred had but twenty-three winters. He had lost all four of his brothers, one prince and three kings of Wessex. We had just buried the last who had died of battle wounds. Alfred was alone."

"So you swore your faith, your life, to him."

"My faith? Aye. Faith was what I swore and he could have refused that from me. But he did not. He accepted what no other man would. If I swore my life's worth to him, he gave it back to me."

She thought of the clever eyes of the handsome young king, eyes that saw what others did not.

"He saw the truth."

The bruised knuckles of his fist held her gaze, skin stretched tight over bones.

"Alfred was the only king who could stand against

the Viking army, and if he failed, there was nothing. The oath we swore to him encompassed all of our hopes. It was given freely. I do not have the words to say what it means."

She touched his hand. He allowed it. She was not sure he even felt what she did. His skin was warm under her fingers. Tight. So strong. So utterly vulnerable to the kind of death that took warriors.

"I do not know how many times I fought that year, how many times we all did. How many raids, open and secret. There were nine pitched battles. At the end of it, Wessex still stood."

His hand moved under hers. She caught it, held him though she should not.

"I did not know what—" She swallowed. "Of course, I heard some of it." At least some of the tidings had penetrated as far as the sanctuary of her father's workplace. "But I did not understand how it was."

He looked up.

"It is not a thing that people should have to live through."

She had not expected him to say such a thing to her. The directness of it, all that it exposed in him, cut through every defense that she had. The hot swell of tears in her throat choked breath. She did not know what she could say to that kind of courage or that kind of sacrifice.

"I wish that no one had to live through such times. That you—" Her voice gave out but at the swift movement of his hand away from hers, she held it, with all her strength. She had the power because the truth was revealed at last. His truth.

"What you have done lives now through this kingdom, through this place, through the very fact that we can be in this room, that you and I can have somewhere called a home. Nay—" She held his hand with both hers.

"It lives through the king's trust, in those people who have shared that last year with you and what came before and will come after. You have that now. You have the king's friendship and the friendship of those who swore the oath with you. It is there. The way this chamber and the great hall and the fields are there."

All the things I cannot be part of.

"You have all that."

He said naught. The acknowledgment of some part of what she had said was in his eyes. She could read it. She could read so much. She could tell herself, if she wished, that she read more in the bright-flecked forest depths, light and dark.

Let there only be light. If such a thing is possible in this world, let it be so for him.

She let go of his hand.

He watched her as she moved back. As she found her kirtle and her tunic. Slid them over her head. He watched her until it was no longer possible for her to hold his gaze and she turned away like something blind and maimed.

"You cannot go in there! Not now—" Her head

turned at the shout outside the chamber. She recognized Boda's voice. She reached for the fastenings of her dress, the wild confusion of her unveiled hair. Then she saw who it was.

"No…" The slight figure wavered in the doorway, Boda close behind him, one overgrown paw dragging at a bony shoulder. Too late.

"Moonwit," muttered Boda as though his charge had been caught in some childish prank. But the look he gave her over the tousled head was totally adult. She could find none of the condemnation she expected.

Edgefrith went chalk-white. Wide eyes stared at her unfastened dress, at her streaming hair, at the bare feet half-hidden in the rushes. Then he looked towards the bed.

Ashbeorn was blessedly still. He did not try to hide as she did. His gaze was utterly direct, as one man confronts another.

"Edgefrith." The deep voice was as open and straightforwards as his gaze but behind it was such understanding that she thought Edgefrith's control would crumple. Ashbeorn moved in the wreckage of the bedcovers and the thin body had turned instinctively towards him. But at the last moment Edgefrith held back. His head turned.

"You have lain with him."

The words were directed at her with a suddenness that took breath. Guilt and confusion and fear of the distress behind the white, closed face took the power of thought. She could hear Boda muttering saints' names.

"Edgefrith…I—"

"I know it is true. I am not a fool." The words flailed at her, vicious with the distress boiling underneath. Out of control.

"I am not a fool and I am not a child." His voice soared, cracking. "I know how things are. I'm a bastard, after all. I should know what—"

"Edgefrith…"

The words stopped. Her brother turned back to confront Lyfing's image in the bed.

"Are you going to marry my sister?"

"No."

She thought the directness of that was brutal, cruel beyond anything Edgefrith merited. But as she watched the shock and then the sudden controlled focus in his eyes she thought perhaps that was the only way he could deal with what had happened. His face changed and she could see the determination that had made him survive Erik's imprisonment.

"Why?"

The directness matched Ashbeorn's. But the question held more than its surface belligerence. The key to the wall of silence was there.

Ashbeorn watched him as though he sensed that.

"Because it would not be right for your sister. Because she could find a better man than I am, and she has the king's protection and his reward of land, as do you." She watched the steadiness of his gaze on her brother's face, heard the gift of the fair spoken words. She saw her brother's hands clench and unclench.

"There are things in my past that I cannot change and that I would not wish on your sister. I would not tie her to that and she would not wish it."

"But she does wish it. She cried after they set your hand. She was crying for you. You have the king's favour now. Everyone knows it. You could marry her if you wished. But you will not."

"Edgefrith…" But her strangled whisper seemed not to carry across the chamber. And he did not hear. His attention was solely and utterly fixed on the man in the bed.

"It is because of me," said Edgefrith. "I am to blame."

She saw the startled reaction in Ashbeorn's eyes but Edgefrith seemed oblivious. His voice went on.

"It is my fault. Because of what I said. I called you a coward and a betrayer. I did not believe you were true and when we went to the West Saxons I shouted it out in front of the Viking so you had to kill him and then Erik— You could have died. It was all my fault."

"No—" It was her cry that matched with Ashbeorn's deeper voice. Edgefrith did not turn. He watched the figure in the bed that was at once Ashbeorn and the memory of Lyfing and perhaps also the remoteness of her own father, all the fathers Edgefrith had ever wanted to love him.

The locked pain inside her would shatter because the boon Edgefrith craved could never be here, either. He could not demand it of Ashbeorn. Yet the desperation was something he could not stop. The unfairness and the impossibility of it cut through her heart. She moved forwards with her hand outstretched. But it was not her hand Edgefrith saw.

"Edgefrith, it was not your fault," said Ashbeorn. "It was Erik's."

It was all that the desperate child needed, what he craved. The small form flung itself onto the bedcovers, incoherent with the tears that must have been inside him since Erik had dragged him away from her at Offleah, perhaps since Lyfing had abandoned his son.

He buried his face in the dark woven wool of the bed-covers. Ashbeorn let him. The large hands, whole and shattered, settled on the thin, heaving back. Edgefrith sobbed, the sound childlike and complete.

Gemma knelt down beside the bed, softly so she would not break the spell before it had to be broken. She caught the loose folds of Edgefrith's sleeve, wanting him to know she was there, yet almost afraid to touch him.

Awareness of Ash took her like a flood. Yet they did not look at each other, and he did not speak. He just sat with the desperate child, the way his father perhaps might have sat with him in this room.

When the tears stopped, she felt the shaft of tension that went through Edgefrith's body at the realization of where he was and what he had done.

She knew the effort it took for him to face that. If she could but— Her hand fell off his sleeve as he moved and she realized how many things her brother had faced in ten winters.

"I am sorry." The childish voice was carefully formal, like one man apologizing in honour to another.

Her brother scrubbed the tears from his face with a movement that was vicious. She reached out, but he twisted away, brushing her hand aside.

"Edgefrith—"

"Leave me." His voice choked. She thought he would turn, flee.

"Please." Her voice choked off. But it was Ash who stopped him.

He used his broken hand. Necessity? Or the same kind of rapid understanding that had thought past all that was in her mind and Erik's in the first moment?

Transfixed she and Edgefrith stared at that linen-strapped hand. Edgefrith could not move a muscle.

"Lord…"

"I chose all of my actions and I knew what the consequences would be. That is how things are."

Fast mind. It held all the power of the way he had turned to her in this room and let her see what had been done to him, with no shield for the damage beyond acceptance.

Not just fast mind. Generous heart.

"But," said Edgefrith, who thought not so quickly, but just as hard, "Lord," he said, struggling with the protection of formality, "I did not—"

"There is naught," said the lord Ashbeorn, "in all that

has happened for you to be sorry for. What you said was done in honour. I would not reproach anyone for that. I would not have struck out at you if there had been any other way. You showed courage. Any man would be proud to have you as his son."

Her brother's face flushed scarlet. His eyes, the image of Lyfing's and so hauntingly like Ashbeorn's own, held disbelief and hope and a thousand emotions warring in their depths. She saw the harshness of his breath, the unsteadiness round his pinched mouth.

"But you do not love us," blurted out her brother with the brutal simplicity that belonged only to the young.

She felt the shock of that basic statement through skin and bone and sinew, through every last hidden place of her heart.

She did not look at the brilliant, fierce, vital creature in the bed. She could not. She wanted to flee in her turn, to escape the soft warmth of the chamber, run and never stop running if only she could be alone when the pain claimed her for its own.

No, I do not.

It was as though she could already hear the deep resonance of his voice, the stark directness that would answer Edgefrith.

I do not.

"There are other things besides love."

She was so close, she heard the faint rustle of the bedclothes as he moved. She almost sensed the vibration of his voice across her skin. That was what he chose to say, the man who sought truth and had always been denied it. Her heart leaped and the blood beat painfully through her veins.

"There are other things besides those that we wish," said her lover.

"But they are not as strong." Her voice spoke before she had the time to will it. The sound cut across the deep richness of his voice, filling the fine chamber so that Edgefrith turned, and even the motionless shape across the room that was Boda looked up. The very air in the long-dead bower seemed to wait on what she said.

The words came out without staying.

"There is nothing as strong as love that is true."

She had nothing in the stark reality of what had been said and done to justify her words, only what she felt. The feeling was as inexplicable and full of power as it had been the first day she had seen Ash in the deserted forest.

There were the masks that had to be shown to the world and the truth behind.

"Such love is stronger than right or wrong, past or future." Her heart tightened. The words she had shared with him in the darkness of her poor bower at Offleah poured into the air. "It is stronger if we trust it."

Her gaze found his. She did not want to beg, to place an unsought burden on him like Edgefrith. If she was wrong about the many faces of his truth, if she sought what she should not...

And then it did not matter. The magic was there. Just as it had been beneath the shadows of the trees, a spell beyond the power of mortal thought or time's reckoning. A force with its own truth.

Her breath caught and her eyes filled with tears. She could see all the haunted corrosive pain of the past in the deep earth colors of his eyes, the bedrock strength and the light like spring leaves. She thought the last deathly grip of the pain dissolved, or perhaps it was the tears marring her sight.

She touched him. Or he touched her. His good hand closed over her shaking fingers, warm, filled with strength and covered in the small scars she had once despised. A hand that protected, that would protect her. Always.

Edgefrith stared at their joined hands in doubt, bewildered by the change, by all that had been said without words.

"Does—does that mean you will wed?"

"Aye." It was Ash who spoke, the word final and complete.

"But—but will I…"

The broken hand slid down to guide Edgefrith's grubby fingers across theirs.

"Can you count that?"

"Three?"

"Perhaps." The bright gaze flicked to the far corner of the room, then sought hers in inquiry.

If it was possible to smile and cry at the same time, she did.

"Not three," said Ashbeorn. "Four." Something emerged from the shadows muttering a catalog of Mercian saints.

"I am not—"

"Boda?" The eagerness in Edgefrith's voice was not something that could lightly be resisted. The shape took a couple of steps but hung on the edge of the light.

"Aye. I fear so. I might need him to teach me spear fighting. Or how to deal with Vikings. I seem to need assistance."

Edgefrith glanced uncertainly at the bandaged hand and then at the lumbering shape.

"From *Boda?*" The sound was no more than a whisper but the shape heard it. Gemma distinguished an offended sniff.

Ash's expression did not alter in its gravity.

"Unless, of course, he admits I could teach him."

"Vainglorious Wessex boaster," said Boda. He stepped into the circle of the firelight and Gemma knew that for him the barrier into manhood had been passed forever. For Edgefrith that moment was still to come, but the step would not have to be taken alone. He would have someone to stand at his back in a father's place.

Always.

"You might have to get used to living in Wessex," said Ashbeorn the thane. "We all will." She could feel the warm pressure of his hand on hers, the promise in it. "Here."

WHEN THEY HAD gone, new man and happy boy, she lay in his arms in the bone-melting warmth of the great bed.

"Are you so sure that you meant what you said?" The dark heat of his breath whispered across her skin. "Are you truly so sure?" She could feel the slight hesitation in that whispered breath as though it were her own.

"Yes." It was so hard to shape words out of the intensity of what she felt. She held on to him. She could feel the wild beating of his heart under her hand.

"I am sure. And…and you?"

"I know what I feel. I have always known it. But I thought—"

"You thought what?"

"That you are so fine and so beautiful and so accomplished that you could have exactly what you said that first day."

"What—what did I say I could have?"

"Any man you chose."

"But I just said that to—"

"Put me in my place. Aye." He glanced away.

"But it was true, what you said. I knew it. I did not see how you could wish anything more with me than belonged to the need of a moment. I could not see how everything that I was, even everything that happened in that last disaster at Offleah, could ever be wiped out."

Her body touched his, softly, everywhere she could. The closeness given and taken like two halves of a whole.

"I have told you," she said. "None of that is as strong as love, if it is shared. I wanted to say that before. But

I was frightened. I did not want to be a burden to you, to force feelings you might not have. I did not want to steal your future."

"Future? I had none. That was the one thing I could not see."

"Yet it was there, waiting for you. Its shape lies in this place, in the brotherhood of those who share your oath." She took a scorching breath. "I would never ask you to turn aside from that."

His hand caught hers, molded round it. The warmth of their flesh fused, just as it had in her workroom. Strength doubled because it was shared.

"No one knows the weaving of fate," he said. "But I do not believe all will be lost."

"No." If she felt fear of dangers unknowable, she also felt the warm strength of hope. The hope was what she spoke to. It was what he needed and what she would give.

"For my part, I believe all that you have given your strength and your dreams to will come to pass. I would not have been allowed to restore the sceptre otherwise." The simplicity and the conviction of that in the warm room seemed absolute.

She felt powerful muscle ripple.

"So much is owed to your skill."

She would have denied that, but he was still speaking.

"I would never wish to take you from your *cræft*. If you could work here, perhaps travel sometimes if you wished, but always come back. I would find everything that you would need. I think the whole world would come here to see what you create."

"I could want nothing more. Here is where I would want to be."

"But here—"

"—would be my home. As it is yours."

"Aye. It is my home and it waits for me, but the only peace I can know comes from you. You hold my heart." She felt the tightness of his breath. "Nothing is as strong as what I feel for you."

"Then grant me the same feeling."

Her hand moved gently over his skin, as though she could soothe the harsh beating of the heart beneath. As though she could find for him the peace he needed. Her heart swelled, but she refused to weep. She wanted only the light for him, all the things life had taken from him such as the simplicity of happiness and joy.

"Besides," she said, letting her hand press harder against his skin, "it had better be so. There were two witnesses to what you offered."

The ripple of breath under her hand was lighter, like the small, unexpected store of laughter in him that never had the chance to come out.

"Aye. So there were. I would not like to be brought to account by either of them."

She smiled. She would bring out the laughter in him. She wanted to do that.

"No, not with Boda being such a skillful fighter, and

Edgefrith—" Her voice caught, despite all her intentions, and some of the tears fell out against the gleaming rise of his skin. "You are what he needs."

"I would never willingly let him down."

"I know that. So does he."

He said naught to that, but she knew enough of his hidden thought-hoard. The power of the past and the power of the future fused together at last.

"Just as you are what I need."

"As you are all that I love."

"Truly?" Her heart seemed to stop.

"I knew that from the first. When I opened my eyes out of the darkness and you were there, like a spirit. I would not admit it, but it was there, strongest when I tried to deny it."

She thought the tears would choke her because she understood each bitter reason why he had tried to deny it, for her sake. She stroked the smooth, heavy luxury of his skin, the dark hairs across the width of his chest. She felt the quick reaction inside him. The tears seemed to thicken.

"I pretended to myself so hard that I cared naught for you. Because I was afraid. I am such a coward—" Her tears choked the words off. She felt his arms tighten.

"Nay. Not so." His voice held all the light she wanted. Like the sun. "It is only that you are not so skilled at deception as me. I would have seen through you straightaway if I had thought to pay the slightest attention."

She raised her head. "The slightest—"

"Mayhap when you crawled into bed with me and claimed me for a husband should have given me a clue. Or when I found that disgusting dog's tooth under the pillow because you wanted me well enough in your bed to— Ouch."

She had found a bruise. She was quite glad. There were a number to choose from. He should remember that. She tried to ignore the blinding sensation of his mouth in her hair.

"You were not supposed to see the tooth. Besides, it belonged to a fox. I thought a wild beast would...suit you."

He had found her neck. Perhaps she would swoon.

"A wild beast," she said. "A savage." She heard the catch in his breath and used the advantage.

"It is as well," she said, running her fingers down to his leg, reveling in the deeper sharpness of his breath. "It is what I need. For I must be a savage myself." She slid her hand onto the heated skin of his thigh, the flaring shape that had driven her into madness the first time she had seen it.

She let her hand rest there, not moving, just knowing his warmth. "I cannot help how I love. It is beyond right and beyond limit. The very life of it is yours. It could find its home in no other."

He held her close, wordless. The gift of warmth in his body and the gift of acceptance in his mind. Outside the shadowed space of the bed lay the peace of the bright chamber, the beauty of the hall and the endless stretch of the fields. Unseen. There.

Always.

HISTORICAL NOTE

King Alfred who ruled so long ago (871–899) is an inescapably romantic figure. He is the only English ruler to have been given the title "The Great." When the twenty-three-year-old king was crowned at Wimborne Abbey, his small realm stood alone against the might of the Viking invasion. Wessex and King Alfred never gave in. The king managed to preserve his land and wrest most of southern England back from the marauding Danes.

My interpretation of Alfred's life is just that: an interpretation.

The figure of Alfred—warrior, scholar and law giver—attracts legends like a magnet. In one folktale, the king disguises himself as a minstrel to infiltrate the Danish camp and learn their battle plans. There is no historical proof for such an incident, but a ruler like Alfred would have been surrounded by hearth-companions brought up to value bravery. And disguises are fascinating.

A story was born.

With the exception of King Alfred and his archen-
emy Guthrum the Dane, all the characters in this story
are fictitious. The sceptre of Cerdic's kin is an inven-
tion.

* * * * *

*Turn the page for an exciting preview
of Helen Kirkman's next dramatic novel*

DESTINY

*A sweeping tale of love, honour and redemption
set in Dark Age Britain*

*coming March 2006
From HQN Books*

Kent, England
The Andresweald, A.D. 875

ELENE HAD TWO ADVANTAGES—desperation and a spear. The man had a sword. Light glittered off his chain mail, off the deep gold fall of his hair. It sparked from him as he moved.

The warrior's sword, gold-hilted, rune-carved, was as yet undrawn, as though he thought he did not need it. She balanced the seven-foot shaft of grey ashwood in her hand. The leafed blade at the tip was strong enough to pierce the hand-linked steel across his chest.

He was shouting. Elene did not heed it. She would deal death rather than be in another man's power.

He ran, closing the gap between them, lithe as a grey wolf, fast. He was huge, a shape of strength and threat. His shadow was black. Behind him was the open space in the half-built wall of the fortress. Behind that was the forest.

She tightened her grip on the smooth wood. The distance between her and the warrior narrowed at a speed that defied thought, closed. Striking range.

He did not unsheathe the sword. *Why?*

No weapon. She would have to spear a man un-armed. The world closed to the glittering moving shape, the death-black shadow. But she was close enough to sense fast breath, heat, living muscle, the courage to face killing steel. For a critical instant she held back.

Her breath choked. She would have to strike him or she was gone. Back into hell. A captive. She could not bear that again.

He swerved. Left.... She tried to follow with the spear point. He yelled, his voice harsh, so strong like him.

He lunged.

The madness made her strike, the point of the spear aimed true, straight at where his heart would be, locked to his movement—it was a feint. She realised too late. The twist of his body, supple despite his size, was too swift to follow.

He took her feet from under her. The spear scraped metal, ripped out of her hand. The point pitched into the dust. He caught her before she could follow. His arms imprisoned her, a solid leg pinned hers.

The feel of his body was pure heat, hard metal, heavy muscle, size. Such size. Weight. It was the way Kraka used to hold her. She struggled, insane.

"...keep still, woman...." The words came through, Danish mangled by West Saxon. She hit, her fist jarring on metal, on flesh hot with sun and exertion, fine skin.

"...*hell-rune*...." Hell-fiend, sorceress. It came out in English, equally mangled. She realised what his accent was and went still. She swore. The language she used was the same, only the dialect was different, the pure Mercian that belonged farther north, in the broad midlands.

"You are English, then." The deep, richly accented voice, held a thread of amusement, exasperation, the fierce intensity of the shared struggle. He was breathing hard.

"Will you stop now?" he inquired. She swallowed with a dry throat. The spellbinding shape of his voice had no significance. East Anglians were dead meat, anyway, their rich, open landscape lost forever to the Viking army, to raiders like the ones she had lived with.

"Well?" demanded the dead East Anglian.

She did not know why he was interested in her word. He could kill her one-handed. He knew it. Her chance was gone.

For now.

"Aye."

He loosened his grip. The fingers of her left hand were tangled in the bright mass of his hair beneath his war-helm. She had pulled bits of it out. She unclenched her fingers. Threads of pure gold stuck to her flesh. When he breathed, the solid wall of his chest pressed into her, metal and padding, and beneath it strong life. His hands, huge, heavy, eminently capable, burned her skin through the bedizened inadequate gown.

He shifted a dense, thickly muscled thigh. His hands moved briefly across her back, the curve of her ribs, under her arms. Shivers coursed over her skin. Her half-clothed body slid down the metal-clad length of his, hardness and heated flesh. Her skirt caught between their tightly pressed legs, lifting. She yanked it down, vicious with fright. He moved. The material came free, dropped, covering the revealing flash of skin, the bright red shoes.

But he had seen the strumpet's dyed shoes of cheap leather, the curving shape of hidden flesh bared to the knee. He had touched her. She read the flare of heat in his grey eyes, beyond anger or vengefulness, deep as instinct. Male. Her breath hitched.

He caught her arm, his hand warm, alive, the touch direct, shockingly intimate, more so because of the brief, naked moments when they had fought between life and death. Close. Deep inside her, sharp feeling uncoiled like a snake waiting to strike.

It was anger, the bitter melding of rage and fear like a killing frost. Rejection. He kept his hand where it was. The heat of the feeling, the solid living touch of him, mocked her.

Her feet lighted on the ground and the dizziness hit her. She felt ill with exhaustion, the mad, fey strength of the struggle gone beyond recall, spent. Her belly clenched. No food, no money, no hope of anything. All lost like her freedom. She made herself stand up straight. Not the freedom, that was not lost, not that. She would do whatever it took.

"Lord, you have caught her—"

She stiffened with shock. She had not seen the others, or even realised they were there, that anything existed beyond the man who held her. She turned her neck on tight muscles.

The garrison of the unfinished Kentish fort surrounded her and the East Anglian warrior like a circle of carrion birds after the battle. Near her feet on the dusty ground lay the lost throwing-spear. Beside her captor's large boots lay the scratched linen bag of pilfered food, the leather bottle of clean precious spring water. Someone's ration of dried meat spilled onto the ground.

"She is dangerous, lord. We could have shot her, but..."

She saw the man with the arrow ready on string. The bow was still bent. *But the East Anglian with the flashing armour, the one referred to as the leader, had flung himself at her with a wolf's speed, shouting.* Her foot grazed the deadly spear shaft. The *lord* held on to her, a tightening of iron fingers on her bare arm, like a warning.

Like a sign of outright possession.

"She is a thief," insisted the man who could only be the garrison commander. The speech, thickly Kentish, alien to the richness of East Anglia, brought sullen murmurs of agreement.

"Of the armoury?" The lord's voice was flat. The captain of the garrison flushed. Elene should not have found the throwing-spear. They had been unforgivably careless.

"She speaks Danish."

This time her belly clenched with fear. The accusation was true. She spoke across them, shouting. "I am not Danish." She nearly spat it. She sought for calm, reason, for her voice to ring with conviction. "I was living in the forest. The Andredesweald."

"An outlaw, then. And—"

A *hor-cwen*. The appalling scarlet dress clung to every curve of her body like a second skin. Her flesh spilled out of it, her arms bare past the elbow, the curve of her shoulder exposed, the tops of her breasts. The material was thin, now travel-stained, ripped at the hem and—heaven knew what she looked like after fighting a warrior built like Beowulf the monster-slayer. It was only the iron grip of his hand on her arm that held her still. The strength seemed to pour from him in hot waves. He did not speak, but her accuser suddenly stepped back, bowing his head.

But it did not stop his vengeful gaze, the mixture of anger and thwarted lust. The same look, the same resentful fire lived in the eyes of every man in the tight circle that hemmed her in, trapped her from escape. She had made fools out of them all. She was a Danish whore. She consorted with those who had raided their land and killed their kindred and taken their families as slaves. Kent had suffered badly, ravaged by horrors.

It was nothing to what had happened in East Anglia. The relentless pressure of the massive hand on her arm increased. The fierce strong body with its merciless courage moved.

"I will deal with this."

She could feel the unslaked anger in the company of men around them, the resentment of her. There were a score of weapons. But the unexplained right over them the East Anglian lord possessed, the command, the unbreakable strength of his will was enough.

"My lord Berg."

Berg.

The packed ranks of men opened in a sunlit path that led straight into the heart of the fortress.

"Come," said the man called Berg.

Question, command or offer. It did not matter. The choice was clear—him or the pack of angry bated hounds on the scent. The lord in the brilliant armour did not spell it out. No need.

She tossed her head. The whore's dress rustled as she walked.

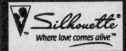

helen kirkman

| 83629-5 | FORBIDDEN | ___ $6.50 U.S. ___ $7.99 CAN. |
| 77017-0 | EMBERS | ___ $6.50 U.S. ___ $7.99 CAN. |

(limited quantities available)

TOTAL AMOUNT	$ _____
POSTAGE & HANDLING	$ _____
($1.00 FOR 1 BOOK, 50¢ for each additional)	
APPLICABLE TAXES*	$ _____
TOTAL PAYABLE	$ _____

(check or money order—please do not send cash)

To order, complete this form and send it, along with a check or money order for the total above, payable to HQN Books, to: **In the U.S.:** 3010 Walden Avenue, P.O. Box 9077, Buffalo, NY 14269-9077; **In Canada:** P.O. Box 636, Fort Erie, Ontario, L2A 5X3.

Name: _____

Address: _____ City: _____

State/Prov.: _____ Zip/Postal Code: _____

Account Number (if applicable): _____

075 CSAS

*New York residents remit applicable sales taxes.
*Canadian residents remit applicable GST and provincial taxes.

HQN™

We *are* romance™

www.HQNBooks.com

PHHK0805BL